DEATH AT A
PARIS HOTEL

BOOKS BY VERITY BRIGHT

DEATH AT A
PARIS HOTEL

VERITY BRIGHT

bookouture

Published by Bookouture in 2025

An imprint of Storyfire Ltd.
Carmelite House
50 Victoria Embankment
London EC4Y 0DZ

www.bookouture.com

The authorised representative in the EEA is Hachette Ireland
8 Castlecourt Centre
Dublin 15 D15 XTP3
Ireland
(email: info@hbgi.ie)

ISBN: 978-1-83618-816-2
eBook ISBN: 978-1-83618-815-5

To Paris, the City of Love, and all the hopeless romantics who love her.

1

'And to think this is only the beginning!' Lady Eleanor Swift whispered from the balcony of her hotel suite. In front of her, the evening lights of Paris sparkled like a diamond necklace, the illuminated Eiffel Tower piercing the skyline like a burning beacon.

She shook her head in disbelief. Only three days? It was hard to believe. Three days into her new dream life, and she was more excited than she'd ever been.

'But also rather daunted, if I'm honest,' she whispered to the warm April breeze.

Which was more of an admission than all of Paris could ever know given the extraordinary life she'd led so far. First as plain Eleanor Swift and then as *Lady* Eleanor Swift, after inheriting her uncle's title and estate.

And now she was married. She flung her arms out, as if trying to capture all the joyous times that promised to lie ahead. Or, a mean inner voice whispered, in case the bubble burst before she'd got used to the shining wedding ring on her finger.

She shook her fiery-red curls. No! Her first marriage might not have lasted through no fault of her own, but this time she had got it right. Of that she was certain. All she needed to do now was to convince herself it was actually real. Along with learning the art of avoiding trouble, she mused with a wince. For that was something she had proved peculiarly adept at getting embroiled in over the last few years.

She looked down at her heavy-set bulldog and nodded. 'You're right, Gladstone, old chum. None of that unpleasantness! We're honeymooning in Paris, after all. Nothing could be more romantic.'

Her thoughts were interrupted by the sound of cheerful humming. And then the far-too-handsome and divinely long-legged form of her new husband. Any evidence of Scotland Yard's permanently over-worked, sleep-deprived detective chief inspector had vanished. His chestnut curls framed his lean cheeks, bringing out the warm brown of his eyes, which shone with joy and love. Hugh Seldon was clearly a very happy man.

Wrapping his arms around her, he nuzzled her cheek. 'How is my beautiful new wife?'

'Truthfully? Covered in pinch marks under these silken sleeves, Hugh. From having to check we're finally married.'

'After five tortuous years of the most awkward courtship any pair has ever unintentionally put themselves through.'

'You missed out fraught and fractious.'

His rich chuckle made her smile. He dropped a cufflink into her hand and rolled back his shirtsleeve.

'You too!' She ran her fingers over his reddened skin. 'How did either of us miss that, though? After all, our clothes have spent more time on the floor than on us.'

Seldon's cheeks coloured as he stared into her green eyes. 'Eleanor, why do I have the feeling that even after we've been married for thirty years, you'll still have the knack of making my toes curl?'

She took the two ends of his black bow tie and tried to create something akin to a presentable result. 'I didn't realise that's what I've been doing in our beautiful four-poster through there.'

'Precisely my point!' Seldon shook his head helplessly as his colour deepened. 'I meant you mentioning unladylike topics. But yes, you definitely have,' he ended in a whisper.

They gazed out at the shimmering lights of the city. He linked his fingers in hers.

'Honestly, Eleanor, I still feel like I'm dreaming. With a recurring nightmare that I still hadn't actually found the courage to propose to the most unorthodox lady of the manor ever born.'

Her breath caught as she remembered another nightmare.

You were almost widowed before you were even married, Ellie!

Two days before the wedding, a malicious figure from her past had tried to poison him. They'd failed by only a whisker. She shuddered at the horrific memory of having come so close to losing him.

He pulled her tighter into his side. 'Cold, my love?'

This was no time to dwell on the unthinkable that almost was. 'Just hungry,' she said with extra gusto.

'As always.' He smiled, clearly as amused as he was still amazed by her robust appetite.

She tossed her curls. 'The world's best surprises make some of us girls hungrier than ever, Hugh. And since you sprung the perfect one by secretly rearranging our honeymoon destination to Paris, it'll be your fault when I devour unseemly amounts of everything this evening!'

'Much to your butler's horror.'

She beamed up at him. 'Absolutely! You know, Hugh, it really was too thoughtful of you to include Clifford. You've no idea what it means to him.' She rolled her eyes affectionately. 'And never will, because you chaps are so dashedly reserved about letting slip even an inch of feelings.'

He smiled. 'It didn't feel right to leave him behind. He's so much more than just your butler. He's a very precious link to your beloved late uncle. And you think the world of him.'

She laughed. 'Along with often wanting to strangle him with his over-starched collar for being an infuriating fusspot.'

He nodded. 'That too. Yet I still don't know him very well at all.' Before she could point out her butler was still something of an enigma even to her, he pulled her closer. 'And this is my only chance to change that, as I'll be up to my neck in case files the moment we return home. Plus, I want to thank him for managing the impossible task of keeping you safe since you returned to England.' He grinned. 'And, if I'm really honest, listening to you two endlessly squabbling is too entertaining to miss for a fortnight.'

She flinched at the sudden peal of church bells. Perhaps the famous Notre-Dame chimes themselves?

'Sounds like we're already late for dinner,' Seldon said. 'And neither of us has finished dressing yet.'

She tutted. 'I know. Honestly, the mess you've made of tying your bow tie, Hugh, tsk!'

He chuckled again as he steered her gently inside with Gladstone leading the charge at the word 'dinner'.

The interior of their honeymoon suite couldn't have been more perfectly Parisian in its decor. Nor more romantic. Each panel of the damask wallpaper resembled one of the famous pictures in the Louvre, while pairs of doves and swathes of roses adorned the ivory sections between. And all so lifelike, she still felt the need to reach out and touch them, even after three days.

'Is it really alright?' Seldon ran an anxious hand through his curls, gesturing around the room.

'No, Hugh. It's far from alright. It's too special for words.' She meant it with every fibre of her skipping heart. 'Especially for the gruff and brooding policeman I mistakenly thought had no ounce of sentiment or romance in him. Although, maybe that was mostly because he used to threaten to arrest me each time we met.'

He shook his head, a smile playing around his lips. 'Pointlessly, since it never stopped you.'

She sighed blissfully. 'Button me up, please, darling?'

'Permanently? With pleasure, my lady,' he said in a remarkable imitation of her butler.

'I meant my gown, you rotter!'

2

Eleanor was still smiling as she and Seldon descended the double-width marble staircase arm in arm, Gladstone lumbering eagerly beside them. Normally, he was inseparable from the cheeky ginger tomcat she had adopted a few years back. But Tomkins had injured a paw during their wedding festivities and needed to recuperate at home, fussed over by her staff.

In the hotel's elegant marbled lobby the porter, liveried in a braided crimson uniform, stood to attention. Next to him was a breathtaking display of a hundred long-stemmed ivory lilies ringed with five bands of pearl-white hydrangeas. Along the walls, between glass cabinets of objets d'art, walnut bureaus held copies of the iconic fashion magazine *Vogue*, and the two leading French newspapers, *Le Figaro* and *Le Monde*. Despite a copy of the latter tucked under his arm, however, her butler appeared to be engrossed in a book.

'What ho, Clifford!' she called, causing Gladstone to charge over and offer licky kisses as he scrabbled up her butler's legs.

Clifford closed his book, ran a hand of greeting over the bulldog's head and exhorted the exuberant beast to at least try walking to heel as they stepped over.

'Good evening, my lady. Sir.'

She pointed at his book. 'Is it tedium of a scientific or philosophical nature that you're devouring this time, my insatiable boffin?'

He tutted. 'To an enquiring mind, my lady, neither are ever "dull". But since you ask, I am reading a historical novel. Penned by the notable French *écrivain*, Alexandre Dumas, in 1844. Much of which is set here, in Paris, during the 1600s.'

'*The Three Musketeers*,' she read out. 'Even I seem to remember hearing of it.'

'Ahem.' His lips pursed as he glanced pointedly at the magnificent gilt pendulum clock dominating the reception area. 'Perhaps I mistook the time you intended to dine? However, I have asked the maître d' to hold your table, just in case.'

Eleanor turned to Seldon, shaking her head. 'Oh dear, Hugh. You were duped. You secreted my butler aboard the ferry from England as the cherry on your wonderful honeymoon surprise for me. But during the crossing, they evidently swapped him for a stuffed goose!'

Clifford's expression softened at her genuinely heartfelt delight he was there.

She smiled. 'Now, I see you've pitched up looking more dapper and distinguished than ever in your dinner togs. Are we to assume that it is purely for the benefit of all the female guests you can't deny are batting their lashes at you from every corner? Or have you deigned to join us for a proper feast, Parisian style?'

His hand strayed to his bow tie. 'If you mean accepting the chief inspector's gracious invitation to toast your nuptials, then yes, my lady. It is an honour worthy of bending the rules for.'

Seldon cocked his head. 'Although I did add a postscript, remember, Clifford?'

'Quite, sir. Safety in numbers. Two against one. In the face of likely innumerable faux pas from a certain member of our party.'

'I know!' she said innocently. 'Gladstone's bound to show us up somehow. So, no point putting it off. Race you to the dining room, chaps?'

Seldon spoke no French at all, Eleanor knew. His previous time in that country having been spent in the trenches during the war. Her own command of the language was gleaned only from hated school lessons, where she had paid scant attention. Even the few words and phrases she'd picked up while stationed in France as a nurse during the conflict she'd purposefully forgotten, in order to block out the awful memories of that time. But she abhorred rudeness of any kind, especially when she was a visitor in a foreign land. Hence, she had been overjoyed to find a potted history of Paris with an English-to-French phrase book in her suitcase. The work of her ever-thoughtful butler, she'd guessed. She patted her beaded evening bag, where it was now nestled.

They entered the dining room, which was already filled with elegantly turned out couples, businessmen, and a few larger parties, all at various stages of their meals.

'Bonsoir,' she said cheerily to the moustached man in black suit tails eyeing her and Seldon like children entering class long after the last ding of the bell. The maître d', she guessed.

'Monsieur Clifford, une autre fois, essayez plus fort, s'il vous plaît!'

'Désolé, monsieur,' her butler said in a contrite tone, giving her a sideways glance.

'What did I miss, Clifford?' she whispered.

'The polite version of the maître d's ire at having his table bookings schedule hurled to the wall,' he murmured back.

She grimaced. She never meant to be late. Distractions just seemed to impede her arriving on time.

The table the maître d' led them to made his displeasure

even more understandable, set as it was under the very centre of the exquisite atrium. Painted on the glass roof panels, peacocks, flamingos and indigo-blue herons looked down, the gold coronet they each sported glinting in the reflection of the chandeliers. Clearly, this was one of the most prestigious tables available, granted in honour of them being honeymooners.

The room itself was a breathtaking octagon which rose the height of two floors, made all the grander by the additional ten feet of the atrium. It was presided over by the hawk-eyed maître d' and his regiment of white-aproned waiters. She smiled at the life-size marble statues dotted in the alcoves. In true French form, they were all nudes. So wonderfully un-English, she thought, not one for prudishness herself.

How can two neighbouring countries be so diametrically opposite in their attitudes, Ellie?

The tables were set with layered ivory linen which cascaded to within an inch of the floor. 'Merci,' she said to the eagle-nosed waiter holding out her chair. She didn't need to look up to know that her two male companions would be chivalrously waiting for her to be seated. And then, despite Seldon having no pretensions about class, Clifford would respectfully wait for him. Before sending silent apologies to his butler brethren for sitting in front of his mistress and new master.

'Champagne, monsieur?' The waiter gestured at the gold-embossed *carte des vins* he had placed before Seldon.

Seldon smiled at Eleanor. 'Naturally! We can't toast our marriage with anything less.' An expectant silence followed. 'Ah, but which one?' he murmured.

After a moment, she caught Clifford spreading three fingers on his napkin, as if appreciating the quality of the linen.

'Hmm, a bottle of Bollinger,' Seldon said to the waiter, reading the third on the list.

'And I'll be ages choosing my meal,' she added, having to

abandon speaking French. 'So may we have ten minutes' grace while we start with the toasting?'

To her surprise, this seemed to be the perfect response as the waiter gave her an appreciative bow. 'Bien sûr, madame. To hurry when dining is a crime!' he said fervently, before gliding away.

Looking abashed, Seldon nodded to Clifford. 'Thank you. I've got a lot to learn.'

'If you say so, sir. Though with a long-experienced butler now in your service...' He left that hanging.

Seldon's expression made it clear, however, that he assumed no claim on anything Eleanor's inheritance from her uncle had bestowed on her just because they were finally married.

'We've all got a lot of change to get used to, Hugh. Wonderful change, though.' She waggled a finger at Clifford. 'Now, you scallywag, help me decipher the menu so I can decide what to eat.'

After a few moments of discussion, she sighed. 'I mean, how can I choose between the trout mousse with black truffles or the chanterelle mushrooms in whatever that word is? They're just the appetisers! There's the sublime starters and mouth-watering mains to choose yet.'

She paused as the waiter arrived with the champagne. Evidently the flourish with which he opened the bottle met with her butler's meticulous standards, given his nod of approval. As the waiter poured them each a glass, her eyes swept over the table. The crystal glassware and silver cutlery sparkled, all bathed in the soft glow from the art nouveau lamp that defined Parisian style; the brass base a resplendent pineapple from which a miniature glass parasol patterned with rose tulips sprouted.

'Now, as you're struggling to choose from the menu, Eleanor, how about we decide what we want to do tomorrow first?' Seldon said.

Her eyes lit up. 'Go up the Eiffel Tower, definitely. The glimpses we got today while strolling along the Champs-Élysées were too tantalising. And let's take a romantic boat ride down the Seine. Plus, umm...' She see-sawed her head, unable to choose between the multitude of wonders Paris offered.

'View the wealth of treasures housed in the world-renowned art museum, the Louvre, perchance?' Clifford said in a hopeful tone. 'Or marvel at the architectural splendour of the Notre-Dame Cathedral and also of the Sacré-Coeur Basilica in Montmartre?'

Normally, art and architecture rarely featured on her must-see list. But here, in Paris, how could she not?

'Perfect! And I've decided on the trout, followed by duck pâté, then guinea hen *à la Richelieu.*'

'Bravo. An inspired selection,' Clifford said.

Seldon shrugged, his dedication to his police work having long ago elbowed aside regular eating habits. 'Is it? I'll have the same then.' He reached for his champagne. Raising it aloft, he nodded as she and Clifford followed suit. 'To living, loving and laughing together, forever, Eleanor. No matter what surprises life drops in our laps,' he said ardently.

'Hear, hear!' she cried. Tilting her head back to take a long sip, she stiffened, staring up at the atrium. Was it a trick of the light that made the painted heron seem to move? No! Her eyes widened in alarm, her cry lost in the ominous boom of the roof exploding inwards. She covered her head as a chaos of shattered glass and broken metal struts rained down onto the table, the mass of jagged shards glinting like blades.

And among them, the body of a man.

3

Stupefied silence filled the restaurant. Then the screaming started. Galvanised into action, Eleanor whipped the draped tablecloths over the man's body to shield him against the last daggers of broken glass still raining down. Caring nothing for those falling on her, she hunched over his head, willing life not to have left him.

'Can you hear me?' she said, cursing the continued cacophony of shouts and screams from the other diners. She peeled the stricken man's thick black woollen hat from his ear, releasing an unexpected tumble of collar-length dark waves and tried again. 'Can you hear me?'

Nothing. But his eyes were open, pools of striking blue locked onto hers as if they shared a... connection?

She shook herself. The man's eyes widened, as if reliving the horror of falling through the atrium roof over again. Imploring her to catch him. To save him.

Leaning in closer, she held her cheek so it almost brushed his lips.

There, Ellie! Shallow, erratic breathing.

'Hugh! Send for a doctor. Quickly! He's alive. Just. Take

Gladstone with you. And calm everyone in the room, please!' Her war nurse's training kicked in. 'And, Clifford, carefully move his lower jaw up to open his airways. But without moving or tilting his neck. It may be broken. I'll check his pulse again.' She wasn't giving up hope. Not yet.

Seldon ducked under the table and then shot away towards the reception area with Gladstone tucked tight to his chest.

Clifford started in on her instructions while she stared in horror at the crimson stain spreading across the ivory tablecloth. A glass shard had probably pierced his back on impact. Or several. She tried to see under the poor man but didn't dare move him. All she could see was what looked like a dusty imprint near his shoulder blade on one side. She bit her lip. Ignoring what she could do nothing about, she checked for other injuries elsewhere.

'Possible fractured wrist,' she muttered, spotting his awkwardly held fist, then frowned. His jacket and shirt must have been ripped by the jagged edges of the broken atrium struts. His inner arm was exposed, the skin looking to be only scratched, not cut, which otherwise could have been a severed artery. But what was that patch of black she could see? A bruise from a previous injury? Peering closer, she realised it was actually a tattoo of some kind of animal. Ignoring it, she willed her fingers not to tremble as she eased the torn cloth further apart to feel for his pulse just above the inner crease of his elbow. Her fingertips, however, strained to detect much more than a faltering beat.

'You're alive and breathing, friend. Stay with me,' she said, far more calmly than she felt. Silently counting the barely noticeable beats, she spotted Seldon hastening back. Despite his lack of French, his authoritative tone soon helped quell the panic in the other diners.

Eleanor's insides tightened. The man's already frail pulse seemed to be weakening further, the light in his eyes waning.

With her other hand and her most encouraging smile, she reached down to gently cup his still clenched fist.

'The doctor will be here soon.'

Glancing down, she registered for the first time he was dressed in a grey cotton twill smock coat. One so dark as to look almost black in the subdued light from the table lamps. Likewise, his thick canvas trousers with deep patch pockets down either leg and rubber-soled deck shoes.

She looked up to see the hotel manager hurrying towards her table, pursued by the gabbling maître d'. Both were staring up at the devastation to the atrium roof. She shivered, not with the cooler air rushing in, and only partly with shock. The restaurant's lights were casting shadows up on the smoke-grey clouds behind the gaping chasm of missing glass. Making it seem ghostly faces were peering in like ghoulish spectators.

'Mon Dieu! Qu'est-ce qui s'est passé?' the manager cried, his slender, almost feminine hands flying to his face.

'Never mind the roof damage. Has the doctor been called for?' To her horror, the manager shook his head.

'Monsieur Pronovost!' Clifford said in a commanding tone, still carefully holding the fallen man's jaw to aid his impeded breathing. 'Urgent medical attention is the only matter of immediate importance.'

The manager's insipid grey-green eyes narrowed. 'I have made the call, since I do not need to be told my duty. But I telephoned not for a doctor. But for the police!' His lip curled as he glanced over the fallen man's face. 'As I suspected on hearing of the calamity from Mr Seldon, this man is not one of the hotel guests. He had no right to be up on the roof. And certainly not to crash through it like a drunken elephant!'

Still trying to focus on the patient's pulse, Eleanor fought the urge to grab Pronovost by his oh-so-neat lapels and shake him. 'The reason for him being on the roof is immaterial at the moment,' she said, teeth gritted. However, the manager's words gave her a fleeting pause for thought. 'I am a guest. And I demand you find a doctor. Now!'

With a barely contained sniff, the manager clicked his fingers at a waiter and barked something that sounded as though her request had finally been heeded.

'Any minute now, you'll be in the best medical hands,' she said reassuringly to the man. Glancing questioningly at Clifford for an update on the state of the patient's breathing, he discreetly see-sawed his head. She nodded back. Momentarily, the pulse beneath her fingers strengthened just enough to give her false hope before it waned again.

Seldon had drawn the waiters into a huddle and now mimed for the shocked diners to be removed. That done, he joined Eleanor, his concern for her clear in his eyes. The diners' exodus was interrupted, however, not by the doctor she had been praying for, but by two policemen. There was no mistaking their midnight-blue uniforms and tall pillbox caps with the small braided insignia above the stiffened peaks.

'Ah, la police!' Monsieur Pronovost said with evident relief.

Suddenly she felt the arm she was still monitoring for a pulse flinch. Fleetingly, the fallen man's gaze widened beseechingly. Was he trying to tell her something? The fingers of his hand creaked open and he pushed something weakly into hers. She glanced down and gasped. Then frowned in confusion. She looked back at his face. As she watched, the last of the light in his eyes faded. His pulse stopped.

Swallowing her anguish for the life lost, her fist closed over the item he had pressed into it. Hastily, she slid it into her evening bag, her head spinning.

4

Surely your mind is just playing hideous tricks on you, Ellie? A moment ago, your new husband raised a toast to lifelong happiness. And now...

Pronovost was gabbling in French to the taller of the two policemen, who was staring at Eleanor intently, despite nodding as if listening to the manager.

It was only then she realised she had her fingers pressed to the fallen man's arm. She started to remove them, but somehow it felt like taking away the last chance she might be wrong. In her heart, however, she knew she wasn't.

'I'm so sorry I couldn't save you,' she whispered. 'Whoever you are.'

Seldon gently tucked a swathe of her red curls behind her ear and dabbed at her cheek with a napkin. Only then did she realise it was painful. A shard of glass must have grazed her as she'd tried to nurse the fallen man.

'I'll be alright, Hugh,' she muttered numbly. 'Unlike this poor fellow. He was far too young to have died. He only looks my age.'

Maybe that's why you felt some sort of connection, Ellie?

She glared at the manager. 'May I ask why the welfare of this man sprawled on the table here doesn't seem to be your priority?'

Before he could reply, the taller of the policemen turned to her. 'I am Gardien Thierry Hacqueville of the *police municipale*. And you may ask. But the answer you know already.' He pointed up at the gaping hole in the atrium. 'He was a thief! Climbing onto the roof in an attempt to sneak into the rooms of the guests to steal what he can. And he got what he deserved when he fell through as he was trying to signal to his accomplice below.' He jabbed a finger at her. 'You! And these two men helped also.'

'What? I don't even know who the poor fellow was!' she cried, sure now she was trapped in a feverish dream.

'How dare you accuse my wife of such a thing!' Seldon growled.

Hacqueville gripped the stout black baton hanging on his belt. 'It is no use pretending this is not the case. This man falls onto her table. And after it is clear he is dead, she still nurses him. No matter she is injured herself. Why would she do this if this man is not one she knows? And not one who she is working with in crime?'

'It's called selfless compassion,' Clifford said crisply.

Eleanor noticed the second, shorter policeman hovering beside Hacqueville. He nodded to her. 'Madame, I am Gardien Luc Bernier, also of the *police municipale*. And I am sorry that you are caught in the wrong place at an unfortunate time.' He turned to his colleague. 'Hacqueville. There are much easier ways to get into the rooms and suites of this hotel than to climb like a monkey across the roof! I believe also, these people are strangers to Paris.'

Her attention was distracted by the stomp of boots. The newcomer, a square-jawed man with a no-nonsense cut to his crown of russet hair, looked uncommonly strapping compared to Hacqueville and Bernier, with their narrow waists and hips; a formidable oak among saplings. His unbuttoned calf-length dark-chocolate overcoat revealed a conker-brown worsted suit underneath. The smart salutes he barely acknowledged from Hacqueville and Bernier confirmed he was clearly the officer in charge now.

The six-strong troop of men marching in behind him were all in police uniforms, too. But those of a more exalted division, Eleanor guessed, given that theirs were embellished with red piping which ran the full length of their smart silver-buttoned jackets. The leather pistol pouch attached to their wide black belts also spoke volumes. Disconcerting ones. English police rarely carried guns. Even as a senior police detective back in England, Seldon only carried a revolver in the direst circumstances.

Casting a wary eye over the new arrivals, Hacqueville's previously confrontational manner was nowhere to be seen as the manager hurried up to the square-jawed officer like an agitated mouse.

'Je suis Monsieur Pronovost, directeur de l'hotel.'

'Inspecteur Gripperel, Police Nationale.'

Far from the gravelled deep bark she had imagined, his voice sounded like slow dripping honey. After a brief exchange she couldn't understand, Gripperel beckoned Hacqueville and Bernier to join him. Seldon squeezed Eleanor's arm.

'Now a detective has arrived, we should be free to leave any minute.'

'Not quite so, monsieur,' Gripperel said, without turning around.

Eleanor and Seldon stared at each other as he dismissed Hacqueville and Bernier with a curt nod. Only then did he turn to face them. He smiled thinly as he ran his hand over Gladstone's head.

'Madame, you and the rest of your party will accompany me, please.'

Seldon's jaw tightened. 'Inspector, I fully understand the job you need to do. But you'll have to make do with just me. My wife has suffered an extreme shock. Clifford here will escort her upstairs.'

Gripperel looked quizzically at Eleanor. 'The lady looks very far from any chance of falling into a faint. Nevertheless, we will have cognac ready in case. And all three of you will come with me.'

She touched Seldon's arm. Her motto was always to get something over and done with, rather than delaying it. And she felt an overwhelming urge to find out even a snippet about the man who had fallen onto her table so tragically.

'I'm fine, Hugh, really,' she murmured.

He hesitated, then threaded his arm tightly through hers as they followed Pronovost and the inspector, Clifford his ever respectful two steps behind. But as she caught his reflection in a gilt mirror they passed, his no-longer inscrutable expression gave away that he, too, was troubled by more than just the man's death.

5

The gold lettering on the door Pronovost opened announced it was his private domain as the hotel manager. He ushered them inside the high-ceilinged room lined with heavy crimson flock wallpaper. Distressingly, the pattern reminded her of the blood seeping into the tablecloth from the dead man's wound. She sank into a chair, wondering how she could surreptitiously ask the questions itching on her lips.

Seldon pulled his seat close to hers, while Clifford placed Gladstone in Eleanor's lap and stayed standing. Gripperel perched on the corner of the green leather-tooled desk. Pronovost stifled a sigh as the inspector's prodigious frame knocked over several neat piles of papers. Clifford gave him a sympathetic look, his own fastidiousness equally nettled.

Gripperel placed his bear paws together, his gaze travelling languidly between Eleanor, Seldon and Clifford.

'Where to begin, I wonder?'

'Our names, perhaps?' she said more sharply than intended, fighting the first shivers of shock.

Gripperel smiled thinly. 'Those I can get from Monsieur

Pronovost later. He will have your passports, or other identity papers, in his safe.'

Clifford stepped forward. 'And besides, the lady requires that promised cognac before answering.' He turned to the silver tray on the polished walnut bureau and poured two double measures. Passing one to her, he offered Seldon the other.

'Not just now, thank you, Clifford.'

Gripperel reached over and took it instead. He waited while Eleanor sipped hers, then savoured a long swig himself.

'Now, madame, if you feel sufficiently recuperated to tell me what happened, please begin.'

She composed herself. 'The three of us were raising a toast. Hugh and I are newlyweds. I looked up and saw...' she swallowed hard, 'saw that poor man crashing through the glass roof. He... he landed on our table. Clifford and I tried to help him, while Hugh did an admirable job of alerting Monsieur Pronovost and then calming all the diners and waiters. Then Constables Hacqueville and Bernier, I think it was, arrived. They will have told you the rest.'

There was a knock at the door.

'Entrez!' Gripperel called.

One of his men strode in and whispered in his ear. Gripperel nodded and motioned for the policeman to leave. He turned back to Eleanor.

'So, madame, please tell me, did the man who fell say anything to you before he died?'

She shook her head vehemently, hoping he wasn't going to delve too much further into anything else the stricken man had done. She fought the urge to clutch her beaded evening bag tighter. The one that held the item he had pressed into her hand. She had recognised it. *But how?*

'No, Inspector, he didn't speak. I believe the poor fellow had broken his neck. Which is often accompanied by paralysis, as you're probably aware.'

'Perhaps,' he replied ambiguously.

She bristled slightly. 'I've answered your questions. Now I'd like you to answer mine. Tell me what you think happened? And if what Constable Hacqueville said about him being a thief is true?'

Gripperel threw Seldon a knowing look. 'You see, I was right about the lady. She is quite composed.' He eased himself off the desk. Holding his cognac up to the light, he looked at her through the glass. 'The man was a thief, yes. But he was not trying to rob this hotel. He had already robbed the Musée d'Art Contemporain. It is only a few streets from here. This is why he was hiding on the roof of this hotel. Because he knew me and my men were looking for him.'

'What did he steal?' Seldon said.

Gripperel lowered his glass and shrugged. 'At this moment, I do not know. The constable has searched the body and there is nothing to be found there. So he must have hidden it. Or... passed it to an accomplice.'

It took all of Eleanor's concentration to keep her expression neutral. Thankfully, Clifford stepped forward.

'Inspector, is it a common occurrence for men of dubious character to use this hotel's roof as a getaway?'

'Certainly not, Monsieur Clifford!' the hotel manager cried before Gripperel could reply. 'Never before has this happened.'

Clifford turned to Seldon. 'Then I suggest, sir, we can probably consider any recurrence unlikely.'

Seldon frowned. 'Hmm, well, I'm far from convinced we should continue staying here.' He scanned Eleanor's face, his expression softening. 'But I'll let my wife decide what she wishes to do.'

'Please keep in mind that I will need you to be available should I have more questions later,' Gripperel said. 'But for now, thank you. You can continue with your evening. I must learn what has been stolen. So, it is to the *musée* I will now go.'

'That sounds the perfect distraction!' Eleanor said quickly, to Seldon's obvious surprise. Gripping her bag, she leaped up. 'Inspector, I simply must escape from the hotel to stop dwelling on the poor man's death. May I, and my entourage, accompany you?'

Gripperel took a step back and rubbed his chin. He eyed her curiously as if she were as hard to read as the *Mona Lisa* which hung not far away in the Louvre.

'I can think of no reason why you, and your party, cannot come with me, madame. My car is outside the front entrance.'

He strode from the room, with Pronovost scurrying after him.

Seldon sighed. 'I shan't ask why we're going along, Eleanor. But at least let me run up and get you a coat.'

She smiled and gestured around the otherwise empty room. 'Where do you think Clifford has gone, Hugh?'

'What? I didn't even notice him leave. He's stealthier than a ghost!' Seldon muttered.

'I know. Neither of us saw him pour the extra glass of cognac each he's left us on the desk either.'

As they reached the hotel's revolving door, Clifford was waiting. Eleanor slipped into her jade wool wrap with the comforting velvet collar and cuffs and Seldon into his broad-shouldered blue wool overcoat. Clifford helped Gladstone into his tweed dog jacket, while eyeing her sideways.

'Yes, thank you, Mr Thoughtful. I'm feeling better.'

Looking unconvinced, he carried Gladstone through the revolving door as her ever-exuberant bulldog had not mastered the art of walking through it at all. Although it was also partly Clifford's horror at the smeary nose marks the bulldog left on the glass.

'The inspector is already installed in his vehicle and waiting, my lady. Shall we?' he said, as if her request to accompany Gripperel had been the most natural thing in the world.

As they pulled away from the hotel, Eleanor stared out of the window. A man under a streetlight caught her attention. In his fifties, she estimated, he was of short height and wearing a thick black coat and hat.

She nodded towards him. 'You should strike up an acquaintance with that chap, Clifford. You'd get on like a house on fire,' she said teasingly, trying to pretend she wasn't feeling the after-effects of shock.

Her butler tutted. 'There is nothing to be sniffed at about being prepared for every eventuality, my lady. And everything to be gained by it.'

Seldon leaned over Gladstone's head to peer through the window. 'What am I missing, you two? He seems perfectly ordinary to me.'

'Yes, Hugh. Save for the umbrella he's carrying. There's not even a hint of rain in the air and it looks big enough to cover him and half the pavement when unfurled. But I bet if you searched Clifford here, you'd find an ingenious folding version somewhere about his person. Along with everything else one couldn't possibly imagine needing.'

'But indubitably will,' Clifford said drily.

Seldon shook his head ruefully. 'Well, after this evening's unexpected events, I'd say there's no knowing what one needs to prepare for. Or carry protection against!'

6

The Museum of Contemporary Art was surrounded by a high wall, its grand arched entrance guarded by one of Gripperel's men. He leaped aside with a salute on seeing his superior. Waving them through, he gave Eleanor and her two companions a quizzical look, but said nothing. Beyond lay a sizable rectangular courtyard with uneven cobbles underfoot, most definitely not designed for Eleanor's embroidered satin heels. Nevertheless, she strode after Gripperel as if her ankles weren't threatening to twist with every step she took. This was no time to highlight the incongruity of her arriving at a closed museum, late in the evening, in an emerald evening gown with her exuberant bulldog in tow.

She tried to memorise the layout as she walked. The thief had been here less than an hour ago. But now he was dead...

Her expression hardened with determination as she hurried after Gripperel.

On either side of the courtyard, a narrow two-storey wing ran down to join the main pavilion. A rather masculine and grandiose edifice, she thought, given the heavy-browed stone arches protruding over the regiment of windows across its four storeys. Even the relief-carved friezes were of battling warriors.

She caught her butler's enraptured sigh from behind and murmured, 'We're not here to appreciate the architecture, Clifford.'

'Pity, my lady. For I would conjecture this is a rare example of High Renaissance making the acquaintance of early Mannerism. Evident in the exquisite pediments, cartouches and intricacy of the entablature throughout.'

Seldon turned and stared at him.

'I know, Hugh,' she said quickly, fearing he might question exactly why she had been so eager to come there. Particularly straight from the shocking scene she had witnessed. 'How does he contain so much twafflesome knowledge under so neat a bowler hat?'

Clifford sniffed. 'Might one dare hope the building's elegance and poise will set the tone for this endeavour, my lady? Whatever it may be,' he added quietly.

At that moment, her heel caught in the gap left by a missing cobble. She flew forwards, her flailing arms only just regaining her balance in time to save herself from falling face first.

'I think you can take that as a no, Clifford,' Seldon said wryly.

With a toss of her head, she joined the now bemused-looking Gripperel, who had paused to talk to the police constable guarding the imposing front door.

Stepping inside, she shivered. Even with the comforting warmth of her wool wrap, the five-or-ten-degree difference felt positively glacial compared to Paris's mild evening temperature outside. Clifford tightened her bulldog's lead around his hand. 'Best behaviour, Master Gladstone.'

They had entered a vast oval hall. A rainbow of silk banners hung down from the domed roof, each printed with a half-obscured image. Evidently, these were intended as a tantalising taste of the current exhibitions on display. The walls were clad in grey-veined rose marble, the floor in mosaic tiles forming a concentric whorl of pearlescent shades through sand, beige and bisque. The pattern was so intricate it had the mesmerising effect of the floor itself spiralling downwards. But it was broken up sporadically by circular panels of blue-green glass set in iron frames. Looking down through the nearest one, she could make out someone moving below, but their features were lost to the blurring effect of the thick coloured glass.

'A peculiar way to treat such an exquisite floor. Almost vandalism in a temple to art, as this clearly is.'

Clifford nodded. 'However, a very necessary act of practicality, I imagine, my lady. Providing much needed light to the basement. Also serving as an expedient release of heat and smoke for the fire brigade, should the unthinkable occur. Since a single calculated blow with an axe will smash the entire panel.'

She shuddered this time. 'Perhaps we won't think about shattered glass raining down?'

All three of them nodded vehemently, stepping carefully around the panels on the way to the semi-circular stairs split down the middle by an ornate bronze handrail. Not so Gladstone, who was finding everything much too exciting to be mindful of anything.

'This way,' Gripperel called, heading towards a heavy oak door marked *Pas d'accès!*

More stairs. Leading down this time. They ended abruptly at a set of double doors panelled in burgundy leather. Gripperel entered without knocking.

Instead of the art academic's study she had expected to find, they stepped into what seemed to be a large warehouse. The high walls were filled with runs of racking, housing a profusion of framed paintings and sketches and a few ceramic sculptures of myriad sizes. Confusingly, along with what looked like everyday household items. Looking again, she realised there was a handwritten inventory pinned below each group. And what she had initially thought was a series of workbenches running down the centre were actually record cabinets, given the brass numbers gracing each drawer. Several of the nearest had been left open, revealing tightly packed yellowed index cards. Wheeled access platforms with steps up the side stood idly by.

They were the only suggestion of inactivity, however, as a near constant stream of men in buff-brown overalls and matching peaked caps hurried in. As they did so, they shook their heads and handed a large sheet of paper to a striped grey-jacketed man with his back and balding crown to her. Then they took a new sheet held out to them, before hastening out again.

'You have news for me on what has been stolen, Omfroy?' Gripperel called out.

The man in the grey jacket spun around. Eleanor's eyes widened. From each cheek sprouted a wide bush of grey-black hair, fanatically groomed and sculpted to end at a fine point level with the stiffly padded shoulders of the man's jacket. In combination with the thick walrus moustache, an avant-garde cravat, vibrantly patterned in geometric shapes, adorned the man's neck. She batted away the thought that the owner of this astounding feat of facial hair could have made a comfortable living in a Victorian sideshow.

Unaware of her assessment, he mopped his deeply furrowed forehead and balding pate as he looked her and her two companions over.

'I repeat, have you discovered what has been stolen?' Gripperel said.

'Yes, Inspector. *Nothing!*'

Gripperel frowned. 'Nothing?'

The museum director threw out his hands. 'Oui! Nothing except an item of... minimal value. Taken from one of the painter's studios that we have reconstructed.'

'Which painter was it?' Eleanor said, hoping it sounded like a natural question.

'Christophe Ury, madame. A little-known post-Impressionist at his death twenty-six years ago, but now recognised as one of the greats!' Omfroy replied ardently.

'I haven't heard of his work,' she said apologetically.

'Or any others,' Clifford murmured for her ears only.

'And have you caught the thief then, Inspector?' the man said agitatedly.

Gripperel rubbed his chin. 'He caught himself. By falling to his death. Onto this lady's dinner table.' He waved at Eleanor.

The whiskered man gaped at her.

She nodded to him over Seldon's unhappy huff at Gripperel's insensitivity. 'Bonsoir, Monsieur...?'

The man frowned disapprovingly. But not at her, at Gripperel, she was pleased to see. The inspector ignored him and introduced the moustachioed wonder.

'Lady Swift. This is Monsieur Eustace Omfroy. Director of the Musée d'Art Contemporain.'

She smiled. 'Pleased to meet you, Monsieur Omfroy. I am—'

'Not supposed to be here!' Omfroy said in a pointed tone. 'This room is out of bounds for visitors. Besides, the museum closed four hours and' – he regarded his watch 'forty eight minutes ago.'

She caught Clifford's eye. 'A man after your own heart where timekeeping is concerned,' she murmured.

Pretending not to have heard, her butler half bowed. 'S'il vous plaît, pardonnez notre intrusion, monsieur.'

Omfroy nodded stiffly.

Gripperel tapped the director's clipboard to get his attention again. 'Monsieur Omfroy, please do not tell me you are still checking for what has been stolen?'

Omfroy threw his arm out. 'Mais oui, Inspector! Naturally,

my staff checked all the most valuable paintings and sculptures
first. Then they started on the lesser exhibits. We have a lot of
the personal effects of the artists as well as their work.' His eyes
took on a dreamy look. 'This is not an ordinary museum, mais
non! The Musée d'Art Contemporain is an experience. One
which aims to leave every visitor a changed person. And to
achieve this, the collections number over three hundred
wonders of modern art set in captivating context.'

'And still your security is lacking,' Gripperel grunted.

Eleanor was delighted but surprised the inspector was
speaking English, even to the director. It could only be for her
benefit. But in truth, it added to her bafflement that he had
agreed to let them accompany him.

'Send me the man who raised the alarm. And quickly,'
Gripperel said.

'His name is Alain Rion and...' As Omfroy scanned the
small brigade of buff-brown overalls and peaked caps in the
room, his brow furrowed in puzzlement. 'And he has
disappeared!'

7

A movement at the far end of the room caught Eleanor's attention. A wiry man in head-to-toe dark blue slid in, as if trying to hide among his colleagues.

'Ah!' Omfroy exclaimed, clicking his fingers. 'Ici, Rion!'

Eleanor noticed the man's face paled. But who wouldn't worry when summarily summoned by their boss?

But then again, Ellie, where had Rion been?

Up close, she fought the uncharitable thought he had something of a ferret about him; beady black eyes and an angular, narrow nose, from which the rest of his face raked back under his tufty raven hair. Despite no hint of grey, she estimated he was in his mid-fifties. Before he could speak, Omfroy gestured to Gripperel.

'L'inspecteur, Police Nationale.'

'Oui, monsieur?' the newcomer said to Gripperel, seemingly engrossed in studying his boots.

Gripperel frowned. 'Tell me what you saw of this thief who has caused all the trouble tonight. In English as best you are able.'

'En anglais?' The newcomer's eyes flicked questioningly

over Eleanor's face, then those of Seldon and Clifford. He turned his lips down dismissively. 'I only see the thief too late. When he is climbing out from one of the windows of the museum on the ground floor. I do not see him break in.'

'Who saw him break in?' Gripperel called to the rest of his staff. They all shrugged and shook their heads.

In French, Rion said something in an urgent tone to his boss. However, the nod he received came from Gripperel. Clearly relieved, he darted out the way he had come in.

'How did the thief get in then, I wonder?' Eleanor mused, as if to herself.

'My men will find out very soon,' Gripperel said firmly. 'They are only now beginning to look into this. Because before, they were busy chasing him. Then with taking away his dead body from your dinner table.'

Seldon's jaw tightened. 'Inspector, enough, please! As I have already pointed out to you, there is no need to refer to the event in such unnecessarily vivid terms in front of my wife.'

Gripperel held his gaze with an ambiguous smile. 'Then I will point out to you, sir, that your wife is only in front of me... because she asks to be.'

'It's alright, Hugh,' Eleanor said hurriedly, fearing either Gripperel or Seldon would start fussing she should leave. She turned to the museum director. 'Your men must have an enormous task to check through such a large trove of modern art treasures, Monsieur Omfroy?'

'This is exactly so, madame,' Omfroy crowed, glancing at Gripperel. 'Why don't you wait in my study until I am finished here?'

Gripperel nodded and waved Omfroy away with a frown and a reminder that he didn't have all night. Something the overall-coated men clearly agreed with as they scattered at Omfroy's barked, 'Recherche! Vite! Vite!'

Omfroy's study was exactly the sanctum she had expected

of an art expert. Especially now having met the fastidiously whiskered man himself; leather tomes, archive files, endless art periodicals. And everything stacked and ordered just so. Except the half-drunk coffee abandoned with a half-eaten biscuit on the coffee table. And next to it, a half-smoked cigar, almost burned down to the red and gold band, the ash perilously close to spilling over from the ashtray. She caught Clifford's shudder.

'You're itching to deal with those, aren't you?'

Before he could reply, Gripperel turned his gaze on her, his eyes scrutinising. 'So, madame, is this how you usually spend your holidays?'

'Oh, but this is our honeymoon, Inspector,' she said, sidestepping the question. 'Which is why there's just the three of us. Plus Gladstone there. But after travelling alone for so long...'

His eyes glinted. She realised she had inadvertently piqued his interest.

Dash your runaway tongue, Ellie!

'Travelling alone before you were married, madame? I see now why you ask to come with me here to the museum. You are a lady who is excited by a mystery and likes adventure, yes?'

'I suppose a few people might say that,' she said airily. 'Although one can never rule out the coincidence of simply happening into things.'

Gripperel looked unconvinced, but nodded to Seldon. 'And you are the man who thinks he has thrown reins around this lady with a wedding ring?'

'Not one bit, Inspector,' Seldon said without hesitation. 'My wife is free to do exactly what she chooses. Now, and always.'

'And what is it you do for a living, monsieur?'

Eleanor's insides clenched. If Gripperel learned Seldon was a senior police detective it would make him even more suspicious of her asking to accompany him to the museum.

Fortunately, Seldon seemed to be thinking along the same lines.

He shrugged. 'I mostly beat my head against bureaucracy, Inspector. And waste hours compiling reports which make no difference to anyone.'

'Ah!' Gripperel said. 'But I think the boredom of your job will be forgotten now you are this lady's husband. Because you will also be caught in the tails of her liking for adventure and mystery, I think.'

'Mystery! Pah!' Omfroy's voice cried behind them. He hurried over, looking perplexed. 'It is... *incroyable!*'

Gripperel looked at him sharply. 'What is "incredible"? You have discovered what has been stolen?'

'Yes, Inspector. *Nothing!*'

She gave the director her best winning smile. 'Monsieur Omfroy, our planned visit to your renowned museum tomorrow was to be the highlight of our honeymoon. But as it turns out, unforeseeable events have overtaken our agenda and we shan't have any other chance than tonight... as... as...' She was foundering. 'As we will be leaving Paris tomorrow now, you see?'

Omfroy's forehead furrowed. 'I do not understand?'

Seldon looked at her blankly. Clifford, however, came to her rescue.

'Monsieur Omfroy, her ladyship has long awaited this exalted cultural experience. A chance to explore the wonders of the world famous Musée d'Art Contemporain in Paris!'

Omfroy seemed moved by her butler's words, but still he shook his head.

Seldon slid his arm through Eleanor's, seemingly catching on. 'I really can't take my wife back to the hotel yet, Monsieur Omfroy. Not after the gruesome scene of a man falling to his death at her table.'

Gripperel seemed to be trying to hide a smile. 'Monsieur Omfroy, my men and I will be here for at least another hour. What harm can it do to let this lady satisfy her hunger to look around your collections?'

Omfroy hesitated, but finally nodded. 'Alright, if you absolutely must, madame.'

Inwardly, she sighed with relief.

Perhaps, now, Ellie, you can find some answers for what you saw tonight!

But when she found them, how was she going to explain to the others something she barely understood herself? That she had an unshakeable certainty that she recognised the brooch the dead man had pressed into her hand? And that when he had done so, it was as if he was... returning it to her!

'Thank you for backing me up just now, chaps,' she said quietly once they were back in the entrance hall, Gripperel and Omfroy having left them to it.

Seldon shook his head. 'Don't thank me, Eleanor. It was the last thing I wanted to say. But all I could think of on the spur of the moment, blast it! And since Clifford was clearly in on this mysterious caper of yours, as usual...' He left that hanging with a quiet sigh.

Clifford gave a respectful cough. 'If you will forgive the correction, sir, I am equally in the dark. However, where her ladyship is concerned, sober experience has taught that acquiescence invariably proves the less painful option.'

The pair of them shared a sympathetic look.

Having the support of her two favourite men in the world meant everything to her. Especially at this moment. Her thoughts would never settle if she failed to follow her heart on this. But quite where it was leading, she didn't know.

Having consulted a plan of the museum, Clifford led them to the second floor.

'This way looks quietest. Though, regrettably, we will miss the work of sculptors influenced by such luminaries as Rodin, Degas and Matisse.'

She shrugged at Seldon's questioning look. 'Not a clue, Hugh.'

They hurried through endless miles of echoing passageways and expansive gallery rooms. Clifford finally brought them to a stop, gesturing reverently ahead with the printed guide. 'As requested, the gallery of Impressionists.'

Seldon grunted. 'What makes a man spend his every waking hour locked up in a garret smearing paint on paper, anyway?'

Clifford's lips quirked. 'Ahem, to paraphrase Alexandre Dumas's character Athos in *The Three Musketeers*, you may take them as heroes or madmen. Two classes of imbeciles sufficiently resembling each other.'

She roused herself. 'Come on, chaps. Seriously, we haven't got long before Omfroy, or Gripperel, throws us out, I'm sure.'

'Whatever it is we need time for,' she caught Seldon murmur to Clifford.

She had to admit, however, the vibrancy of colour and bold brush strokes of the paintings here were undeniably striking. The subject of many of them seemed to be leisure; boating scenes, carefree picnics, families strolling along the beach, all blithe and gay.

Seldon stepped up to her as she reached one particular painting. He gestured at the depiction of an elegantly dressed couple waltzing barefoot on golden sand.

'That should be us, Eleanor. Given this was supposed to be our honeymoon.'

She gazed up at him apologetically. 'That will be us, Hugh. Very soon, I promise.'

He smiled. 'Whenever you're finished doing whatever it is you can't let lie here, it will be. But whatever that is' – he pressed his finger gently to her lips – 'I can wait until you are ready to tell me. Whenever that may be.'

He couldn't have said anything she needed to hear more than that right then.

'Thank you, Hugh,' she whispered in relief.

She poked her head inside the next door. Yes! The first painting was signed Christophe Ury. It evoked a feeling she hadn't experienced in the other displays. A feeling she couldn't quite put her finger on. The topics and style were not too dissimilar to those she'd just seen, but the brush strokes struck her as having been made with that extra bit of passion. And... she shook herself. Like with the brooch, she had the strangest feeling of... déjà vu?

Someone's next door, Ellie!

She stepped quietly over, fearing it would be one of Gripperel's men. It wasn't. The room housed the recreation of Christophe Ury's studio. And Rion, the guard, was rubbing a polishing cloth over one of the glass cases. What a stroke of good fortune! Here was the very man who had spotted, and reported, the thief to Omfroy. She'd been desperate to speak to him earlier, but with Gripperel present she'd fought down the questions burning on her tongue.

'The artists' studios have been so fascinating, let's see Christophe Ury's,' she called brightly to Seldon and Clifford, stepping into the room.

And hopefully find out why a man plunged through your hotel roof to his death, Ellie.

8

'Bonsoir, monsieur!'

Rion stared back at Eleanor like a startled rabbit. In a blink, his expression turned. To one of wariness.

'Excusez-moi, madame, but the museum is closed.'

She smiled sweetly. 'Yes, I know. But your director, Monsieur Omfroy, was an absolute darling and said that we could take a quick tour even though it's late. We'll be leaving with Inspector Gripperel, I expect.'

At the mention of the inspector, Rion hung his head with a forlorn sigh. 'I feel bad that I could not stop the thief. This museum is home to important art. I wish I would have caught this man.'

'Well, you did your best by raising the alarm,' she said soothingly. Glancing around, she took in the overall ambience of the room. Unlike the previous ones, where she'd gained a sense of the artists having been theatrical personalities, here she felt something different. Something... more... authentic? More genuine? There was also a tinge of wistfulness about the space.

Her eyes fell on one of the glass display cases. Its front was smashed, the brass lock hanging open. She skipped over the

French and Italian language sections of the sepia-inked label on the front to the English version:

RING OF PEARLS PENDANT BROOCH.

The only painting Christophe Ury sold in his lifetime was to a rich, anonymous widow. When she offered to buy his painting – *Dansant sous les arbres fanjan* – he told her to give him what she thought it was worth. Without hesitation, she gave him the most expensive piece of jewellery she was wearing at the time – a pearl brooch. Even though he was all but penniless, Christophe vowed never to part with this one token of recognition his genius inspired while he was alive.

For some reason, Eleanor's heart clenched at the thought of Christophe losing the brooch.

But why, Ellie?

Not wanting to arouse Rion's suspicions, she quickly glanced at the next exhibit, a little black sailboat, and stepped away. In between all the displayed items were several unfinished sketches.

'Will these wonderful works get completed by Mr Ury's hand, I wonder?'

'Mais non! Christophe Ury is dead, madame. Like all the painters on display on the second floor here,' Rion said.

'Oh, I see. Poor chap.' She wondered why it seemed you had to be dead to be famous enough to have your pictures hung in the gallery.

Seldon was idling through the catalogue of Ury's other paintings, which she knew he had no interest in. As an overworked policeman normally mired in the grim underbelly of life, he had little inclination or time for the appreciation of art. Clifford, however, was murmuring snippets of information to

Gladstone who was oblivious, too busy eyeing up the only armchair in the room for the chance of a comfy nap.

'Well, everything looks securely kept,' she said to Rion.

'Impressionist paintings have come to be worth many times more francs in the last years,' Rion said, with a frown. 'Collectors wish now to buy those of the artists who are growing in fame. Because the ones who are already famous' – he rolled his eyes – 'their paintings are too expensive, even for most art collectors.'

'Well, naturally. Hence, I'm debating potential additions to my current collection back home,' she said airily.

Clifford peered teasingly at her. 'It is most surprising the Impressionists appeal to you, my lady. With their unconventional technique of seeking to focus on sense, mood and feelings rather than the intricate and finely detailed. Indeed, the founding artists of the movement were the rebels of their day. Considered most unorthodox. Reckless even, with their stated disregard for accepted rules.'

Despite herself, she couldn't help smiling. He'd just described the very characteristics in her which frequently scandalised his rigid sense of propriety.

'Watch it, or I'll send you back to sit with that nude painting you avoided looking at until I'm done,' she murmured. 'Monsieur Rion, did I hear correctly? That no paintings of Christophe Ury were stolen?'

'Oui, this is so,' Rion said.

'Well, that's great news. So it was just whatever was in this damaged case that was taken, then?' She peered at the label as if naturally curious. But unnecessarily so, as she had already memorised it. 'You raised the alarm because you heard the thief breaking into it, I imagine?'

Rion hesitated. But whether through worrying he shouldn't be telling her about the museum's business or not, she couldn't decide. After a moment, he said, 'Non, madame.

After the museum is closed, always I make regular tours of the floors. I am very proud of my job to protect the art here. Then, on the third time I check this area, I see this!' He pointed at the broken display case. 'The thief steals only one thing, I think, because he hears my footsteps and flees. He could have stolen many more things if I had not disturbed him!'

'Absolutely! Well done. What did you do then?'

'I rang the alarm. Then I chased the thief. But first I found Monsieur Omfroy to tell to him what happened.'

'Lucky he was working late. Unusually late, perhaps?' she said casually.

Rion hesitated again, then shrugged. 'He is the director.' His voice became more animated, as if reliving the drama. 'He reached straight for the telephone to call the police. Then I shouted for the other staff left in the building to search for the thief!'

'Gracious, and did any of your colleagues see him?'

'Non, nobody saw him. Only me. From the floor above, I saw him running across the ground floor. But too late to catch him. Then I found the window he forced open in the visitors' cloakroom. He must have come in this way, I think.'

'Well, excellent effort. Anyway, we won't disturb you any longer. We'll just continue on our little tour.'

Seldon and Clifford joined her as she headed towards the door.

'Madame, please?' Rion called.

She turned back. 'Yes?'

'As you arrived with the police inspector, maybe you know if they have caught this thief?'

'You haven't heard?' As soon as she'd said it, she remembered. He hadn't been in the records room when Gripperel had told Omfroy.

Rion shook his head. 'I have not left my post here since I

reported the thief running away. Only one time to speak with Monsieur Omfroy. But I am worried this thief will try again!'

'You've no worry about that, monsieur. You see, the thief won't be stealing anything else.' She felt a wash of sadness. 'He is... dead.'

Rion's jaw dropped, but he quickly snapped his mouth closed. 'Dead?' he muttered, glancing away.

Something in his tone struck her. 'Monsieur, did you recognise the thief?'

Rion blanched. 'I... I did not.'

He's lying, Ellie.

She stepped over to him with a sympathetic look. 'Please forgive me for continuing to speak to you in English, monsieur. I fear my French will let me down in offering proper condolences.'

His beady black eyes stared back at her. 'This last word I do not understand, madame?'

'What I meant is, I am sorry about the death of the thief who stole the brooch from here. I didn't realise you would be upset. I should have told you he'd died more sensitively.'

He stiffened. 'Upset? But why would I feel this?'

'Well, because you knew him,' she said, as if it was obvious.

Rion slowly shook his head. 'Madame, I told you before. I do not know the man.'

'Really? I was just speaking to your director a moment ago. Perhaps I should talk to him again?'

Rion's eyes widened. 'Please, madame! I...' His shoulders slumped, but his ferret-like expression remained taut. 'Okay. I confess, I had seen this thief before. But only one or two times. And I do not know his name. Sometimes he sells his paintings on the railings of the boulevard along the Seine. But I think he sells one only when his chicken grows the teeth!'

'A French idiom for an event which it is assumed will never occur, my lady,' Clifford translated.

'Why do you say that?' she asked Rion.

'Because he looks like the hungry dog who has not had a meal in many days. Like most of the artists,' Rion scoffed.

Her thoughts flew back to the man as he lay dying on her table. He had been gaunt in the face, now she thought about it. And his grey twill smock coat and canvas trousers had hung loosely about his sprawled body.

'Poor chap,' she murmured.

Rion cocked his head. 'Madame, it is strange for a lady on her holidays to be interested in a nobody from Paris, I think? Especially when he is a thief.'

Seldon stepped forward. 'Whatever he was, he died a tragic death. My wife did everything to try and save him.'

Rion bowed his head contritely. 'Then, monsieur, I apologise. And, madame... thank you for what you did.' He looked up. 'Now, I must get on with my duties, or Monsieur Omfroy will be displeased.' Touching his fingers to the peak of his blue cap, he darted away.

'Interesting,' she muttered to the others as they retraced their steps. 'Were either of you convinced by what he said?'

Seldon and Clifford both shook their heads.

'Me neither. And did you notice how scornful he was when mentioning that thief, who also seems to be a painter, never sold anything?'

Seldon nodded. 'It's unusual to be so vehement about someone you hardly knew.'

'Exactly. And why did he thank me for helping someone he hardly knew? He's definitely hiding something. And that earns him a place on our suspect list!'

'Madame, where are you?'

Omfroy appeared looking flushed. 'I am sorry. But really, you and your friends must leave the museum now. It is too late. And I need my staff to concentrate on their duties.'

'Yes, of course,' she said contritely. 'I'm grateful you let us stay on.'

Outside, as they crossed the courtyard, Gripperel was talking to the officer at the entrance onto the street. She grabbed Gladstone's lead from Clifford and waved as she let her eager bulldog pull her along.

'Bonsoir, Inspector!' she called, discreetly beckoning for Seldon and Clifford not to get caught in conversation either.

A few yards around the first corner, Seldon pulled her gently to a stop. 'Thank goodness that's over, Eleanor. I've been worrying all the way around that infernal museum that Gripperel would realise.'

'Realise what, Hugh?' she said tentatively.

He held her gaze. 'That the very item stolen from the museum is in your handbag. As it has been since the thief pressed it into your hand just before he died.'

She stared between him and Clifford. 'I didn't think you'd seen?'

'Think again,' Seldon said earnestly. 'You're always telling me I'm one of the best policemen in England.'

'The best, Hugh.'

'Perhaps. And I know you well enough to make the connection with your interest in that broken glass case.'

Clifford nodded soberly.

'I'm sorry, chaps, truly. But I didn't say anything because something is very wrong about everything we've been told tonight.' She failed to hide a shiver. 'You see... the thief didn't fall through the roof. He was pushed!'

9

On the corner of a cobbled street, the yellow glow of a late-night café shone out like a beacon. Perfect! She simply couldn't bear to spoil the honeymoon any further by tainting their suite's romantic ambience with anything to do with the evening's hideous events. Café Bohème looked just the spot for the difficult conversation she couldn't put off any longer.

Inside, she wasn't disappointed. The reassuring aroma of freshly roasted coffee mingled with the soft strains of a *musette*. The player, an old man with a large black cat on his knees, sat at one table, a murmur of voices coming from the other few occupied seats.

Behind the bar, a grey-templed man in a green ribbed wool waistcoat looked up from polishing a collection of glasses. 'Bonsoir à vous. Et bienvenues,' he said with a flap of his white cloth, his welcoming tone leaving his words in no need of translation. Clifford gestured respectfully to Seldon, who led Eleanor to a table while he stepped up to the bar.

Among the clusters of simple wooden chairs and small round tables, a few padded benches offered more intimate nooks. Having slid into the one in the quietest corner, Eleanor looked around, trying to get her thoughts in order. Only then noting the cosy lighting was subtly reflected in the large wall mirrors, which had been painted with images of women in 1880s-style crimson plume-feathered hats and gold bustle-puffed skirts. In one of these she could see Clifford had finished ordering and was now restraining Gladstone's eager hello to the *musette* man's black cat. Evidently, her bulldog was missing his inseparable ginger friend, Tomkins. She semaphored to the barman in the mirror, waving three fingers.

The man smiled and nodded.

Seldon was settling in beside her as Clifford came over with Gladstone.

'It was good of you to order our drinks,' Seldon said. 'But I didn't suggest you might like to join this trip to Paris so you could act as a butler. It's supposed to be a holiday for you, too. As a thank you.'

'Too kind, sir.' Clifford peered sideways at Eleanor. 'Rest assured, this is turning out to be every inch the expected "holi-day", Lady Swift style.'

'Good point,' Seldon said ruefully.

She groaned. 'I know. And I'm sorry that this trip has taken a rather troublesome turn, chaps. Or rather, I've veered us down it, I admit. But, Clifford, it would help enormously if you could bear to bend your rules for the duration of this holiday? For Hugh's sake, if not mine?'

'Of course, my lady.' With a quiet sigh of resignation, he took the seat opposite.

An uncontrollable shiver overtook her.

Seldon hastily shrugged out of his evening jacket and tucked it snugly around her shoulders. 'Blast it, you are suffering with shock, Eleanor.'

The barman arrived a moment later with a tray of steaming black coffees and warmed cognacs. Along with a plate of what looked like the most divine hot toasted sandwiches covered in a browned thick sauce. Clifford opened his mouth to politely protest he had only ordered for two, she knew. But the barman clapped him on the shoulders with a grin and jerked his head at her. Placing a bowl of water in front of Gladstone, he smiled as he gently tweaked the bulldog's wrinkled jowls and then delighted him with the end of a baguette. 'Bon appétit!' he said and wandered back to the bar.

Over the sounds of Gladstone's crunching, Seldon pressed a glass of cognac into Eleanor's hand. Then held a hot coffee up for her to take in the other. 'When you're ready to explain your startling statement, Clifford and I are more than ready to listen, Eleanor.'

Never one to put things off, she nodded, feeling the cognac warming her throat, the coffee chaser doing the same for her insides. She mustered her thoughts.

'The truth is, it was only because I tipped my head back to sip my champagne at your wonderful toast, Hugh, that I saw what I did.'

Catching her shoulders slumping with remorse, Hugh gave her hand an apologetic squeeze.

Clifford ducked down, under the auspices of helping Gladstone make less mess with his baguette.

Seldon took her butler's thoughtful cue and tucked one of her curls behind her ear. 'Eleanor,' he whispered. 'I married you with no illusions, or hopes if I'm honest, that life would be in any way normal. Or predictable. It's just that I rather hoped all that might start *after* the honeymoon.'

She grimaced. 'I wish with all my heart none of this had happened at all. But I can't ignore what I saw.'

'What did you see?'

Clifford sat upright, his fixed gaze betraying his curiosity.

She tipped her head back and closed her eyes, reliving the scene she'd witnessed. 'I saw a man... the thief, as we now have to assume he was. He was leaning over, peering down through the atrium. I saw his face. And either side of it... his hands were pressed to the glass.'

Seldon and Clifford both stiffened.

'But if he had his weight on the glass already, he wouldn't have suddenly fallen through it like he did,' Seldon said slowly.

'Exactly, Hugh! But a fraction of a second before he fell, he lurched forward and did crash through the atrium. And hurtled down and landed on our table. Where I... I failed to save him,' she ended quietly.

'Eleanor, don't torture yourself. Especially after doing so much more than you had any obligation to do,' Seldon said gently.

She bit her lip. How could she explain that she felt so much more obligation to save him than to a... a stranger, which is what the man had to be, surely?

Clifford nodded. 'Misplaced regret will certainly not help the gentleman now, my lady.'

She shook her head. 'But that's just the point! I feel I have to... help him. If not in life, then in death, at least. He was pushed. I'm certain of it! And also because' – she fumbled with the clasp of her beaded handbag – 'he gave me this.'

Trying to quell the tremble in her hand, she unfurled her fingers to reveal the ring of pearls pendant brooch the thief had pressed into her palm in his last moments.

Clifford's brow flinched, but he said nothing.

Seldon peered at it. 'Were you telling Gripperel the truth when you told him the thief didn't say anything to you, Eleanor?'

Only with his eyes, Ellie.

'Yes, Hugh. He didn't *say* anything. But even if he'd wanted to speak, I don't think he could have. Poor fellow.'

If he had, what would he have said, Ellie? Would he have been able to explain her feeling of déjà vu? Not only with the brooch, but also when seeing Christophe Ury's paintings for the first time?

Seldon took the brooch, his fingers wrapped in his handkerchief. Turning it over, then back again, he looked at her questioningly.

'He died to get that, Hugh,' she said earnestly. 'But the fact he stole it is mostly the reason for my horribly strong feeling Gripperel wouldn't act on what I saw if I told him.'

Seldon nodded. 'And he would be right to do so, in my professional opinion.'

At her horrified look, he held up a placating hand. 'Eleanor, I can't imagine the Paris police have any less of a nightmare than I do in London; too few men, too little funding, too much crime! You have no firm evidence of what you saw. And the height of that atrium roof must be thirty-odd feet from where you were sitting.'

'Thirty-two, sir. If you will forgive the correction,' Clifford said.

Seldon shook his head wearily. 'I shan't ask how you know, Clifford. Because splitting hairs isn't going to change the facts. My wife, as I've only just managed to make her, withheld important information and a vital piece of evidence from a police inspector. And, to make it worse, one in a foreign country, where I don't even speak the language so I can't plead on her behalf if it comes to it.' He let out a long breath. 'Which I would do in a heartbeat, because... I think you're right to have done so.'

10

For a second, Eleanor was lost for words. Then she shook her head slowly. 'Really, Hugh?'

He nodded resolutely. 'Yes. As a man. Not as a policeman, though.'

'Which you aren't at the moment. You're—'

'A honeymooner. And the sooner we can get back to that the better. But I don't need to have been in as many unpleasant matters with you as your poor beleaguered butler here has, to know one thing.'

She frowned. 'What's that?'

He sighed. 'You're too compassionate and selfless to be able to let the matter rest until you are sure justice has been done for this fellow. Thief or not, he didn't deserve to die. If he was murdered, that is. Which, if your eyes and intuition tell you he was, then I've learned by experience not to doubt it! So we'd better get to work finding evidence of the crime if we're ever to get justice for him. And our honeymoon back,' he ended quietly.

She caught Clifford nodding readily in agreement and felt her shoulders relax.

'Thank you, both. That means the world.'

Clifford held up the plate the barman had brought. 'If I might suggest, perhaps a recap of what we know after restoring some of the energy lost to shock, my lady?'

She nodded. 'Only if you join us. We all missed dinner. And a toasted sandwich won't kill you if you eat one in front of me, just this once.'

Clifford's lips quirked. 'Indeed, it will not, my lady. For these are, in fact, croque monsieur, originating, like the school of Impressionism, from here in Paris. The bread is toasted and buttered on one side before the generous addition of Dijon mustard. Then spread with layers of ham, grated Gruyère and Emmental cheese, plus béchamel sauce, with' – he held up a finger – 'the traditional nutmeg. The final stage of being oven baked until crisp and golden gives the dish its signature finish.'

'So, it's a fancy ham and cheese toastie with an amusingly pretentious name?'

His lips quirked. 'Most assuredly, my lady.'

'Well, it's sublime!' she said, savouring a mouthful.

Seldon nodded. 'Delicious!'

She swallowed another bite. 'Now, we'd better jot down what we know.'

'Thinking I was off duty, I didn't pack my police notebook,' Seldon said wryly. 'Clifford, I don't suppose you, umm...?'

'Naturally, sir.' He slid his hand inside his jacket. But not to produce his slim leather pocketbook as she expected. Instead, he pulled out a small parcel, wrapped in pretty sage-and-moss-green tissue paper. He passed it to Seldon, who handed it to her.

'It's only a tiny gift, Eleanor, but I couldn't resist buying it.'

She started to unwrap it. 'And Clifford had it, because...?'

'Because you were supposed to be engrossed in admiring the Arc de Triomphe, or whatever it's called, while I bought it.

But you seemed more engrossed in your new husband! Fortunately, Clifford arrived just in time and I sent him off to get it.'

'Oh, Hugh, it's gorgeous!' She ran her finger over the silk-covered notebook with the image of a carefree young woman flying along on her bicycle. 'She's even got a doggie fellow in her basket.'

'I know. That's why it reminded me of you the moment I saw it. That and the fact her curls are all over the place.'

'And her skirts,' Clifford murmured.

She laughed. 'Very droll. But, Hugh, it's too lovely to use for a murder investigation.'

He shook his head. 'Don't worry. I'll buy you another one to take home.'

'Right, so let's keep munching on these grandly named toasted sandwiches and get to it.' She accepted Clifford's fountain pen with her one free hand.

Seldon's expression was thoughtful as he chewed. 'So, the thief broke into the museum and stole that brooch you have in your bag. I imagine even if the pearls aren't the finest, it's worth a pretty penny.'

She added a note. 'And the guard, Rion, said he saw the broken display case and raised the alarm. He alerted Omfroy, the museum director, who telephoned the police.'

'Meanwhile, the few staff on duty searched the building.'

She paused in writing. 'I remember Gripperel mentioned the police station isn't very far from our hotel, which means it can't be far from the museum. But still, it means the thief must have been trapped inside the museum for a while. Likely hiding from the staff he could hear running around after him.'

'Why?' Seldon said.

'Think about it. Rion told us he saw the thief escaping from the window in the visitors' cloakroom but only after he'd found Omfroy and told him what had happened. Omfroy must have told Gripperel's men which way the thief was heading for them to have tracked him to the hotel. Otherwise, the thief would have simply vanished down a side street and not been forced to hide on the roof of our hotel to escape.'

'Good point,' Seldon said appreciatively. 'So, it must have taken a little time for Gripperel's men to appear, even if the police station is just around the corner.'

She nodded slowly, still frowning. Laying down her pen, she looked thoughtful. 'I suppose after he did finally get out, the reason he was on the roof of our hotel was most likely a spur-of-the-moment decision?'

Clifford cleared his throat. 'It strikes me, my lady, that perhaps the thief had intended to climb onto the hotel roof all along? Although that is pure conjecture.'

'Go on, conjecture some more,' she coaxed, pen poised.

'He may have planned it as a predetermined hiding place until all the fuss died down.'

Seldon shook his head. 'Bad choice, if he had. It didn't turn out to be very safe!'

Clifford winced. 'Quite, sir.'

'Or,' Seldon continued, 'he may have pre-arranged to meet someone on the roof? An accomplice, maybe?'

'Which is me, Hugh, according to Constable Hacqueville!' Eleanor grumbled. She noted down their points. 'If your suggestion about an accomplice is right, Hugh, it seems logical to think it was that very accomplice who pushed him through the atrium roof! Because who else would have known he was there?'

'A literal falling out of thieves?' Seldon rubbed his chin. 'Very plausible. *If* there was an accomplice.'

A movement reflected in the mirror opposite caught her eye. Out on the street, two *police municipale* were loitering on the corner. She slid over Seldon's lap, leaving him looking confused and not a little embarrassed. She stared in the mirror. 'I thought so!' she hissed to the others. 'It's Hacqueville and Bernier.'

'What! Are they following us?' Seldon said.

Her brow creased. 'Why would they? Hang on. A fancy car has just drawn up and Hacqueville, I think it is, has hurried over to it. Now he's leaning in the rear window having an intense-looking chat with someone I can't see.'

After a few moments, Seldon hissed, 'What's happening, blast it?'

She turned away from the mirror. 'Looks like the meeting is over. The car has driven off and Hacqueville has rejoined Bernier and they're both walking off down the road, talking.'

'Mmm. So it doesn't look as if they were necessarily following us. But we can't rule it out. Whoever was in the car may have warned them off for the moment.'

She slid back to her seat and drummed her fingers on the table. 'Well, I can't deny it seems suspicious.'

Clifford finished the last sip of his coffee and fed Gladstone the last half slice of croque monsieur. 'Perhaps, my lady, you might feel today has been eventful enough to retire to the hotel for the night?'

'Yes. Absolutely,' she said, an idea forming.

Seldon stood up. 'Good. We'll regroup tomorrow then.'

'Although it is technically tomorrow, now, sir.'

As Clifford went up to the bar to settle the bill, Seldon turned to Eleanor. 'Well, whichever day it is when we wake up, my darling wife, somehow we are going to have something of the honeymoon we dreamed of! No matter what else happens.'

'Absolutely, Hugh.' She slid her arm through his. 'There is, however, just one tiny thing we need to do before we retire tonight...'

11

———

'At last!' Eleanor hissed, ushering Clifford into her suite. She pointed at the tray of vols-au-vent he was carrying. 'And this?'

'Immaterial, my lady.' He set it down on the coffee table.

'I see,' she muttered, not seeing at all. 'Well, are we all good to go, my intrepid scout?'

His brow flinched. 'As good as can be, given the proposed endeavour, my lady. The guests have all collected their keys and not stirred from their rooms in the last hour. And aside from the night porter, all the staff have retired.'

'And Hugh and I located the door to the service stairs earlier, so we're set once he returns.'

Clifford slid his pocketbook from his inner jacket pocket and opened it at a double page, bearing a detailed inked diagram.

She sat and examined it. 'Ah! That's the atrium roof, looking up from the dining room below, yes?'

'Indeed, my lady.' He gestured over the sketch. 'Here is the location of the table at which you were sitting. And here are the missing three panes of glass, along with the broken support struts resulting from the thief's fall. Although, it is the remaining struts we are mostly interested in. After all, we do not wish to re-enact the thief's last moments, hmm?'

'Gracious, no!' She studied the sketch, trying to imagine how it would appear from the roof looking down. 'Top-notch thinking, thank you. But how did you draw this without seeming suspicious, my infallible egghead?'

'Mixed compliment aside, it was easy. Once the two remaining staff had been dispatched to cater to the whims of my mistress's untimely evening appetite...' He indicated the vols-au-vent.

'Very amusing. We'll eat those on our return.' As she finished speaking, the door opened again and Seldon slid in. She rose. 'Good. We're all here now. So, let's go!'

At the top of the enclosed, whitewashed service staircase, she lifted the iron bar and pulled.

'Locked, dash it! Clifford, I don't suppose you packed your... ah!' she whispered in relief as he patted his jacket front.

A moment later, he slid his picklocks away and lifted the iron bar, recoiling from the force of the wind, which tried to whip the door from his grasp.

'The roof being enclosed on three sides, it is channelling the wind, I believe. Care needed.'

Seldon nodded. 'And we need to ensure we aren't spotted by guests above. There are only balconies at the front but one of them may be having a quick cigarette before bed with the sash thrown up.'

He stepped out onto the roof first. Eleanor followed, relieved to see Clifford wedge the door open with a metal pail. If the door closed behind them, and a diligent member of staff locked it, they would be trapped up there. She wondered fleetingly if the thief's accomplice was one of the staff. If so, they could have left the door unlocked that evening so the thief could escape down into the hotel.

Raking her wind-blown curls from her face, she willed her

eyes to adjust. The hazy luminescence of Paris's night illumina-
tions made the roof darker still. She couldn't even see her feet
properly to tread carefully.

Suddenly, only a yard away, a shaft of light shone up from
the dining room below, ruining what little night vision she'd
gained. She froze. One or more of the staff must be up!

Seldon and Clifford clearly had the same thought.

'We'll have to wait until later, Eleanor,' Seldon whispered,
gesturing at the door they'd entered the roof from.

'No, Hugh,' she whispered back determinedly. 'It's actually
a lucky break. We wouldn't have even half as good a chance of
finding anything by torchlight alone. And we might never have
the chance to sneak up here undetected again.'

He shared a resigned look with Clifford and reluctantly
nodded. 'Only please, be careful. That's all I ask,' he murmured,
waving her in front of him.

Shielding her eyes from the flare of the dining-room's lights,
she stepped forward. Her limited night vision slowly returned
enough for her to make out a narrow-tiled walkway running
along the side of the atrium.

*Of course, Ellie. There has to be some means of getting
around the outside of the atrium. It could never be cleaned or
checked otherwise.*

She spotted the cautious sweep of Seldon's partially
obscured torchlight, his long frame hunched over his knees as he
scrutinised the tiles.

Reaching the atrium itself, she noted the bottom glass panes
ran up straight, then pitched increasingly inwards to create the
captivating effect she had admired in the dining room below. It
took all her fortitude to fight off the image of the thief crashing
through the glass and hurtling towards her.

She rallied herself to focus on the matter at hand, noting the
support struts ran just as Clifford had sketched them. The only
thing his diagram hadn't captured was the strip of lead flashing

attached along the join where the flat panes met those that sloped inwards. A rain gulley, she assumed.

On the glass in front of her was one of the painted indigo herons she'd seen from below. A few inches away was a similar shimmering flamingo. She understood now why they'd created such a stunning impression from the restaurant. They were as tall as she was!

She turned back to the others and whispered, 'I think we need to be around that next corner.'

Clifford's inked diagram appeared over her shoulder with the light of his torch partially covered. 'Indeed, that is the side from which the thief fell,' he whispered. 'At a point nine to ten feet from the corner, in my best estimation. However, I also estimate the most significant danger of weakened struts lies three feet on either side of that. If we do not proceed with extreme caution, I fear a second body may hurtle to its demise below!'

Eleanor swallowed hard. With Clifford's words of warning making her insides knot, she edged to the corner. But instead of sliding around it, she beckoned for the others to hurry and join her.

What had caught her attention was not the rail running along the outside of the walkway, but the telltale metal handholds betraying the presence of a fixed ladder.

'Assuming that leads to the ground, I would hazard a guess that's how the thief got up here.'

'Absolutely,' Seldon said. 'It would have been safer than trying to go through the hotel. But we can check that tomorrow.'

She shook her head. 'Not necessarily. It might end outside the kitchens where the staff will see us if we wait until morning. Or worse, the manager's office window!'

Before she could hitch her skirt up to investigate, Clifford darted backwards over the top of the handrails. He disappeared down the ladder with the agility his many years in the army with her uncle had instilled in him.

Time being short, she left him to it; every minute they were up there increased the chance of them being spotted. Stepping around the corner of the atrium, she hesitated. She was acutely aware that as soon as she reached the gaping hole in the roof, whoever had turned the dining-room lights back on had only to look up. And they would see her clearly!

Under the cover of the painted peacock beside her, she pressed her eye gently to the glass. For a moment, the dizzying effect of looking down thirty-two feet made her heart falter. But then she spotted Pronovost. There was no mistaking the hotel manager's slender frame and pointed features, nor his darting movements. She blinked. She hadn't expected to be able to see someone's face so clearly from this height.

Hmm, what was he doing at this time of night? The very man who had to be harangued into calling a doctor to stop a man dying, Ellie! Could he be our thief's murderous accomplice?

12

Clifford reappeared, slinking like a cat over the top of the ladder. She stepped over to him, with Seldon huddled in close.

'What did you discover?' she whispered.

'That this ladder is obviously the maintenance access point to the roof. It is bolted to the wall all the way to the ground, but for the last six feet.'

'What is there after that?'

'Air, my lady. However, having let go of the last rung and dropped to the ground, I was easily able to jump up and grip it again and thus swing myself back onto the ladder. Before I did, though, I ascertained I was in the walled kitchen yard. There is a door into the kitchens, while the yard can be entered from outside via a seven-foot high gate. Beyond which lies an alley which runs behind the hotel to join the side street which leads in the direction of the museum.'

'Good work, Clifford!' Seldon cheered quietly. 'So the thief could have come in through that gate and swung himself up onto this ladder. And then onto the roof, exactly where we are.'

She nodded. 'Yes, Hugh. And the murderer could have

followed him. Then escaped the same way.' She frowned. 'Surely the yard gate was locked, though, Clifford?'

'Tonight, yes, my lady. But it may have been unlocked yesterday evening as the kitchens were open and the staff working. It is of the barred metal variety, so easy to climb.'

'I shan't ask how you know that, Clifford,' Seldon said wryly.

She raised her hand. 'Let's discuss this later, somewhere more inviting! I'm going to examine the spot from where the thief actually fell.'

Seldon had started scouring the walkway with his torch again. He leaped up. 'Not alone, you're not!' He gestured for Clifford to take over.

'Alright. But we need to stay down, Hugh. Pronovost was just below a moment ago. He might look up and see us. Or even our shadows.'

Had anyone asked, she would have admitted that creeping towards the jagged scar in the atrium roof was unnerving. At least there was no broken glass to crunch underfoot and alert the hotel manager below if he was still there. That, of course, had all landed inside, down below.

As she reached the edge of the gaping hole, the light dazzled her momentarily. The splintered struts that hadn't crashed down with the thief hung forward into the dining room's lofty void, like twisted arms pleading for help. She shuddered. Or shattered ribs!

With Seldon close behind, she inched along beside the hole. With her eyes shielded against the light, she swept her gaze across the immediate walkway in front of her and then up the jagged edges of glass. She crept along, repeating this operation until the sound of her gown hem tearing drew her up short. Yanking it free of the jagged edge of a section of lead flashing, she sighed. They had found nothing to prove there had been anyone else around the vicinity of the atrium when the thief fell. Let alone any clue as to the identity of that person.

She nudged Seldon, motioning reluctantly that they were done. Starting back in the same slow hunched manner to ensure they weren't spotted, she realised everything looked just that bit different from this angle. The shadows cast a different perspective and highlighted sections in greater detail.

The lights in the dining room went out.

'That's one blessing,' Seldon murmured in the sudden blackness.

'Hugh!' she hissed. 'Just before it went dark, I caught a small splash of... something. Your torch, quick!'

In the covered torch beam, Seldon's frown gave him an eerie look. 'Pronovost might not have actually left the dining room yet,' he whispered, his mouth close to her ear. 'There's still one lamp on. It's too risky.'

'It's too risky we won't ever get the chance to see this again!' She took his torch and held her breath as she dared to sweep it slowly up the bottom panes of glass. 'There! It's blood!'

Seldon peered at the congealed smear. 'True. But it just shows us exactly where the thief fell from.'

She jumped as Clifford's silent form appeared beside her. Evidently having crept around the full perimeter of the atrium roof the other way.

'With respect, sir. The thief cannot have fallen from that spot.'

'Why, Clifford?'

'Because, just before the thief fell through the glass, her ladyship mentioned she had seen the painted heron above her move.'

'He's right, Hugh!' She pointed to where Clifford was crouched. 'That's the end of a peacock's tail. The birds are about two feet apart. Which means the heron I thought I saw would have been just where your knee is now.'

Seldon rubbed his chin in the eerie torch light. 'So, unless the thief arrived at this point the long way around—'

He broke off at Clifford's headshake.

'Most unlikely, sir. There are a series of large cowled air ducts which made the route I took to join you a far more laborious and slow one. Especially for a man looking for a speedy escape.'

'Then it must be the blood of whoever was up here with him,' Seldon said.

She gripped his arm. 'Yes, Hugh! And I think whoever it was leaned against this rail behind us to press their foot... no! Both feet actually, against the thief's back. I remember seeing what looked like a dusty mark near the poor man's shoulder. I'm sure now it was the imprint of a boot! That's why he lurched forward the way I saw him do just before he crashed through the glass.'

Seldon's voice became more animated. 'Good work, Eleanor! So we've confirmed to our satisfaction there was another person up here who pushed the thief to his death.'

'Most likely the accomplice we already conjectured about,' Clifford said.

Seldon studied the blood smear again. 'Probably. But I can't see the two of them having fought up here to the point of drawing blood. There was too much chance it would draw attention. The murderer must have known the police were chasing the thief.'

Clifford tutted.

'What?' Eleanor hissed.

'I merely noticed you have torn your gown, my lady. How, I cannot imagine.'

Seldon's eyes widened. 'I can!' He shone his torch along under the blood smear. 'The underside of this lead flashing is damaged here. And razor sharp.'

'That settles it,' she said. 'We need to look for a murderer with a slash to the bottom of his trousers.'

'More likely those would have ridden up as he lifted his legs to kick the thief in the back, my lady.' He demonstrated quickly, revealing long black socks covering his ankles and shins. She shook her head.

They must go up to his knees, Ellie.

'Well, since most men wear somewhat shorter socks, Clifford, I'd wager we're looking for a murderer with a fresh gash up the front of his shin.'

'Which is actually better than looking for one with ripped trousers, Eleanor,' Seldon said. 'They're too easy to destroy.'

Back at the door leading down the service staircase, she paused. 'Thank you for believing in my idea, chaps.'

Clifford half bowed. 'A pleasure, my lady.'

Seldon grunted. 'Yes. Now all we have to do is create a list of suspects and ask them all to roll up their trousers. Or if they're ladies...' He coloured.

She spun around. 'Exactly, Hugh! What if our murderer is a woman? How will she hide such a scar?'

Seldon swallowed. 'More to the point, if she is, how in blazes are we going to ask her to show us her legs!'

13

Eleanor squinted at the ornate porcelain clock on her bedside table with bleary eyes.

'Not quite quarter-past five. Perfect,' she whispered.

Had Clifford heard her, he might have blanched. Early mornings and his mistress were normally strangers. Especially this morning, as she and Seldon hadn't fallen through their suite door wrapped in each other's arms until gone one a.m. And it had been over an hour later they had finally slept. After all, they'd both wordlessly agreed, not all their honeymoon plans needed to go by the wayside! Blowing her still fast asleep husband a kiss, she slid out from under the bedcovers and crept into the dressing room. Her eyes raced along the row of filled hangers before settling on just the right ensemble. Not a pairing she would normally choose but her cream blouse with its lace cape collar and wide wrist cuffs, teamed with her sleeveless, moss-green tunic dress would hopefully be less intimidating. And going alone would help. Something even beyond her innate sense of justice was driving her this time; the unfathomable connection she felt to the dead man. And, even more unexplainably, to the brooch he had entrusted her with in his dying moments.

Having dressed, she tiptoed past her snoring bulldog in her sensible Oxford flats. Pausing only to scoop a prettily patterned tin from the mahogany bureau into her wrist bag, she slipped out of the honeymoon suite. As she carefully closed the door, the irony she would never have pulled off such a covert move back home at Henley Hall made her smile. Uncannily, Clifford always seemed to know the very moment she stirred, and would have been waiting before she reached the bottom of the stairs.

Instead of taking the main staircase down to the reception area, however, she turned left along the corridor, then slipped down the staff stairs. She had observed first-hand the keen fascination hotel employees had about guests. Especially in luxurious establishments such as this. And that curiosity led to gossip.

The stairs ended in the basement and a maze of drab grey corridors. Working down here would feel too much like being in prison, she thought with a frown. Turning on the spot, she sniffed the air. From the left, tantalising wafts of the impressive guest buffet breakfast being prepared made her stomach gurgle. From the right came the heady mix of cleaning products mingling with the pungent smell of laundry whitening. And the sounds of whispered conversation. Thinking that whispering and secrets often went hand in hand, she walked along the corridor, but as she got closer, to her dismay, one of the voices sounded upset.

Torn between needing answers and not wishing to intrude, she was about to tiptoe past when the door opened. A slender girl of barely nineteen with red-rimmed blue eyes blinked back at her in alarm. Her hands leaped to her white maid's apron, like a mouse caught in the hot breath of a poised cat.

Eleanor gave a warm smile and offered a pristine handkerchief from her tunic dress pocket. 'Excusez-moi,' she said, floundering for more French, given she was groping to know what to say in English.

The maid stared at the handkerchief, shook her head apologetically and darted back inside. Eleanor followed, ducking under several lines of wet sheets to find the maid hissing pleadingly, 'Jules!'

Eleanor's eagle-nosed waiter from the aborted dinner of the previous night appeared from behind a tower of stacked laundry crates, his arms holding a large basket of gentleman's shirts.

'Hello,' she said. 'Please forgive me if I'm interrupting?'

He shared a worried look with the maid. Now she was face to face with him and not distracted by trying to choose from the dinner menu, Eleanor realised he was a lot younger than she had thought. With his dark hair untamed by its previously stringent combing and without his smart white waiter's jacket and black bow tie, he couldn't be much over twenty.

'Madame, I think perhaps you are finding yourself lost?'

She nodded genially. 'Do you know that happens a lot? Although, as my ever-pedantic butler repeatedly insists, "finding oneself lost" is a contradiction.'

The waiter's worried expression relaxed somewhat. 'You mean Monsieur Clifford?'

'That's him.'

'Ah, then I understand. You wish to collect your laundry that he sent down yesterday? But guests usually telephone housekeeping to deliver this when it is ready?'

Grateful for the excuse she'd unexpectedly been thrown, she flapped a hand. 'I didn't want to bother anyone when I've got legs perfectly capable of managing the stairs. Gracious, I know how hard you all work, er, Jules, is it?'

'Oui, madame.' He nodded towards the maid, his arms still encumbered by the loaded basket. 'And this is Sophie.'

'Bonjour, Sophie,' Eleanor said.

'Bonjour, madame,' she replied tentatively.

'Les vêtements en le nom du Seldon, and aussi brodé avec le nom de Lady Swift, Sophie?' Jules prompted the maid.

'Ils ne sont pas prêts!' the girl stammered, wiping away another tear with her hand.

Eleanor gathered the conversation had something to do with her washing not being ready. She held out her handkerchief again. But again, Sophie shook her head.

Jules grimaced. 'It is kind, madame, but she cannot. If she is found taking even so small a thing which belongs to a guest, *oh la la*! The extra work will never end for her for the rest of the year.'

Eleanor silently cursed her blunder, fearing it might seem insensitive. But she had to ask.

'Extra work? Is that how staff are punished here for any mistakes or perceived wrongdoing?'

'Except for stealing expensive things. That is punished by being thrown to the street. But all mistakes or breaking of anything mean more hours added without pay,' Jules said. 'That is why Sophie is crying. She was punished with three more hours each day for a week because a sheet was torn. But she did not cause the damage.'

Eleanor was appalled. Life down here must feel even more prison-like than the drab grey walls already suggested. 'That is terribly unfair. Une grande... injuste!' she tried for Sophie's benefit.

'Thank you, madame.' Sophie dabbed at her eyes.

Eleanor raked her now steam-dampened curls from her forehead. The heat and fumes were making her skin feel raw and prickly. And her new husband might wake up at any moment and decide to find out what his wife was up to.

'I'm so pleased I found you here, Jules. Because I wanted to check how you are. After that awful scene in the dining room last night, I mean.'

His eyes looked haunted. 'It was a terrible shock, madame.'

Sophie nudged him and said something Eleanor couldn't understand.

'She says she thinks you are the kindest lady to have tried to save the man who fell,' he translated.

'I'm sure anyone would have done the same.'

Except Pronovost, Ellie.

She addressed Jules again. 'Perhaps among you all, you've heard something about the poor man? Maybe, his name?'

Jules shook his head firmly. 'No, madame. Nobody here knows. The *police nationale* found nothing in his pockets to give his name or any idea where he lived.' He shrugged. 'The inspector was not happy.'

'Inspector Gripperel? Why?'

'Because his men found nothing at all. Cass heard him say later.'

'Cass?'

'J'arrive!' another male voice called, making her jump. A pair of braided crimson trousers appeared, followed by a tousled head of straw-fair hair, framing questioning grey-blue eyes. The matching crimson porter's jacket swinging by the side of his long frame gave away what his job was.

He stared at Eleanor for a second, then smiled awkwardly. 'Bonjour, Lady Swift. I hope you are not too upset from last night?' He looked genuinely concerned.

'I'm fine, thank you. Unlike poor Sophie.'

Noticing the girl's tear-stained cheeks, his face fell. 'Pas encore, petit?' Stepping over, he hugged her.

Jules poked the porter's arm. 'This is Cassin, madame. Or "Cass" to his friends.'

'Bonjour, Cass,' she said. 'You're just in time, actually.' She rummaged in her bag. 'I want you all to help me with these.' She pulled out the tin and popped off the lid. 'If I eat all these chocolate biscuit fellows, my new husband won't recognise me! Please, say you will?'

Sophie's eyes lit up. The others too. Cass licked his lips.

With little more persuasion on Eleanor's part, they were all soon savouring the delectable chocolate and hazelnut mousse-wrapped wafer rolls.

'Lucky you heard us talking about you, Cass,' Eleanor said, leading the conversation back to where she needed.

'I heard my name only. What was Jules telling you? That I am the more handsome of us two?' Cass grinned and posed like a photographer's model, evidently the joker among them.

Even Sophie giggled, Eleanor noted with delight.

'Sorry to disappoint you, Cass, but we were discussing how you overheard Inspector Gripperel being cross with his men because they found nothing to identify the poor dead man.'

He let out a long whistle. 'This I did hear, madame.' Cass lowered his voice. 'But he was more cross with Monsieur Pronovost just after this. They were shouting together!'

'Inspector Gripperel and the hotel manager? Golly, I wonder what about?' Eleanor said, spotting Jules pressing his last two biscuits on Sophie.

Cass beckoned them all in closer. 'I heard only part of the argument. But I heard Monsieur Pronovost accuse Inspector Gripperel of being responsible that the man fell to your table. He was very certain the *police nationale* were the reason for this and so should pay for the repairs to the dining-room roof.'

She filed that away. 'And how did Inspector Gripperel respond to that accusation, Cass?'

'With very strong words that Monsieur Pronovost himself was to blame!'

'What reason did the inspector give?'

'He said it was too easy for the man to get on the roof. Almost as if Monsieur Pronovost had wanted him to.'

'And just before the man fell through the roof, where was Monsieur Pronovost?'

Jules said something to the other two, who shrugged. He

turned back to her. 'We do not know. He told Cass later he was in his office and did not want to be disturbed unless it was an emergency.'

She frowned. 'Is that normal?'

He nodded. 'Yes. Especially when there is an awkward guest he is trying to avoid!'

Before she could ask another question, she jumped in unison with the others at the nasal bark from the doorway, 'Que se passe-t-il ici?'

The sheets parted. Pronovost pointed a bony finger at his staff and barked again. His words were lost on Eleanor, but his abrupt manner left no doubt that punishments aplenty had been handed out.

She stepped forward. 'Monsieur Pronovost. I want to pass on my sincere commendations for your staff. Particularly, these three here.'

Pronovost's eyes slid to the others, before coming back to meet her keen gaze. 'Well, that is pleasant music to my ears. What exactly have they done that has impressed you so, madame?'

'They have each gone above and beyond to make my honeymoon stay here truly perfect, particularly after the distressing event in the dining room last night.' She looked Pronovost firmly in the eye. 'Now, kindly guarantee that rewards will be forth coming to them? And reassure me, this is not one of those disgraceful hotels where staff are punished by being made to work extra hours without pay? Because I have heard such barbaric tactics are employed in some Parisian hotels. And if this were one, I would have to rethink recommending this hotel to my social circle. Which would be a pity, as Paris is on all their agendas for this spring or summer.'

Pronovost smiled tautly. 'You have my assurance... on both, madame.'

'Lovely. Now, let's go to your office.'

Out in the corridor, he turned to her. 'I answered your requests. Why do we need to visit my office, madame?'

'For discretion,' she whispered, herding him towards the staff stairs. 'After all, the poor man died in your dining room.'

'But it was not my fault!'

She feigned horror. 'Then you must believe the *police nationale* are guilty!'

'I do,' he said defensively.

'Gracious, have you told Inspector Gripperel you think one of his men acted maliciously?'

'What?' he cried. 'Non, madame. I meant only that they were responsible for the thief falling because they chased him up onto my dining-room roof. Why did they not simply surround the hotel and get him down safely?'

That is an excellent point, Ellie! Why didn't they?

Leaving the baffled manager staring after her, she waved an adieu and bounded away up the stairs. Her thoughts were reeling. Had she unearthed their second suspect? One among the *police nationale* who was part of the fatal chase, and the thief's accomplice as well.

'And murderer!' she murmured.

Or was their first suspect, Pronovost, artfully deflecting suspicion off himself? To answer that question, she would need help. But not from the hotel's employees this time.

As she emerged through the swing door of the staff stairs, a disapproving cough came from behind her.

Ah, Ellie, just the man you were looking for!

14

Turning around, Eleanor was met by her butler's admonishing gaze.

'Ah! A new game of trumps you've conjured up, I see, Clifford. Count me in. Ready, steady, go!'

She tossed her head of steam-bedraggled curls while mirroring his stiff stance and pursed lips.

'My lady?' he said with a quizzical look.

'What? Keep up, Clifford. It was your idea to play best imitation of a constipated duck, but...' She slapped her leg in pantomime disappointment. 'You win! I can't compete with your years of practice.'

His eyes gave away his amusement at her teasing.

One of the desk clerks appeared, adjusting his suit jacket as he hurried towards his post. He jerked to a stop on seeing them.

'Is everything alright, madame?' he said hesitantly.

'Perfectly peachy, thank you.' She hoped he wouldn't ask what on earth she was doing by the door to the staff stairs.

'That is a "yes". Merci, monsieur,' Clifford added at the clerk's confused look.

Once he'd gone, she tugged Clifford by his sleeve into the guests' reading room, earning herself a round of tutting.

'Stop fussing, Clifford, do. I'm bursting to tell you my news. And to give my thoughts some logic and order.'

'Hmm, a second new experience this morning, m'lady? The first, seeing a clock before noon.'

Ignoring the quip, she quickly filled him in on everything she had learned from her conversation with Jules, Sophie and Cass. 'But Pronovost also gave me pause for thought. Why didn't Gripperel order his men to catch the thief safely?'

Clifford's brows twitched. 'Offhand, I do not know, my lady. However, despite the dismaying tactics employed in venturing below stairs, bravo on making headway with the investigation. And if I may now be permitted to try my hand, I might have an explanation forthwith?'

Saying nothing further, he glided away. She watched as the door closed behind him. Then stared down at her side.

'What the...?'

How he had slid a book under her arm without her noticing, she couldn't imagine. She rolled her eyes at the title: *The Ladies' Book of Etiquette*. Turning to the page from which her butler's familiar leather bookmark poked, she laughed. 'Chapter Four. How To Behave In A Hotel.' She started reading as she paced the floor.

How many minutes passed before Clifford returned she had no idea, but accompanying him was the welcome sight of a tray of divine-smelling coffee. And a plate of dainty breakfast pastries, offering tantalising wafts of chocolate, apricots and butter.

'Very thoughtful, thank you.' She dropped onto the burgundy-velvet settee.

'Actually, these come with the compliments of Jules, my lady,' Clifford said. 'Who mentioned my mistress's kindness to him and his colleagues. Which, distressingly, however, seems to have occurred in the laundry room.'

'Hence my soggy hair, which you've been dying to ask about, I know. But goodness, it was the least I could do. In fact, I'd appreciate your help in working out how I can do more.'

'It will be my pleasure, my lady.'

'Good. Now.' She eagerly accepted the coffee he held out. 'Ready to tell me what scallywag ruse you've just returned from then?'

'Tsk! In my defence, I can assure you that no scallywaggery was involved.'

'Shame.'

'Most assuredly,' he agreed, making her laugh again.

With a flourish he placed the generous selection of pastries before her. 'I went to speak to *les vitriers*. Or glaziers, to you and I. Having overheard—'

She halted his flow with a wave of a pain au chocolat which coated his impeccable shoes in a dusting of pastry flakes. 'Oops, sorry about the crumbs. But I simply have to ask. When did you suddenly become so fluent in French?'

'That is far from a claim I can make, my lady. However, I included a translation dictionary in my travelling valise. And also, coincidentally, happened to have elected to renew my study of the language recently.'

'Hmm? "Recently" being when Hugh confided in you that he was secretly planning to whisk us here for our honeymoon, was it?'

Clifford mimed buttoning his lips.

She smiled. 'Alright, I shan't press you any more on that because it was the most wonderful surprise. Please continue with your news.'

'As I was saying, my lady, I overheard just before we retired last night that a specialist firm of glaziers had been hurriedly instructed to repair the roof. The foreman particularly is extremely knowledgeable in regard to glass grading relative to tensile strength and soundproofing qualities.'

'Clifford?' she interrupted. 'Given it's barely six in the morning and my head should still be filled with fluffy dreams, maybe you could save me the technical side until later?'

He nodded apologetically. 'Noted. Salient facts only. In short, in his expert opinion, the damage must have been caused by the thief falling heavily against the glass to have crashed through in the way he did.'

'He's absolutely sure?'

'Categorically so, my lady. To the point, he annotated my pocketbook sketch of the roof as seen from the dining room below made last night. To make up where my hastily crammed French for all things glazing in the small hours of this morning failed me.' He opened his pocketbook and tapped the now familiar inked diagram.

She peered at it, understanding nothing of the neatly added notes. 'Very helpful of him. All the while, he was thinking you were just an egghead fascinated by the roof's architectural design and construction, I assume?'

'Regrettably so. That not being much of an accolade on which I wish to hang my bowler hat, as it were.'

She finished the last of the pastries and washed it down by draining her coffee cup. 'Top initiative on your part, Clifford. But where does that leave us—'

'Ahem, I have more to impart, my lady.'

'Gracious. Impart away!'

'The man also mentioned that Inspector Gripperel told him the thief tripped while running across the roof. Which is why he must have fallen through the atrium roof with such force.'

'What! Clifford, I know he didn't trip. I saw his face up against the glass just before he crashed through it.'

'Quite so, my lady. A fact neither the chief inspector nor myself doubt for a moment.'

'But then Gripperel must be lying! But why? Unless...'

'Unless he is the murderer?'

'Possibly.' She frowned and tapped her forehead. 'You know, my thoughts keep churning back to the museum guard who raised the alarm on seeing the thief, though.'

'Monsieur Rion?'

She pointed at him. 'Well remembered, thank you. Is it just me, or did he seem particularly perturbed when I told him the thief had died?'

'No, it seemed that way to me at the time also.'

'You know, I can't stop wondering if he knew the thief better than he said? After all, he denied recognising him at all to begin with. Is he mixed up in this, I wonder?'

'I concur again,' Clifford said. 'However, Monsieur Rion did also state he never left his post at which we found him from the time he reported seeing the thief running away.' He held up a finger. 'Actually, my error. He noted he left briefly when he went to check with Monsieur Omfroy in the records room.'

'Ah! He had to say that because we saw him there ourselves. Either way, Rion is a man we definitely need to question again. With a little bit of pressure, or guile, he might let something slip. And...' She held her hands up. 'Honestly, it sounds a lot easier than working out how on earth I'm going to look up Gripperel's trouser leg to see if he has a murderously damning cut on his shin!'

Clifford winced. 'I dread to think how. But experience tells me you will find a way. Albeit a mortifyingly less than ladylike one.'

They looked up at the sound of a familiar, rich chuckle in the doorway. Gladstone bowled in with a bemused-looking Seldon following. He stretched, then ran his hand through his chestnut curls, which left them unintentionally mussed. 'Morning, both. I've found you finally. But what's this about my wife doing something unladylike? Is that possible, Clifford?'

'Possible? No, sir. Highly probable, however? Most definitely!'

'Morning, Hugh,' she said, thinking even with him having washed and shaved, he looked even more dashing for being still a little bed-tousled. 'Oof! And Gladstone. Must you offer all your cuddles with such gusto, old chum?' She cradled his top half, which he had just hurled into her lap.

Seldon winced. 'Enjoy it. In your absence, I got your licky morning greeting as well as mine.' He sat down beside her and slid his arm around her waist. 'Eleanor, what on earth are you doing up at this hour? And what have I missed? Aside from the treat of waking up with you?' he ended in a whisper.

She snuggled into him. 'Oh, just Clifford being a total terror in his usual way.' She held up the book on etiquette he had slipped her.

'Ahem! And her ladyship managing to devour a breakfast aperitif large enough to be the meal itself, sir.' Clifford gestured at the empty tray.

Seldon smiled. 'I'm sorry to have missed watching you two squabble. However, I don't believe that's even the half of what you've been up to. But if you want to keep me in the dark,' he shrugged, 'so be it.'

'No, Hugh. It's not that.' Eleanor ardently linked her fingers in his. 'I was only trying not to spoil our honeymoon any more than I already have. So I slid away early to ask a few discreet questions of the staff. And Clifford quizzed the men repairing the atrium roof. So, if we grab an out of the way table, we can tell you everything we've each learned over breakfast.'

Gladstone stopped snuffling up her pastry crumbs on hearing his second favourite word. Sausages being his first.

Seldon squeezed her hand. 'Yes, please, Eleanor. Because if

you're determined to investigate, I want to be right alongside you at every step.'

'Thank you, Hugh,' she breathed, her worries over ruining their time in Paris diminishing a little.

'Now, let's eat and talk, you two. For some reason, I'm famished. And then we'll be free to visit the Eiffel Tower just as we'd planned yesterday, Eleanor. But only after we've taken a trip down the Seine, just you and me, because, well, you'll see...'

15

Seldon groaned. He lowered his voice as the three of them were far from alone in the street outside the hotel. 'Eleanor, Inspector Gripperel is a senior policeman. And one in a foreign country. For Pete's sake, you can't accuse him of murder without a court's worth of evidence. And even then...' He threw his hands up.

She folded her arms. 'A court's worth of evidence is exactly what I intend to get. But we've only just started finding suspects. I'm sure a lot more will emerge out of the woodwork soon. I... I just need a quick chat with these gentlemen first.'

She'd recognised the two policemen passing. The taller of the two was the one who had told Gripperel nothing had been found in the thief's pockets when they had been shown into the hotel manager's office. The other one had also been among those with Gripperel when he first arrived in the dining room.

Gracious, was that really only last night, Ellie?

She stepped over to them. 'Bonjour, Constables. Though that's possibly not the correct way to address you? My apologies. But gracious, have you been on duty all night long?'

'Oui, madame, we have. Bonjour, messieurs.' The box-jawed constable acknowledged Seldon and Clifford with a nod. His expression softened as Gladstone slipped his lead and charged over to say hello.

'Goodness, excuse his lack of manners,' Eleanor said. 'He's decided he's too old to be told off. And he has a thing about being attracted to policemen.'

'Both sound familiar?' Clifford murmured to her.

The square-jawed policeman squatted down, running his hands over Gladstone's jowls. 'He is like the French bulldog. But five times the size!'

'Mostly in terms of girth, sir.' Clifford gestured at the bull-dog's portly tum.

The constable laughed, too distracted to dodge the licky kiss Gladstone planted on his cheek.

'Well, it might have been a long night for you. But at least you're on safe ground now,' Eleanor said.

The policemen shared a baffled look. 'Madame?'

'I mean, you aren't still charging about on that dangerously shattered glass roof of our hotel. And in the dark, it's a wonder neither of you fell through, wouldn't you say?'

The policeman rose with an apologetic pat to Gladstone's head. 'We were not on the roof at any time, madame.'

Her skin prickled. 'None of your other colleagues, either?'

'No. When we all arrived at your hotel, the thief had already fallen.' He gave her a sympathetic nod. 'I am most sorry that this happened on your holiday.'

'Honeymoon,' Seldon corrected. 'But thank you for your concern for my wife.'

'Well, all credit for arriving so promptly after the poor chap fell,' she said. 'Did you come straight to the hotel after Monsieur Pronovost, the hotel manager, rang the police station?'

The policeman shook his head. 'No, again, madame. We were here at the museum because Monsieur Omfroy, the direc-tor, had telephoned. We were chasing the thief when he disappeared around the back of your hotel. We heard screaming from the front of the hotel and Inspector Gripperel ordered us inside.'

'Of course, that makes sense.' Her thoughts were whirling. 'Did you, by any chance, see anyone in the streets between the museum and the hotel?'

The policeman shrugged. 'There were people here and there, of course. This is Paris.'

'Ah, yes!'

'But,' the policeman continued, 'maybe the *police locale* saw someone, madame?'

Before she could stop him, he called out to two other policemen passing on the other side of the street.

Hacqueville and Bernier, Ellie. What are they doing here?

She rolled her eyes to herself. Of course! They'd been the first police to arrive at the hotel, so this was obviously their usual beat.

Hacqueville scowled at her, but Bernier gave her a smile, and, having listened to the *policier nationale*'s question, nodded. 'Yes. I saw someone. A guard from the museum. The one who raised the alarm. I almost knocked him down as we ran into each other on the corner of Rue de Poulignac.'

'Monsieur Rion?' she said casually, her heart beating a little faster. 'I wonder what he was doing out while on his shift.'

Hacqueville was looking daggers at his partner, but Bernier ignored him. 'He must have been chasing the thief also, I think, madame. But was returning to his post because he saw the police had taken up the chase.'

Hacqueville spun his partner around and muttered something angrily in his ear. Bernier pulled back, looking angry himself. 'I am sorry, madame,' he said, addressing Eleanor again, 'but it seems we are wanted urgently elsewhere. Good day.'

He touched the peak of his cap and strolled off with his partner.

Obviously not that urgently, Ellie.

Once they were alone, Clifford pulled a meticulously folded map of Paris and his pince-nez from his coat pocket. She and Seldon joined him around it as if discussing where to go next.

'Good work, Eleanor,' Seldon said quietly. 'That gave us a lot of new information.'

She frowned. 'If what those two *police nationale* just told us is true though, that puts Inspector Gripperel and his men in the clear.'

'And if what Bernier said is also true, propels Monsieur Rion more firmly to the top of the suspect list, perhaps?' Clifford said.

'Given he swore he hadn't left his post after raising the alarm, save for a brief trip to the records room, I'd say so,' Seldon agreed.

'Plus, he lied about never having seen the thief before when we first asked him, remember.' Her brow furrowed further. 'But did Rion get as far as our hotel roof? And was he the one who pushed the thief through it? Could he realistically have done it? You're our time guru, Clifford.'

He studied the map. 'Here is the museum, my lady. And just over here is our hotel. And Rue de Poulignac... is here.' He pointed on the map again. 'So, I would conjecture that Monsieur Rion would have been missing from the museum for at least ten to fifteen minutes.'

'Still a short enough absence for it not to have been noticed in all the confusion, perhaps?'

Seldon rubbed his hand over his chin. 'True. But Hacqueville, and Bernier, also had time to push the thief off the roof before we saw them in the hotel restaurant. And so did Pronovost, especially as he could have used the service stairs to the roof. He'd have access to the keys.'

She grimaced. 'True. We've still so many other unanswered questions. Like who the poor dead man even was?'

If you knew that, Ellie, maybe it would answer the other questions about the brooch and Christophe's paintings running around your head?

Seldon nodded. 'True. But for once, pressing as those and other questions are, they can wait a while.' Taking her by the shoulders, he spun her around, leaving a fleeting glimpse of Clifford melting away. 'We came here for a honeymoon, Eleanor, and if it's the last thing we do in this city, we're going to have one!'

16

The boat ride along the Seine was even more of a treat than she had expected. And not just because she could forget, almost, about murder for a few hours. Seeing Paris from such a different perspective was wonderful. There were even more amazing buildings lining the river than she'd thought, each extravagant enough to be a palace. Seldon was more garrulous and relaxed than she'd ever known him. And Gladstone was his usual entertaining self, balanced on Seldon's lap, woofing at every boat they passed and delighting in the wind fluttering through his jowls.

Having bought return tickets, she was surprised when Seldon looked up from studying both the map and guidebook and pointed at the jetty the boat was pulling into.

'Off we get!'

'But we're only halfway down the river, Hugh.'

'Help a man out by not asking questions when he's trying to pull off something quietly, can't you?' he whispered.

What he had come up with, she couldn't fathom, but that he had thought of a surprise made her shoulders rise with happiness. Still, she was baffled, given they were now walking along the street level with their boat chugging alongside.

'Ah!' he said after a few minutes. 'You need to go and read that plaque and admire that statue of... Well, that statue over there while I... go somewhere.'

'Say no more!' She set off with Gladstone in tow. The statue was of some character from Paris's long and colourful past. But as she couldn't read French, she couldn't work out what he was famous for. Seldon was gone for a while and just as she was starting to worry, his deep voice tickled her ear.

'Right. On we go.'

She spun around, her hands flying to her mouth at what he was holding.

'Oh, Hugh! You've bought a beautiful potted rose tree! A bunch, or even a single stem, would have been romantic enough. We'll have to take turns carrying the gorgeous thing for the rest of the afternoon.'

'No, we won't.'

Without further explanation, he led her through an impressive wrought-iron gate into a park laid with vast expanses of perfectly tended lawns, flower beds, and spreading trees dotted with elegant fountains and statues.

What's he looking for, Ellie?

Or who? She realised, as he stopped by one of the park gardeners on his knees in a flower bed. A conversation entirely in charades followed, which involved her being beckoned over to join them, still none the wiser.

'Un symbole pour bénir votre mariage? Mais, bien sûr, monsieur!' the groundsman said. Beaming, he clapped Seldon on the shoulder and winked at Eleanor. Pointing behind them, he tapped his forehead and his watering can at the same time. 'I can, er... care for this for you,' he managed in English, to his, and Seldon's delight.

Seldon pulled out his wallet, only to have it waved away.

'Pour l'amour toujours, monsieur,' the groundsman said softly.

As they crept through the tall plants into the middle of the flower bed they had been pointed to with a now very excited Gladstone, she turned to him.

'Hugh, have you just arranged to plant this lovely rose tree here in honour of our marriage?'

He nodded. 'Yes. Lucky he was such an understanding fellow. But honestly, if he had said no, I would have done it anyway.'

'And you a policeman!' she teased.

'Not today. Nor for the rest of our honeymoon.' He cupped her cheeks. 'The moment I arranged things so we could honeymoon in Paris as a surprise for you, I wanted to leave a testament to our love here. I've been racking my brains to think of something ever since.' He looked abashed. 'But I'm hopeless at romance, and this is the best—'

'—way you could ever tell your wife you love her,' she interrupted, eyes swimming. 'You hopeless at romance? Never! But we should have asked that chap if we could borrow his spade.'

Seldon shook his head. 'And spoil Gladstone's fun? He's part of our family too, remember?'

The pair of them were soon showered in earth, trying to stifle their laughter at the sight of Gladstone digging with gusto. The tree carefully set in the hole, Seldon slipped two tiny silver hearts in side by side among its roots before filling in the earth. He took both of her hands over the top of the roses.

'Eleanor, my love for you already courses through every fibre of me. And makes my heart fit to burst. But it will grow more every day. Like this rose tree. Which will never be as beautiful as you. Even when we're in our eighties.'

She thought she might explode with happiness as he robbed her of her breath with a tender kiss. And then a passionate one.

He finally pulled away. 'Now, I spotted a bandstand in the guidebook that I'd like to waltz you around. If that suits, my lady?' he said with a courtly bow.

Afterwards, they visited the cosy café in the gardens. As they waited for their tea to arrive, and Clifford, as Seldon confessed he'd arranged to meet him there, she sighed in contentment.

'You know, you couldn't have picked anywhere more perfect for our honeymoon, Hugh. Paris is a truly special place.'

He nodded. 'London probably has some lovely parts in its own way, too. I never have time to notice.'

She grimaced. 'That's because you're normally mired in its grittier side. Up to your neck in the worst of what people can do.'

'Someone has to,' he said soberly. 'But since you've mentioned it. Eleanor, I'm still seriously contemplating leaving the police force now that we're married.'

She scanned his face. 'If it would make you happier, Hugh?'

He smiled ruefully. 'See, you do understand me sometimes. Because the answer, as you've already worked out, is no. I'd feel guilty. Terribly guilty.' He seemed to drift away into his thoughts. 'But you've also solved terrible crimes, Eleanor. And caught the culprit, too. Which has made my heart stop every time, by the way,' he muttered. 'And you've proven the police wrong on more than one occasion.'

'With Clifford's help. And his endless calls of "Prudence, my lady!"'

'All of which your impetuousness has ignored.'

'Not deliberately. Besides, the three of us together have been an even better team. The best! Ha! Maybe you, me and Clifford should start our own detective agency,' she joked.

'I've thought of that. A lot, actually,' Seldon said to her amazement. 'But it would never work.'

'Why not?'

'Because, my darling wife, in the few short hours since we've been investigating this murder alone, you've shown me how likely it is we'd all be arrested every time! And I couldn't get you out of jail if I was incarcerated myself.'

'Arrested for what?'

He hushed her gently and whispered, 'How about, this time for instance, withholding evidence from the police?'

'I know.' She reached for her coffee cup, but pulled her hand back, feeling an inexplicable tremble at the thought of giving the pearl pendant brooch up to Gripperel.

'Cold, my love?' Seldon said, shrugging out of his jacket.

She shook her head. 'No, just wishing I hadn't spoiled our honeymoon by getting us caught up in this awful business.'

'Which your selfless compassion will never forgive you for if you don't solve it.' He pressed his fingers to her lips, stopping her from reminding him they had agreed not to talk about it until later. 'It's fine.' He pointed to the door. 'Here comes Clifford. We can all walk to the Eiffel Tower together.'

'Ahem, sir?'

Seldon frowned. 'Hello, Clifford. What's up?'

He half bowed to Eleanor. 'I thought it might be of interest to mention I spotted a certain Monsieur Omfroy in a gentleman's outfitter not that far from here.' His eyes twinkled. 'I wondered if it might be an opportunity for her ladyship to, ahem, discreetly question the gentleman further?'

Seldon chuckled, rising in unison with Eleanor. 'I doubt if "discreetly" comes into it, but I'm sure she'll have a go anyway!' He dodged her slap. 'Lead the way.'

17

As Eleanor and Seldon hurried after Clifford, Gladstone picked up on the excitement and charged on ahead, his lead at full stretch.

'Restrain yourself!' she chided gently. 'We're supposed to be cutting a sophisticated image.'

'Perhaps I should retire with Master Gladstone for a brief excursion, more in keeping with his interests?' Clifford said. 'Like the nearest bottomless buffet.'

'I thought you were talking about the sausage monster, not my wife,' Seldon said, which clearly tickled Clifford's mischievous sense of humour as he turned away, feigning a cough.

Eleanor laughed. 'Hilarious, you two.'

Seldon put a restraining arm on Clifford's shoulder. 'Hang on, you can't leave me with Omfroy trying to bluff my way through sounding like I know a decent painting from a... a tattooed cat's elbow!'

Clifford winced. 'Wholeheartedly noted, sir. And with her ladyship also needing some assistance in such matters.'

Eleanor waved at her bulldog, who was now trying to yank a

discarded boot sideways through the narrow iron railings of the park alongside.

'I propose when we get inside the outfitters, I simply play the unorthodox lady who dotes on her beloved bulldog's every whim.'

'Though any pretence therein is?' Clifford gestured them onwards.

Before they could reach the gentleman's outfitters, however, they were met by the fantastically sculpted side whiskers and moustache of Monsieur Omfroy emerging onto the street.

He regarded them with a look of alarm. She reciprocated with a genial wave, fleetingly wondering if there was a Madame Omfroy in his life, or if his facial hair was companion enough. Today his jacket was a sombre, single-breasted, striped black and charcoal affair. Conversely, his cravat was an eye-popping riot of fiery-orange sunflowers.

She observed him with a sceptical eye. After all, he was working late the night of the robbery. Unusually, it seemed. And even if he was guiltless, as director of the museum he might be able to fill them in on some background information which might help them catch a killer.

'Madame, I did not expect to see you again after your visit late last night.' His tone was suspicious. 'You insisted, most emphatically, that you were leaving Paris.'

'What a marvellous memory you have, Monsieur Omfroy,' she said airily.

Omfroy's brow furrowed. 'I do not believe you answered my question, madame?'

'Didn't I? Oh, do you see how full my head is with dreaming of the artistic wonders which my collection awaits? I'm so grateful that we have met so fortuitously. And so flattered that someone as busy and in demand as yourself would be willing to take time from your hectic schedule,' she gushed, noting that it seemed not to have had the disarming effect she had hoped for. She clapped her hands. 'Now, some advice, if you would be so kind?'

'Perhaps ask the director of another art museum, madame? Paris has many,' he said weakly.

She tittered. 'What a wag you are! I meant advice on what would best enhance my collection?'

Omfroy blinked hard. 'Madame, are you really asking me to believe you are a collector?'

'Well, why not!' she cried, as if he'd slapped her face. She folded her arms. 'It's because I'm a woman, isn't it? Outrageous!'

Clifford tutted while Gladstone let out a snort that made his jowls flap and Seldon held Omfroy in a firm stare. 'Perhaps you would tell this gentleman just how large her ladyship's collection is, Clifford?'

'The main portfolio currently stands at one hundred and twenty-seven works of art. And then there are, of course, those housed in her ladyship's Irish castle.'

While that was true, she couldn't claim any credit. It had all been included in her uncle's bequest to her. And a fair few were simply paintings of his beloved bulldog, she had to admit.

Omfroy looked down at the pavement as if hoping it might swallow him up. 'Madame, my sincere apology. I did not mean to cause offence. Perhaps you can tell me the most important thing that you seek in a painting for it to be worthy of joining your collection?'

'The artist's story!' she said passionately. 'Just as I have yearned to know since seeing the displays of your Impressionist painters.'

'Ah!' His voice was keener. 'Then I think, for you, my museum has achieved all that I work so hard for it to do. After your visit you were a changed person, yes?'

She put her hands together reverently. 'No, monsieur. I was a *better* person.'

His gaze became wistful. 'And it is of the Impressionists you wish to hear more? Then I will tell you. In the first room, you will have seen...'

She nodded along as he expounded on the painters featured in the museum, making appreciative noises at intervals. But she took little in until she heard one name.

'And Christophe Ury's paintings are displayed next. I am particularly pleased with the reconstruction of his art studio. Such a detailed picture his personal items themselves paint of the brilliant man behind the easel.'

'That's possibly where I had the strongest feeling,' she said thoughtfully.

Especially to one item, Ellie.

'Can you tell me about him?'

'Sadly, he is dead, madame. But when he was alive, ah! What a genius! Especially after he returned to France. From then on, he was a most prolific artist. His paintings I have on display are but a soupçon of all that he created. They are loaned from the Galerie Delorme, where you will find the largest collection of his most-important works still available for sale.'

'And where is this gallery?'

'In Rue Coeur de Lion, in the distinguished Saint-Georges district of the city. Monsieur Delorme is a true connoisseur. And he also knows the story of each artist he displays. He would be delighted to assist you in choosing the very best paintings to enhance your collection.'

'How perfect! Monsieur Omfroy, you've been too good to me.'

He bowed. 'My pleasure, madame. Perhaps you will not think me rude if I continue with my day now?'

'Not at all!'

He shot away down the street.

'Probably gone to lock himself in his office back at the museum until he knows you've left Paris for sure, Eleanor. Poor fellow!' Seldon said.

She laughed. 'Probably, Hugh. And while he does, let's visit this gallery he was talking about and have a word with this Delorme. Any acquaintance of Omfroy's is instantly suspect to my mind!'

18

A few minutes later, Eleanor realised what Clifford was up to. Having all agreed in the lovely April sunshine they fancied walking to Galerie Delorme, he had appointed himself map reader. And impromptu tour guide. With his store of fascinating historical snippets and amusing anecdotes about the beautiful buildings, impressive monuments, and intriguing statues they passed, all thoughts of murder were forgotten. Well, pushed to the back of the mind for a while at least. And replaced with the feeling that, once again, they were finally on a relaxing, sightseeing honeymoon in the most romantic city in the world.

She mouthed a thank you to her butler, who nodded imperceptibly in acknowledgement and tapped his nose.

Ah, he's got something else up his sleeve, Ellie.

At one of the ancient bridges over the Seine, they paused to enjoy the passing ballet of the few remaining steam-powered passenger boats, or *'bateau-mouches'*, as Clifford informed them they were called. Then turned to marvel at the famous Notre-Dame Cathedral, adding it to their list of must return to sights.

Further on, Clifford pointed to a tower. 'That clock on our

left is the oldest in all of Paris. Commissioned by Charles V in 1370. Though the external face was not added until 1419.'

'But that means its workings are over five hundred years old,' Seldon said in amazement, staring up at the striking gold-and-blue timepiece.

'What do the female figurines either side of the clock represent?' she asked.

'Law. And Justice, my lady.'

Now she understood. He hadn't come this way just to indulge his passion for all things clock related. He'd known how reassuring she would find the timelessness of those two symbols. Standing together, as an enduring declaration to every inhabitant of Paris, that evil would be rooted out and punished. Sending each of the figurines a silent plea to help her solve the thief's murder, she turned to thank Clifford, who, however, tapped his nose again.

Ah! Something more up his sleeve, Ellie.

'Look there, Eleanor,' Seldon said a few moments later. 'People are selling their paintings along the railings on this side of the river. Like Rion told us he'd noticed the thief doing.' He scooped her arm in his. 'Come on. You're itching to ask anyone you can about him. And we might find a picture to buy and take home to remind us of our honeymoon.'

Immensely relieved he seemed reconciled to juggling the two opposing strands of their trip, she nodded keenly.

At the riverside, the selection of paintings for sale was as diverse as the ingenuity of the artists in displaying their wares on their few square feet of pavement and railings. The level of skill was universally accomplished; scenes of Paris with her iconic buildings and spectacular skyline abounded. Possibly hoping to appeal to tourists, she thought. Or perhaps Parisians loved their city so much they adorned their walls with its artwork?

There were also numerous still-life studies; bottles of wine, cheese and fruit, all looking tantalisingly real. And several surreal dreamlike-scapes that reminded her of the Impressionist paintings in the museum. Most interestingly, there were copious nudes. Clifford and Seldon chivalrously looked away, which made her smile.

She noticed that lots of people were stopping to look, but few seemed interested in buying. Rion's remark that the thief sold little to nothing flooded back. She dismissed the thought and concentrated on enquiring if anyone knew who the thief was.

The three of them split up. The first artist she asked, however, was so intent on adjusting his display, he ignored her totally. Despite this, she left the money for a selection of hand-painted postcards featuring a cheeky cat and dog stealing fish and joints of beef from the baskets of oblivious shoppers.

The next artist was a bespectacled, earnest young man whose work comprised intricate sketches of architectural columns and arches. He shrugged helplessly at her English. Clifford suggested he try with his more practised French, leaving her free to move on to another artist. This time, one in his late thirties, with a voluminous shock of blond-corkscrew curls that was art enough in itself. And his exquisite paintings of mostly sunrises and sunsets were as engaging as his hopeful smile. Seldon passed with a whispered, 'Good luck!'

'Bonjour, madame. You are English or American, perhaps?' the artist said.

'English,' she replied. 'And I love the imaginative setting of your gallery. I've seen nothing quite like it in London.'

He waved the sketchpad he held. 'It has been the tradition for painters in Paris for ever.'

'And is it always the same artists here?'

'No. It is the first to arrive who can claim the space of six railings for the half-day. This is the agreement.'

That wasn't the answer she'd hoped for. 'Oh, so you wouldn't know then if an artist... suddenly stopped coming?'

He shook his head. 'Not unless I knew him, or the other artists in my commune talk of it. But no one there has made mention of such a thing.'

'Your commune?'

'Oui, madame. Most of us artists stay in communes.' He shrugged. 'We have a different temperament to those who do not see art as the only point of life. Because of this, there are several communes spread around Paris.'

'So, if I wanted to track down a painter who sells his works here, which commune should I start asking in?'

He shrugged. 'Any. Most are outside the centre, in the cheap areas. The biggest one is in Montmartre. What style of painting would this mysterious missing painter favour?'

It was her turn to shrug. 'Er... Impressionism?'

He nodded. 'Then definitely start in Montmartre.'

Clifford arrived with two rolled canvases under his arm, Gladstone trotting beside him. She bade the painter a cheery '*au revoir*' and set off with her butler to track down Seldon. Maybe he'd learned something useful.

Having caught up with him, and pretended she didn't notice he was hiding his purchases under his jacket, they carried on, none of them having found out anything of note.

'Well, look on the bright side,' she said cheerily. 'When we meet this gallery owner he's bound to be convinced we're bona fide art lovers. Given we'll arrive with our hands full of masterpieces.'

Clifford's brows flinched as he peered at her dog and cat themed postcards and light-hearted depictions of Parisians at play. 'Ahem, if you will forgive my offering a contrary view, my lady. I think they may be best hidden from sight.'

From the depths of his coat, he produced a black-cloth shoulder bag with a magician's flourish and unbuckled it.

'A stroke of luck you had that with you, Clifford,' Seldon said, sliding his purchase in without Eleanor seeing what it was.

Clifford mimed buttoning his lips.

She shook her head. 'What my butler is trying to restrain his razor wit from replying, Hugh, is that sober experience told him he'd need it if I got the merest whiff of a shopping opportunity.'

'Alas, the more appropriate four-wheeled sack barrow was unavailable, sir,' Clifford said mischievously.

Seldon's rich chuckle rang out. 'Come on, let's find this gallery. And then we can get on with more honeymooning. And shopping!'

Twenty minutes later, in the upmarket *arrondissement* of Saint-Georges, they found Galerie Delorme. Eleanor's immediate impression was that a daunting world she knew nothing about awaited inside. She gazed along the run of arched gold windows fanning back either side of its gleaming white stone façade. The double front door was an impressive ten foot high forest of sculpted bronze strands depicting something too abstract for her to fathom.

'No point putting it off,' she murmured.

'Indeed, my lady,' Clifford said. 'The inevitable egg on face suffered can be attended to swiftly afterwards, after all.'

'Very funny!'

Seldon stepped forward, looking for a door handle. For a moment, he stared at it in puzzlement. Then stepped back as the sea of bronze parted in the centre as if by an invisible silent force, revealing an acre of pristine ivory carpet beyond.

Clifford hurriedly scooped Gladstone up and followed Eleanor and Seldon inside.

The first thing that struck her was the feeling of walking on air. Air perfumed with vanilla and jasmine. On every wall were paintings set in gilt frames, pearl-white cards embossed in gold lettering mounted centrally beneath each one. The cards listed the title of the work and the artist's name. And the price! Even

given the overall ostentatiousness of this palace of art, the prices
were astronomical. She shook her head. It made no sense. Why
would the thief have risked breaking into a museum packed full
of eye-wateringly valuable paintings like these, and yet seemingly made no attempt to steal any of them? Her hand strayed to
the brooch in her pocket, the same feeling she had in the hotel
restaurant coming back, but more strongly. There was something about it that was... comforting?

But why, Ellie?

If only she could grasp it, she felt the answer might help
explain what exactly she was doing there. And why it mattered
so much.

19

A handful of elegantly suited and fur-trimmed potential buyers were spread across the saffron-velvet settees, each eyeing a painting or two from various angles. In the centre of the gallery, a glass staircase wound up to evidently yet more works available solely to the wealthy elite. It was from there a medium-framed man in a blue silk suit the colour of French banknotes was descending with the demeanour of an emperor. He paused on the bottom step and threw Eleanor a provocative smile.

'Bonjour, madame,' he announced, stroking the eye-catching lilac ruff at his neck. 'I am Monsieur Bellamy Delorme. Welcome to my gallery. You have arrived at the ultimate word in fine art.'

'And what made you assume I am English?' she retorted in her best lady of the manor tone.

'Ah, that would be telling, madame,' he replied with a rakish wiggle of his dark eyebrows. Now he was standing in front of her, she noted his wide, somewhat flattened features. And the greying strands at his temples which he had attempted to conceal by brushing his hair forwards. His scrutinising gaze left her feeling she was being sized up, wealth-wise.

Flicking her hand out to the side, her thumb and forefinger closed on her calling card, which magically appeared courtesy of her ever-ready butler.

She handed it to Delorme, looking around with a slight wrinkling of her nose. Turning to Seldon, she pouted. 'Darling, I'm not at all sure we shouldn't be elsewhere. We agreed on a unique piece and nothing less.'

'I know what you mean, my dear,' he murmured, clearly playing along.

Delorme looked up from reading her calling card with an eager glint in his eyes. 'But, Lady Swift, my gallery is famed for being the pinnacle of the exclusive!'

She sighed. 'Oh, very well! I suppose I might look about for a moment.'

He smiled like a hungry crocodile. 'Perhaps if you will permit me to be your personal guide? Together we will find a work of art to make your little heart sing.'

'Really! I want something to enhance my prized collection. Not titivate my insides.' She clucked her tongue. 'Oh, do explain to this gentleman, won't you, Clifford?'

Her butler beckoned Delorme to one side. 'Sir, her ladyship has deigned to visit your gallery on the strength of a single recommendation; that the owner is a connoisseur of Impressionist art. And neither disappointment nor time-wasting are favoured, trust me,' he ended pointedly.

'Impressionist!' Delorme put his fleshy hands together, revealing an enormous watch on one wrist and an elaborate gold bracelet on the other. 'Ah! Lady Swift, I can promise you are in the right gallery. Please, come upstairs. And I will introduce you to the finest treasures of the Impressionist movement.'

'My wife will judge for herself, thank you!' Seldon said firmly.

'And you will be able to evidence any painting's provenance

her ladyship might wish to purchase? To prove its authenticity,' Clifford said.

Delorme's eyes lit up. 'But, of course! Monsieur Omfroy himself, director of the Musée d'Art Contemporain, has independently verified each work hanging in my gallery as a genuine oeuvre of the artist listed. He is, along with myself I might modestly say, the most-respected expert on Impressionist painters in France!'

She nodded. 'I have met Monsieur Omfroy.' She graciously took his proffered arm with her fingertips as they ascended the stairs.

On the second floor, there was an impressive number of paintings hung along the walls and down each face of the eight ornate pillars. And there were fewer other potential buyers up here, she was pleased to see. Just two suited gentlemen and a woman with an eye-catching feathered fascinator, along with a hunched figure in a black coat and hat, seated on a saffron banquette seat. He was leaning on his elbows, apparently absorbed by the selection of sculptures in front of him. As she stepped past him, she stiffened. It was the man with the uncommonly large umbrella she had teased Clifford would be the perfect companion for him, given their clearly shared obsession with being prepared for the worst. For a moment, she felt unnerved. She had first noticed him while in Gripperel's car en route to the museum. Was he following them then? And now?

She glanced discreetly at him again. No, he hadn't even registered she was there, his gaze still transfixed on the works of art.

Perhaps just a rather unorthodox-looking art aficionado, Ellie?

Deciding she was being over-fanciful to think anything else, she refocused on the job at hand. Homing in on one particular painting at random, she stepped slowly towards it, with Seldon and Clifford following. Cocking her chin, she pretended to study it.

'No, after the first impression, this, like the others so far, falls short.'

'Both in derivable significance and emotions evoked, perhaps, my lady?' Clifford added.

'Well, naturally, in both. But mostly the former.' She tutted dismissively as if he had noted it was oxygen they were breathing.

'But you did so want to invest in a work of art while we were passing through Paris, darling,' Seldon said indulgently. 'Keep looking, just in case. I can't bear you being disappointed.'

Delorme's grey-attired assistant appeared holding out a tray of four filled champagne flutes.

'Alright.' She glided on around the walled displays with her glass of bubbles, Delorme trailing in her wake as if not wanting to interrupt her focus. Out of the corner of her eye, she spotted Clifford had peeled off to the central section. A moment later, his quiet cough reached her.

Ah! It seems that's where we should be, Ellie.

She continued on around, feigning increasing disillusionment. As she neared the central section, she let out a cry. 'Oh, now maybe... Christophe Ury! I believe these works might be his?'

'You are right, Lady Swift,' Delorme purred from behind.

She joined Clifford, quietly swallowing her incredulity at the price. Gratefully, she listened to his murmured words, then repeated them loudly. 'I like how Ury's influences from Renoir are so subtly cached. Hints of mid-period Van Gogh, too. And a delightful soupçon of Monet's earlier works,' she said, as if that were her everyday topic of conversation.

Delorme's nodding told her that her butler had helped her drop just the right names.

'A not entirely unworthy choice of works from which to

choose a complement to your Pissarros and Courbets, perhaps, my lady?' Clifford said.

Delorme failed to hide his gasp at the suggestion she owned such treasures.

'Let's get Hugh's view. Darling?' she called.

Seldon joined them, his champagne in hand. 'Hmm,' he said thoughtfully, cocking his ear to catch Clifford's murmured prompts to him this time. 'Interesting composition. Tone and palette in sympathetic harmony, too. Not too long a mile from that Degas we're still thinking of buying.'

'True. But we couldn't possibly decide without knowing more about the artist,' she said.

Delorme joined them, holding an open champagne bottle, eyes animated. He topped up her glass.

'If I might be of assistance, Lady Swift. But first, perhaps you will permit me to say you have a fine eye. Because Christophe Ury's works are sitting poised to soar further in value.'

'Well naturally, Monsieur Delorme. I wouldn't be considering purchasing one otherwise,' she said tartly. 'But what of Ury himself? I know a little, naturally. But I need to know if he is worthy of a space in my collection.'

He held his hands up. 'Ury was a creative genius until he died in 1899. He was inspired at the beginning of his career by the years when he lived on a tropical island. After some time, he returned to France. To Paris, or near Paris.' He checked himself and hurried on. 'His early works I do not have on display.'

'Why not?'

'Because they are inferior to his later masterpieces, Lady Swift. They are a period of experimenting, of perfecting his Impressionist style. Needed, to be sure, to reach the transcendent standard of those I do have on display.' He waved a hand reverently at the paintings.

For the next few minutes, he talked about technique and

form or some such things she hadn't come to find out about. Each time she steered a question back to Christophe Ury, the man, however, Delorme turned it on its head. Relating his answer to a different one of his paintings, which he led her to. It was soon obvious he knew little else of Ury's background. She switched tack.

'It was Monsieur Omfroy himself who recommended I visit your gallery,' she said. 'The robbery was terrible news. I'm surprised I didn't meet you there last night, now I think of it.'

The gallery owner's manner was suddenly less effusive. He ran his hand over his brow as if trying to smooth out the frown that now dogged it. 'I had no reason to be there, Lady Swift. Last night, like usual, I was here until late. Working alone. I heard only of the theft later.'

'But surely you were concerned about the paintings your gallery has loaned the museum? Any one or more could have been stolen.'

Delorme fiddled with his lilac neck ruff. 'Monsieur Omfroy telephoned me late last night and reassured me all the paintings and personal effects I have lent the museum were accounted for. Only one trifle of little value from Ury's past life was stolen, I believe.'

Inexplicably, she bristled, as if she had been personally insulted. 'You call a pearl brooch of little value?'

He laughed. 'Compared to the value of a single painting, yes. Besides, the pearls are false, of course.'

She stiffened. Then forced herself to relax.

'But the sign I read next to the empty display case said the brooch was given to Christophe Ury by a rich widow. She wouldn't have given Ury a fake?'

Delorme tutted. 'Of course not! But Ury was practically penniless his whole life. I imagine he sold the pearls immediately, and swapped them for imitations, but kept the brooch for some sort of sentimental reason.'

'I assume as an expert on Christophe Ury, you're most likely to know who the thief was?'

'Me? I have no idea who it was,' Delorme protested, rather too quickly to her mind.

'When did Monsieur Omfroy telephone you?' she said.

'Oh, I cannot remember.' Delorme's smile returned as he tugged his right jacket cuff down. 'As you can see, Lady Swift, I do not permit a clock to hang on any wall of my gallery. This is a temple for art only.'

Hmm, what about the swanky watch he's covering up, Ellie?

He lowered his voice. 'You will forgive me saying, but talk of robbery is not a conversation I naturally wish my clients to overhear.'

She looked around. Everyone but them had left. Even the umbrella man had abandoned his seat.

'But we're alone. Save for your assistant over there.'

Delorme shook his head. 'This building has many echoes, Lady Swift.' He raised his voice again. 'Let us talk more about Ury's paintings. Because, oh la la! The interest in his work is increasing every minute we are standing here looking to decide. And with his being dead, he cannot paint any more.'

Seldon frowned at him and took her arm. 'Monsieur, my wife will not be pressured into buying anything!'

'Indeed. I believe we are done. Thank you for your time, Monsieur Delorme,' she said, steering Seldon towards the stairs. It was only then she realised Clifford had disappeared with Gladstone.

Delorme hurried after them. 'Lady Swift, I was not trying to hurry your decision!' he flustered. 'I am stricken with shame you think I, Bellamy Delorme, would try such a thing. Let me make a gift of an apology to you.'

'Such as?' she said indifferently.

'Tonight, I am invited to an exclusive cocktail reception in Gustav Eiffel's "secret" apartment at the very top of the Eiffel

Tower. Few people even know it exists. Eiffel would only entertain eminent scientists and engineers there. But he died just
over a year ago. And the new owner, as a true art lover, is much
more enlightened. Unfortunately, neither my partner nor I are
now free to attend. Would you consider taking our place?'

The idea of seeing a hidden part of Paris's iconic landmark
filled her with excitement. The views would be incredible. And
so romantic!

'Well, perhaps we might find time for it, darling?' Seldon
evidently thought the same.

'Alright, thank you for your kind offer, Monsieur Delorme,'
she said graciously. 'We shall return tomorrow to let you know
which of Ury's paintings I may be interested in.'

'Parfait!' he declared. From his pocket he produced a gold-
embossed invitation card.

As she and Seldon stepped out of the gallery, Clifford was
waiting on the pavement outside.

'Thank you for bailing me out in there,' Seldon said to him
once they were around the corner.

'And me!' she added gratefully. 'What we learned about
Christophe Ury might help solve a part of this mystery in the
future. You never know.'

Clifford cleared his throat. 'If you will forgive the correction, my lady, I believe you may be wrong.'

She and Seldon looked at him in surprise.

'What you learned may help solve part of this mystery right
now,' he continued. 'You see, whilst you were concluding your
business with Monsieur Delorme inside, outside, ahem, the plot
thickened considerably!'

20

'Listen!' Eleanor said as patiently as she could manage after she was steered past a third café. 'Much as I truly appreciate your chivalry, I won't fall into a fit of the vapours if there's sawdust on the floor and no tablecloths. When I made it around the world on my bicycle, I just had to make do with what came along. And I didn't have room for luxuries in my meagre panniers. Goodness knows, I barely had enough changes of under—'

'I don't doubt that,' Seldon interrupted hurriedly. 'But "making do" was before you became my wife.'

'And I, your butler, my lady,' Clifford added. 'However, perhaps that establishment might be a reasonable compromise, sir?' He gestured to a pretty tile-fronted café with red-and-white cane chairs set around the three outside tables.

In the most tucked away corner inside, and with their order given, she leaned forward. 'Now, before I'm even more compelled to beat your head against this table, Clifford, tell us what you meant about "the plot thickening considerably", please?'

'Very well. I was informed of a most surprising fact, my lady.'

'By who?'

'A mysterious voice,' Clifford said enigmatically.

Her reply was interrupted by their coffees arriving along with a bowl of water and a handful of meat scraps for Gladstone.

'Merci beaucoup,' she said sincerely.

Once the waiter had gone, she spread her hands on the table. 'Clifford, what voice? You met us in the street right outside the gallery. Well, just a few yards from that funny little green structure—' She caught his and Seldon's cheeks colouring. 'Oh, I see! I didn't realise it was a gentlemen's, um, stand-up facility. So someone came in behind you then, Clifford?' She suppressed a smile at his shudder. 'But naturally, you couldn't turn to find out who it was. Sorry for almost pressing you for the, er, finer details.'

Clifford briefly closed his eyes. 'If we might move on, my lady?'

'Good idea,' Seldon agreed readily. 'What did the voice say?'

'That "the dead man the lady is asking about is—"'

'Yes?' she couldn't help interrupting.

'"Emile Ury!"'

She gasped. 'Ury? That can't be a coincidence!'

Seldon rubbed his chin thoughtfully. 'Assuming it's true?'

'Dash it! I hadn't thought of that.' She shrugged. 'Suppose for the moment it is. And that whoever told you... I assume it was a man?'

'The only sliver of a silver lining in the otherwise ignominious encounter, yes,' Clifford said, clearly horrified by the alternative.

'Right. So, if we assume he was telling the truth, do we also assume he was a friend or a foe?'

Seldon's brow furrowed. 'Hopefully a friend. Because the fact that someone knew to deliver that message to Clifford means we haven't been as discreet as we thought!'

'You mean I haven't, Hugh.' She sighed, not wanting to hear what she imagined was burning on his tongue.

Clifford melted away, pretending to admire a particularly drab framed photograph no one could be interested in.

Seldon held his hands up. 'Eleanor, I'm not going to plead that you be cautious, careful or anything else I know is the opposite of the captivating and beautiful way you're made. Because I promised a while ago I would stop doing that. But I waited an eternity to be able to spend the rest of my life with you, as my wife. So, remember, I'm hoping for it to be a very long and happy one, please?'

She nodded. 'Of course, Hugh.' That peculiar sense of loss she'd felt on seeing what the thief, Emile, as she now knew, had pressed into her hand washed over her again. 'But it felt like he reached out to me in his final moments. And I... I just can't let him down.'

'*We* won't,' Seldon said gently. 'The three of us have proved quite the team on exactly this sort of unpleasant matter before, as you mentioned earlier.' He looked up apologetically as her butler rejoined them. 'Although goodness, sorry, Clifford. I didn't mean to speak for you.'

'I would not countenance anything other than doing everything I can to assist, sir,' Clifford said ardently. 'In fact, the words of the eminent French writer, Alexandre Dumas, have been ringing constantly through my thoughts. "If you wish to discover the guilty person, first find out to whom the crime might be useful." Though the irony in this case is that the police believe the deceased to be the criminal. A Monsieur Emile Ury, it now seems.'

'That's because they're focusing on the wrong crime; the robbery, not the murder!' she retorted.

'Indeed, my lady. One thing strikes as likely, regarding the identity of the mystery messenger though.'

'That it wasn't the murderer?'

He nodded.

'I agree,' Seldon said, tapping his fingers on the table. 'Whoever murdered the thief had no reason to then come forward with his victim's name.'

She nodded as well. 'Well, at least we think we have a name now. So we can find out more about him.'

She was certain she'd never heard the name Ury before coming to Paris. But now he had a name, she felt an even closer connection to the poor man.

'When Rion confessed to recognising the thief,' she continued, 'he admitted he had seen this Emile trying to sell his paintings along the river. So it seems Emile was a painter as well, as we suspected. Maybe it runs in the family?'

Clifford unfolded his map on the table. 'The artist you talked to along the Seine told you there were several communes around Paris. He mentioned the largest is in the Montmartre district, which begins but a few streets north from here. We could enquire about Monsieur Ury there?' He tapped the map.

'Then what are we waiting for?' she stated, leaping up. Catching Seldon and Clifford sharing a perturbed look, she tiptoed up to Gladstone and whispered, 'I just hope those two can be subtle for once, rather than charging in like rhinoceroses, as usual!'

Seldon laughed. 'If we ever did, we'd have learned the art from the queen of such!'

'Wait a moment.'

Seldon and Clifford paused in rising and looked at her expectantly.

She hesitated. 'The brooch. Delorme said the pearls were fake. I know you both have experience with fake jewellery. In the course of your police work, Hugh. And you, Clifford, in the course of...' She hurried on. 'Could you tell if they are fake?'

Seldon shared a puzzled glance with Clifford. 'Possibly. It depends how well they are made.'

Clifford nodded. 'Usually false pearls are more even in roundness compared to the genuine article.'

'And,' Seldon added, 'if you rub them on your teeth, strangely, you can tell if they are fake often by how smooth they are. Real pearls are a little... gritty.'

They both sat down while Eleanor produced the brooch, having checked they couldn't be seen or overheard.

After passing the brooch between them a few times, and subjecting it to close scrutiny, Seldon shrugged and passed it back to Clifford again. He, in turn, passed it back to her.

'I'm sorry, my lady. If they are fake, they're very good imitations. We'd need to take it to a specialist jeweller to check, but that's impossible.'

She paused in putting the brooch away safely. 'Why?'

'By now every jeweller in Paris will probably have been sent a police bulletin with a description and photograph, I suspect, of the missing brooch,' Seldon answered for him.

She nodded. 'Of course.'

He stared at her oddly. 'Does it matter that much?'

She shook her head. 'Well... I... I just wondered, really. Now, let's get to Montmartre and see what we can dig up on Emile.'

She set off briskly, pretending she didn't see the look that passed between Seldon and Clifford.

How long can you keep on pretending it doesn't matter enormously, Ellie?

She sighed. Even if she did confess how much it meant to her, she still wouldn't be able to explain why.

. . .

Eleanor hadn't expected anywhere in Paris to be so steep. Yet after leaving the café, every step had been such a climb, she felt they must have left France's capital city far below. And that was before they started up the run of almost vertical stone steps, which had gaggles of tourists and older locals pausing to catch their breath.

At the top, the three of them plumped for the right-hand fork of two cobbled pedestrian streets. The proliferation of untamed bohemian beards, neckerchiefs and colourful head-scarves gave the area its own unique feel. The air buzzed with a different vibe, too. Here, art and literature were clearly the dominant passion; painted images and stanzas of poems adorning the exterior walls of buildings and the flagstones of thoroughfares.

In between it all, nature too had found its haven, with thick ivy embracing the façades of the narrow buildings and leafy shrubs reaching out through almost every railing. Even the iron street lamps had been cast with creepers in relief, twirling up their tall posts.

The mix of scents wafting from the art stores, second-hand bookshops and myriad herbalists blended with the aromas of strong coffee and cigarettes tickling her nose. Tiny shopfronts were interspersed with cosy cafés, with chickens roasting in age-blackened rotisseries in the streets. In between, barrels served as stand-up bars with price lists painted on the walls.

She pointed out a wooden windmill set between two buildings.

'I feel like we've been somehow transported a million miles from busy, image-conscious Paris to a charismatic rural village.'

Clifford produced his guidebook. 'An astute observation, my lady. Montmartre was indeed independent of Paris until it was annexed to the city in 1860.'

She looked around at the multitude of people passing. 'Even with the locals being easy to distinguish from the tourists, stopping them at random to ask if they recognise the name "Emile Ury" feels way too hit-and-miss. Some of them could be poets or writers, and not even artists.'

Seldon rubbed his chin. 'Why wouldn't the artists here sell their paintings like the ones we spoke to along the river? Outside, somewhere free, with a captive audience of people passing, too?'

'Indeed, sir.' Clifford consulted his map. 'I believe Place du Tertre is where we need to be.'

She frowned. 'What's a "*tertre*"?'

'A "mound", my lady.'

She shuddered. 'Well, we'll be fine so long as it doesn't turn out to be a funeral mound!'

21

It wasn't, Eleanor thought with relief a few minutes later. The centre of the café-ringed square Clifford's map led them to was filled with artists, not bodies. And all were plying their paintings under the square's leafy green trees. Some were even walking around with sketchbooks offering to complete a caricature in a matter of minutes. The scene was a riot of colour, infused with the hum of animated voices. Gladstone's stumpy tail didn't stop wagging, convinced, as always, that everyone wanted to be his new best friend.

'Fingers crossed some of these artists will know our poor deceased Emile,' she said.

'Assuming that's even the thief's name. I suppose we could split up to find out?' Seldon said, somewhat reluctantly.

'A pincer movement in pairs? Good idea, sir,' Clifford said smoothly, clearly trying to ease Seldon's concern at letting her out of his sight. 'But which partner would you choose on merit?' He gestured between her and Gladstone.

Seldon stroked his chin. 'Hmm, tough choice.' As she laughed, he scooped her arm in his. 'Meet you on the far side of the square and we'll swap what we've learned, Clifford.'

However, it seemed that might be little or nothing as the artists closed ranks. They did learn that Emile was known there. But only because he sometimes came in from outside Paris to sell his paintings. With a little more pushing from her, and diplomacy from Seldon, they also managed to extract the information that he usually stayed with a female friend in Montmartre while in Paris. But no one would tell them her name. Or where she lived.

Just as Eleanor was about to give up, an ancient, whitewhiskered artist wearing a sky-blue beret nodded. 'Emile was a good painter, but he did not have the artistic skill of his father, Christophe.'

So they were father and son, Ellie.

'You knew Christophe *and* Emile Ury?' she said, her breath catching. But the old man waved her away, muttering, 'Au lapin agile!' and turned back to his painting as if she no longer existed.

As they walked off, she turned to Seldon. 'It adds up too, doesn't it? The gallery owner, Delorme, said Christophe died in 1899 and poor Emile only looked around early thirties. My age.'

They rejoined Clifford who shook his head ruefully at their questioning look. 'Extreme reticence was the universal reaction I encountered.'

Seldon bent to ruffle her bulldog's ears. 'Even with Gladstone playing his best irresistible card each time, hey, old friend?'

'Indeed, sir.'

'That's because they don't know we're trying to get justice for Emile!' she hissed. 'If everyone we'd asked knew we were trying to solve his murder—'

'I wouldn't know who to watch out for,' Seldon said gravely. 'Eleanor, we've only got a tenuous list of suspects at present. And no real idea who might have been on the hotel's atrium roof with Emile Ury. It could have been one of his artist friends!'

'Even this woman friend. If only we could have discovered her name,' she said frustrated.

'I believe Master Gladstone and myself may have. Sabine,' Clifford said. 'A sculptress, apparently.'

Her expression brightened. 'Well done, Clifford! You did better than us on that score. All I got was the old chap who told me Emile had a friend, then told me to get lost! Or "Go jump with the rabbits" or something similar.'

Seldon's jaw tightened. 'If I'd realised what he'd said, I'd have taken him to task for speaking to you like that!'

'Ahem,' Clifford said. 'Perhaps, my lady, he said, "Allez au lapin agile"?'

She feigned horror. 'Yes. But tsk! I didn't expect my impeccably starch-collared butler to have mastered the more unseemly French idioms.'

He tutted. 'Au Lapin Agile, or Agile Rabbit, is the name of a bistro and evening, ahem... cabaret, I happened to notice we passed en route to here.'

'Just happened to notice, eh?' She herded him and a now hesitant Seldon forward as a church bell tolled one o'clock. 'Well, if you're lucky, chaps, the showgirls, sorry, agile rabbits, might be sporting their cottontails early. Lead on, Clifford!'

The bistro turned out to be an unassuming two-storey building with faded-green shutters, and a gaggle of bohemians heading inside. Across the cobbled street, Eleanor slid out of her tailored jacket and mussed her red curls into a messy updo with her scarf. Seldon reluctantly removed his tie while Clifford, having removed his, produced a patterned handkerchief from nowhere and knotted it jauntily around Gladstone's neck. She wished she had a box Brownie camera to capture the uncharacteristically less than smartly attired image of her two favourite men as she'd likely never see them so attired again.

Pity, Ellie. Your ladies back at Henley Hall would be in giddy schoolgirl heaven if they could see them now!

As they entered via the old wooden door, a donkey stuck its head through a window on the opposite wall, braying a welcome, she hoped. She paused to scan the large wooden-floored room, gathering her wits. The walls were crammed with paintings, books and musical instruments. Ruched curtains screened off the far end which had steps up to it. Probably the cabaret stage. The only seats were backless wooden stools or long benches, all set at lengthy, unpolished tables. Signs hanging on the three large barrels set on the bar counter read: *Rouge. Blanc. Biere.*

As Gladstone shamelessly sniffed the admittedly tantalising aromas from the plates of those eating nearby, Eleanor wagged a finger at her butler's silent sniff.

'Clifford, you've drunk goodness-only-knows-what with me in far less salubrious dens.'

'Sir! I—'

Seldon raised his hand. 'Whatever my imagination conjures up, Clifford, it will be less shocking than the truth I've no doubt.'

'You two go up together,' Eleanor whispered, glancing towards the rosy-cheeked woman behind the bar. 'She'll be putty with the two of you looking that rakishly handsome.'

As she settled onto one of the benches with Gladstone at her feet, she heard Clifford order three glasses of '*Rouge*', while seamlessly sliding in the name 'Sabine' as if there was nothing unusual about it. She held her breath as the barmaid frowned and looked him and Seldon over, the flush to her cheeks deepening as he followed Clifford's lead in leaning on the bar with a disarming smile. Clifford purred something Eleanor couldn't hear. A few moments later, they joined her with four mismatched goblets of red wine, a bowl of mixed unshelled nuts, and a shared look of mortification.

'So far, so good, my lady,' Clifford said.

'I've just had a troubling thought, though,' Seldon said quietly. 'We agreed that if Emile Ury did have an accomplice on the atrium roof, it could have been anyone as far as we know. Including...'

'Sabine,' she groaned.

'As Alexandre Dumas so shrewdly wrote,' Clifford said, '"Cherchez la femme." Or "Search for the woman. For, there is a woman in everything!"'

'Often true, in my experience,' Seldon said, hurrying on quickly at Eleanor's look. 'That's not the worst of it though! We're pretty sure the murderer must have a nasty cut on their shin from that blood we found on the atrium roof.'

'Which means you'll both have to discreetly stare at a strange woman's legs!' Eleanor teased.

The three of them quickly adopted nonchalant expressions on spotting the barmaid heading towards them. She set down a basket with generous baguette chunks, cut open lengthways. Followed by four small bowls of hard-boiled egg halves, sitting among slivers of roasted ham and mushrooms drizzled in tasty-looking thick gravy. She winked at Clifford as he slid some money on the table.

As the barmaid turned to go, the door opened. Quickly she half-turned back.

'Voilà. C'est Sabine,' she said, waving the newcomer over.

Eleanor's first impression was that Sabine was stunningly beautiful; exquisite dark eyes, high cheekbones, full lips and a heart-shaped face, all framed by a mane of carefree raven waves. And that, hand on slender hip, her manner announced frankly she cared nothing for what others thought.

Hmm, perhaps not quite the sweet and easy sort we hoped for, Ellie?

'No worries about needing to covertly peek at her legs,' she whispered to Clifford and Seldon. 'She's wearing trousers! Is that because she's got a nasty gash on her shin she's trying to hide, I wonder?'

22

'Bonjour, Sabine,' Eleanor said genially. Receiving only a suspicious stare in reply, she gestured to the seat Clifford was holding out. 'I'm sorry my French is shamefully lacking. Do you speak English, perhaps?'

'A little, yes. But I have no reason to sit with you,' Sabine replied, her seductive French accent doing nothing to soften the directness of her delivery. Her gaze moved appreciatively over Clifford, and then lingered even longer on Seldon. 'I do not know any of you. What do you want?'

'To talk to you about... Emile.'

'Emile? He has not mentioned any of you to me,' she said coolly.

Or was she just masking her grief, Ellie?

Eleanor was gripped by a sudden realisation. With the shock of a body falling out of the sky practically into her lap, she'd forgotten it had only been the night before. Interviewing the hotel staff, visiting the Musée d'Art Contemporain, then the Galerie Delorme, and questioning the artists along the river and then up here in Montmartre, had all happened the same day. In fact, it was still only the afternoon after Emile's death. What if he and Sabine had been close? Perhaps even lovers. And she didn't even know he was dead yet?

'Well, we were with him last night,' Eleanor said, keeping her voice as neutral as she could.

Sabine's self-assured poise faltered. 'Who are you?'

Eleanor shrugged. 'Honestly, just three people who came to Paris for a honeymoon and holiday. But instead, got caught up in... in a very unpleasant matter.'

'Honeymoon?' Sabine looked between Seldon and Clifford again, then turned to go. 'Well, I am here only to eat my lunch.'

Eleanor pointed at the bowls. 'We bought you some lunch. I'm Eleanor, by the way. And this is Hugh. And Clifford.'

'And Master Gladstone. With apologies for his lack of etiquette,' Clifford said as the bulldog snuffled up Sabine's trousered legs.

For the first time, her expression softened. She traced her fingers gently over the bulldog's wrinkled jowls.

'Salut, toutou,' she murmured, drawing a besotted look from Gladstone.

'I know you weren't expecting to be met by a group of strangers,' Eleanor said. 'So I understand if you choose not to eat with us.' Sabine nodded curtly and swept up her bowl and goblet of wine. As she turned to sit at another table, Eleanor added, 'But you might think differently if you realised we're only here to help Emile.'

Sabine paused. 'I do not understand this because...' Her self-possession wavered as she tailed off, staring blankly at her meal.

'Because you and I need to speak. For Emile's sake,' Eleanor coaxed.

Sabine's black eyes bore into Eleanor's. 'Not here,' she said finally.

Pulling open a half baguette, she tipped the contents of her bowl into it as an impromptu sandwich and headed for the door.

Eleanor followed with Gladstone at full stretch on his lead, Seldon and Clifford on their heels.

Their new acquaintance didn't speak as she led them across the cobbled street and down a steep set of narrow steps. At the bottom, iron grillework stairs ran up and along each of the five floors of a weathered brick warehouse. Sabine pointed to the top and stomped on ahead.

Seldon scooped Gladstone into his arms and whispered to Eleanor, 'Got a good feeling about this?'

'Well, not a bad one,' she whispered back, following their guide.

At the top, Sabine unlocked a dilapidated wooden door and then aimed a hefty kick at it. It swung open.

'Oh goodness. I didn't know what to expect, but it wasn't this,' Eleanor said honestly as she followed her in.

Sabine shrugged. 'One day, I will have a proper studio. Not this rotten garret with water running down the walls and mouses and spiders running everywhere.'

Eleanor shuddered. 'I can't say I'm a fan of spiders.'

'Neither me. They leave their legs behind in the plaster when it is drying and spoil my sculptures!'

Eleanor noticed buckets of dried plaster on a dented workbench. Rolls of various gauges of chicken wire also lay on it among carryalls full of fine-bladed tools worthy of a modern surgeon. And raw-toothed saws and axes worthy of a mediaeval one. Then she saw the two stepladders set about ten feet apart a little further into the room. As her eyes wandered up to the plank balanced between them, she gasped.

Sabine had mentioned her sculptures, but Eleanor was not prepared for the scale of the one she was looking at. A remarkable representation of a man escaping from an egg. As full size as he was perfectly lifelike. With his bare torso and one leg hooked over the edge of the broken eggshell, there was no mistaking his nakedness either. But it was his haunted expression which made her breath catch. Her thoughts flew back to Emile's beseeching gaze locked onto hers. Then her eyes fell on a shadow on the inside of the figure's arm. Peering closer, she caught the distinct smell of fresh paint.

'Sabine, this is incredibly... realistic.' She stared in fascination at the intricate detail of the sinews in the forearms and knuckles where the man was straining to haul himself out.

Stepping up beside her, Seldon's eyes betrayed his bafflement at what kind of imagination would conjure up such a sculpture. 'I can honestly say I've never seen anything like it.' He hastily looked away.

'Very impressive indeed, mademoiselle,' Clifford said, doing the same. 'Perhaps gypsum is your main sculpting material? Since it is quick drying and the entire Montmartre hill was ringed with mines of such but sixty years ago.'

Sabine nodded, clearly impressed by her butler's knowledge. Walking to the end of the bare brick room, she yanked aside a voile curtain used as a divider. Behind it was a small settee leaking its horsehair insides and a simple wood table and two chairs. On one wall, a rail hung with a few eclectically stylish clothes and underwear. And next to it, a roughly made bed.

Clifford and Seldon immediately looked away again, both seemingly engrossed in something undefined in the far corner of the studio.

Sabine perched on the table. Pulling a sliver of mushroom from her salvaged lunch, she slid it between her lips. 'Well, now what, Eleanor?'

She decided, given Sabine's blunt manner, a direct approach would work best.

'Why did Emile burgle the Musée d'Art Contemporain last night?' She watched the woman's reaction carefully.

For a moment, Sabine didn't respond. Then she shook her glossy tresses violently. 'Emile? You are mistaken! His paintings... are the only interest for him. Especially selling them. That is the single reason he was in Paris last night.'

Eleanor didn't miss Sabine's hesitation. Nor her referring to Emile in the present tense. She threw her a sympathetic look. 'Only his paintings interested him? That must hurt you to say.'

Sabine frowned while picking a piece of egg from the baguette. 'Why do you think this?'

'Because you and Emile were lovers.'

She laughed, but it sounded forced. 'Emile and me. We were never lovers. Only friends.' She dropped the piece of egg on the floor where Gladstone snuffled it up noisily.

Eleanor looked disbelieving. 'Really?' She pointed to the sculpture. 'Your truly arresting representation of the man clawing his way out of the egg is Emile, isn't it? And to sculpt that, you must have known every inch of his body as only a lover could.'

Sabine's eyes flashed dangerously. 'Then you were his lover too, to know this, huh?'

Clifford glided past, pinching the bridge of his nose.

Eleanor held her hands up. 'No! Emile and I never even got as far as exchanging words.'

But somehow you still felt an unexplainable connection, Ellie.

Sabine rolled her eyes. 'You talk in puzzles! Yes. Emile was the model for my work sometimes. I am a *sculptrice*, as you have seen. And unlike you English, we French are not ashamed of the naked body.'

Eleanor switched tack. 'Was Emile like his father, Christophe?'

Sabine frowned in confusion. 'How can I know this? His father died a long time ago. When Emile was young.' Her gaze turned suddenly wistful. 'He talked much of his father's paintings because he had great admiration for his father's talent. Christophe was an Impressionist.'

'Emile too?'

'No. His paintings are a mix of two movements; *Dadaïsme* and *Surréalisme.*' She shot Eleanor a smug look. 'But you don't know what they are, I think?'

'I haven't a clue. But Clifford will delight in wittering my ears off about both of those things you mentioned later.'

'With the greatest of pleasure, my lady,' Clifford's voice drifted in from behind the curtain.

'You told us Emile had come to Paris to try and sell some paintings,' Eleanor said. 'He didn't live here then?'

'No. He does not.'

'How were the police when they came to see you?'

'Police!' Sabine cried. 'They have not come. What reason would they have?'

'Because you knew Emile. And they know he stole something from the museum last night.'

'But this is not true! Someone has pointed the finger at Emile to make it seem they are innocent.' Her eyes narrowed. 'Maybe it is you?'

Eleanor shook her head. 'No. I was busy trying to toast my honeymoon before...'

'Before what?'

She hesitated, then continued as if she hadn't heard the question. 'What did you do last night, Sabine?'

'I sat in the brasserie where you met me waiting for Emile. He said he would be there at eleven. But he did not come.' Sabine's jaw tightened. 'Why are you asking all these questions about him?'

Seldon reappeared. 'Because my wife tried to save Emile Ury's life last night.'

Sabine blinked rapidly, dropping her sandwich onto the table. 'Tried to... save him?'

Eleanor nodded. 'If you honestly didn't know already, we're truly sorry to be the ones to break it to you. But Emile is dead.'

Sabine stood up, tears welling in her eyes. 'It is time you left. Now!'

'Alright. If you want to tell me anything you might have... forgotten, you can contact me at the hotel where Emile died. Or if you just need help.'

As the three of them left, Sabine wiped her eyes and called after them, 'Wait. Still, I do not understand why you came to find me.'

Eleanor hesitated, not wishing to deliver another terrible blow after telling her Emile was dead.

Assuming she isn't lying about not knowing, Ellie. And even if she isn't, there's a killer to catch.

'Because I believe Emile was murdered. That's why,' Eleanor said quietly.

Sabine's face paled. 'Now you are the liar!' she stuttered, her hand trembling as she covered her mouth.

Eleanor shook her head. 'Trust me, I wish with all my heart that was the case.'

'But you were not even his friend. I was, am, his friend! His only friend in the world, except his grandmother. She brought him up as a child.'

'Really?' Eleanor said firmly. 'Then, if you cared about him at all, answer me one last question. Where did he live?'

Sabine folded her arms shakily. 'I don't see why you want to know. But because he was not a thief, and I do not like you saying he was, I will tell you so you can find out for yourself. He lived in Magnes-sur-Oise.'

'Thank you.'

Back down in the street, Seldon looked thoughtful. 'She struck me as a tough-hearted sort. I think she'll be alright even if she didn't already know Emile was dead. But I'm pretty certain she did.'

Clifford raised an eyebrow. 'It must be your many years of

police experience, sir. Because I confess, I left still feeling as unsure as her ladyship.'

Eleanor felt a wash of relief. 'Really, Hugh? Because honestly, when you said so bluntly that he was dead, my heart stopped for a moment.' She frowned. 'As Clifford said, how come you are so confident Sabine knew?'

He slid his hand into his pocket. 'Because, to my shame, I took a leaf out of your butler's book of dubiously learned tricks and swiped one of these from her workbench.'

She and Clifford leaned in to see what he had pulled out.

Eleanor's frown deepened. 'Sabine's business card? But what of it— Oh gracious! Her surname is Rion. The same as the guard at the museum!'

23

The three of them walked down the street in silence. Finally, Seldon spoke.

'Feelings about our conversation with Sabine, Eleanor?'

She thought for a moment. 'Well, firstly, I'm certain she was lying about her and Emile not being lovers. Or at least former lovers.'

'Did you have to start with that?' He ran his hand around his neck. 'I've been desperate, and hesitant actually, to ask why you were so sure that bizarre sculpture of the man climbing out of an egg was Emile? Because he was... you know.'

'Ahem. Unattired?' Clifford said.

Eleanor smiled. 'But that wasn't why, Hugh. You probably didn't see the tattoo on his forearm that I saw when checking the poor chap's pulse?'

Seldon shook his head. 'I was busy trying to calm the guests and getting the waiters to help.'

'Well, the figure in Sabine's sculpture had a dark shadow in the same place, which I believe had just been painted over.' She shivered. 'Though honestly, the haunted look on its face was too similar to Emile's expression in his final moments, too.'

He pulled her to his side. 'Plus, we know Alain Rion knew the thief died within only an hour or so of it happening. Because you were the one who told him at the museum. And Sabine having the same surname, would be an amazing coincidence if they aren't related. So she almost certainly knew Emile is dead. Unless Rion kept it from her for some reason. Hmm? We'd best jot this lot down.'

She nodded, reached into her handbag for her notebook and pen, and started writing:

<u>Alain Rion</u>

- Lied about knowing Emile at first
- Lied about leaving his post
- Was seen coming back from direction of hotel by Officers Hacqueville and Bernier

<u>Sabine Rion</u>

- Lied about relationship with Emile?
- Lied about knowing about Emile robbing museum and his death?
- Related to museum guard (will find out exactly how) – did they plan murder together?

<u>Pronovost</u>

- Didn't appear immediately Emile fell – told staff in office – could have had time to push Emile and then come down service stairs – would have had key
- Refused to send for doctor – maybe hoped Emile would die?
- Tried to put blame on to Gripperel
- Motive –?

Seldon groaned as she then wrote:

<u>Inspector Gripperel</u>

- Lied about thief tripping while running across roof
- Had his men chase thief up on roof? (2 of his men say none went up there)
- Was surprisingly keen to let me go along to museum late last night – keeping an eye on me?

'I can't tell you how much I hope it doesn't turn out to be Inspector Gripperel,' Seldon said. 'He's a powerful man in this city.'

She shrugged. 'Well—' A church bell ringing out the quarter hour interrupted her, reminding her time was moving on and she was neglecting again the very reason they'd come to Paris. 'Anyway, I know exactly what to do next.'

'Which is?' Seldon said.

'Enjoy Paris like it's going out of fashion, Hugh!'

His soft-brown eyes lit up, making him even more handsome than she had thought possible. 'Really, Eleanor? But what about the investigation?'

'It'll keep for a few hours. In fact, until after our cocktail soirée up the Eiffel Tower tonight. What do you say?'

'I say let's go and make some honeymoon memories we'll never forget. For all the right reasons this time,' he said fervently.

She turned to Clifford. 'We'd both love you to join us, but the invitation is only for two. And you might appreciate being free of me for a while?'

He shook his head respectfully, then adopted a sprinter's stance, eyes twinkling.

She laughed. 'Be off with you! And I promise not to ask what you got up to later.'

He tutted. 'Rest assured, there will be no indecorous tales to relate on my part. Unlike those your unruly ladies back at Henley Hall will no doubt have to tell me when I telephone them today.'

'Pity! Send them my love.' She took Gladstone's lead from his hand and whispered, 'You're in liberal Paris, Clifford. In Uncle Byron's spirit, please go and play unchecked. Just like you used to do in the good old days with him. If you wish, meet us at, say, nine at the base of the Eiffel Tower by one of the lifts? I'm sure there aren't that many.'

He gave her a rare smile. 'Certainly. In the meantime, perhaps you might wish to leave Montmartre via the Basilica Sacré-Coeur?' He pointed off to the right. 'The views are known to be spectacular with a particularly captivating one of the Eiffel Tower itself.'

'Where we'll catch up with you tonight,' Seldon said.

With a keen nod, Clifford melted away into the crowds.

Eleanor clapped her hands. 'Where shall we start, Hugh?'

'Right here,' he murmured, linking his long, strong fingers with hers. Closing his eyes, he kissed her.

She gasped, then murmured, 'In front of other people, Chief Inspector? Whatever would English sensibilities say!'

He opened his eyes. 'Frankly, I don't care. I love you, Eleanor. And I want the world to know it.'

She cocked her head. 'I adore this new, impassioned Hugh. But I am wondering what happened to the usually reserved policeman who took forever to stutter out his feelings for me?'

He sighed. 'Oh, he'll be back the moment we hit English soil. At least in public. Because he'll have to be. Which is why I'm secretly wishing we could stay in Paris permanently. And...' He broke off, rubbing his forehead.

'And, Hugh?'

'Never mind. That's for later. Now where was that thing

Clifford said to visit... what the...!' He looked down in surprise and pulled Clifford's map from under his arm.

She laughed and waved the guidebook she hadn't seen her butler slip her either.

'Come on. Let's explore!'

From the dizzy heights of Montmartre, Paris's majestic buildings and parks stretched out below them, the sun lighting the Eiffel Tower as if it were made of solid gold. She turned to look at the white domes of the Sacré-Coeur.

'What an amazing building! According to Clifford's guide-book, after forty-four years, it's not even finished. It was only consecrated on sixteenth of April 1919.'

'Ah, five and a half months to the day before I first set eyes on your irresistible fiery-red curls.'

She laughed. 'I didn't realise you've remembered the actual date we met, Hugh?'

'Well, of course I do. It's in my official police notebook. I threatened to arrest you!'

He led her over to a small café, outside which a cream-aproned waitress was conjuring up what looked like enormous thin pancakes on a large circular black griddle plate. Beside her, a wheeled cabinet was filled with a choice of delicious-looking fillings. Seldon held up two fingers, his lips moving as if trying to remember something. 'Er, deux... of those, s'il vous plait,' he said with a sheepish shrug.

'And deux more for dessert,' Eleanor added eagerly.

The waitress poured a ladle of batter onto her griddle plate. A few minutes later, they were snuggled up together on a stone wall, savouring a selection of delectable savoury and sweet 'crêpes' as they had been told they were called.

She smiled at him, sharing his ham and cheese one with Gladstone. 'Any more surprises coming, Hugh? Because I didn't realise you've been learning French.'

'It felt rude to just keep speaking in English without even

trying to learn a few words. So I've been dipping in and out of that phrase book of yours. Although, I haven't much idea what I'm saying. I probably sound like a lunatic.'

'Yes.' She laughed as he batted her nose with his crêpe.

Their impromptu snack finished, they strolled down the steep hill, letting Gladstone and anything that caught their eye lead their feet. As they neared the bottom, they came across myriad shopping arcades. All of which were exquisitely tiled underfoot, the windows framed in polished brass, and the high-vaulted ceilings hung with shimmering lights.

Seldon looked bewildered. 'What shall we buy for your wonderful ladies back home?'

'Tsk! Spoiling one's staff is strictly against the rules,' she said in a remarkable imitation of Clifford.

'And yet you do it all the time. That and partying into the small hours with them in the kitchen and who knows what else!'

'That's because they all work far too hard on my account, and I'm very blessed to have inherited them, along with Henley Hall.'

His chestnut curls brushed against her cheek as he whispered, 'And they've grown to feel like the family I wish I could make up for you not having.'

She snuggled into his chest. 'Both of my parents are always in my thoughts, just as they have been since they disappeared. But Mother, particularly, has been in them since... the awful matter we aren't talking about for the moment. But you're my husband now, Hugh. That's more family than I dared hope for.'

'The latest addition to your motley household. At least I will be when we get back.' He buried his face in her curls. 'Eleanor, maybe you and I might add to that family one day? To... to our family?' He cleared his throat. 'But that's another conversation for later, too.'

She nodded.

And the biggest, Ellie.

24

The next hour passed with Eleanor and Seldon strolling hand in hand through enchanting arcades of boutiques and covered markets, with Gladstone in doggy raptures at all the new smells. They emerged within sight of one of the majestic stone bridges over the Seine. A collection of pretty cloth bags, printed with Parisian scenes, hung from Seldon's shoulders and a basket bursting with dainty packages swung in Eleanor's hand. They had chosen the souvenir gifts between them, her heart swelling at his appreciation of all her staff did for her.

'And how much they care about you, Eleanor,' he said. 'Now, along with one of these bags each, is that enough for your ladies?' He gestured over the beautifully boxed soaps, hand creams and scented drawer liners in her basket.

She nodded. 'And we've got the perfect present for Clifford.'

In a tiny shop bursting with unusual books, the Dickensian-whiskered owner had delighted in rifling through his shelves to find something that would appeal to her impossible-to-buy-for butler. Finally, he had come up trumps with an exquisite leather-bound book on the history of the clocks of Paris. Making it even more perfect, inset in the front cover was a working replica of the oldest one of all, the striking gold and blue one Clifford had shown them.

Then, to cap it off, the extra special gift she'd been aching to find appeared for Clifford's young ward, an independent young boy named Kofi from the Gold Coast. An incredible wooden model kit of the Eiffel Tower with hundreds of intricately cut pieces. With Kofi sharing Clifford's fascination for all things engineering, the two of them would spend endless happy hours together building the five foot high structure.

In another shop they found a set of hand pruning tools in a woven belt for Joseph, her gardener. They were embossed with French plant names which she knew would tickle his sense of humour over wearing something so la-di-dah, as he would see it. Gardening was his love and his passion. And that they had recognised it would also mean so much to him. Gladstone had even helped in choosing something for his best friend, Tomkins. In truth, he had stolen the toy with its nest of felt mice from the shelf of a pet shop they had found in a charming side alley, refusing to leave without it.

Looking through the bags, Eleanor checked off the last few items. 'Selection boxes of macarons, a range of syrups, two sets of jars of delectable French nut and chocolate spreads and a whole cake of nougat.'

'And these we bought for...?' Seldon held up a stack of nine different coloured berets.

'A fun addition to the nibbles for our party the night we get back, Hugh. It's tradition to extend the trip for another evening and do everything in the style of wherever we've just returned from.'

'I know. You invited me to the one the night you all got back from Egypt, remember?' He rubbed his hands over his cheeks. 'You could have warned me that there would be belly-dancing once your cook's home-brewed concoctions flowed, though.'

'And spoil the surprise?' she said innocently. 'Just imagine what we'll all get up to after Paris!'

They chose a quintessentially romantic Parisian restaurant; red-and-white striped cane chairs with matching tables and clusters of miniature tulips as centrepieces. Their menu choices made, Seldon accompanied the waiter to the wine cellar to select a bottle to accompany their meal. He was clearly enjoying the chance to spoil her, given he'd already ordered champagne cocktails to start.

The *soupe à l'oignon* starter was divine. The *fruits de mer* main course too. A refreshing salad with the lightest, tastiest dressing followed as a third course. To her delight, the pudding options included *café gourmand*; a miniature of each of the five desserts available, along with a rich-roasted coffee. Seldon watched in amusement as she enthused over the Chantilly cream meringue, apricot tart, hazelnut mousse, crème brûlée and chocolate-drizzled Armagnac-steeped pear.

'Time to start back to the hotel to get ready for the Eiffel Tower,' Seldon said, rising to settle the bill.

She nodded. 'I'll meet you outside in a moment.'

Heading off to powder her nose, halfway along the passageway, she passed a set of closed glass-paned doors. Quickly, she ducked back against the wall. Was she seeing things? She peeped through the nearest pane into the small private dining salon beyond.

No, you're not, Ellie. It's Delorme and Omfroy.

It seemed a strange place for the flamboyant gallery owner and elaborately whiskered museum director to meet. Why not in the main salon? Why the need for such seclusion? She peeped again. Omfroy was drinking coffee, Delorme smoking a cigar, the ruby-red and gold band catching the light as he leaned forward earnestly. Sneaking as close as she dared without being visible to them, she strained to hear what they were saying.

Dash it, Ellie! This glass is too thick.

Omfroy was looking agitated now, Delorme seemingly trying to calm him. But whatever Omfroy then said to him angered the gallery owner enough for him to jerk him to his feet and throw his napkin on the table. Delorme pointed the lit end of his cigar in Omfroy's face, then spun on his heel to flounce out.

Eleanor shot away down the passageway. She couldn't spoil the rest of the precious romantic afternoon by telling Seldon what she'd seen. That would have to wait until after the cocktail soirée.

But Delorme seemed so enraged, Ellie... almost murderously so?

25

Eleanor paused to marvel at the iconic landmark silhouetted against the early evening rose-streaked clouds. She remembered Clifford telling her at just over one thousand feet, the Eiffel Tower was the tallest man-made structure in the world. And a testament to mankind's determination to leave his mark, she felt. Sculptured in what looked like intricately woven iron lace, its pattern of graceful girders, struts and trusses held together by thousands of rivets was mesmerising. The elephantine lattice-work base pillars, spanned by sweeping arches, seemed to have sprouted from the very ground she was standing on. Even without the five lifts ascending and descending, the constant streams of visitors surging up and down the staircases, made the whole structure seem alive.

Seldon, head thrown back, stared up at the tower. 'I feel like an insignificant ant.'

Unprepared for such an uncharacteristically philosophical observation from the world's most down-to-earth policeman, she couldn't help laughing. 'Well, take heart, Hugh. You're the most handsome insect I've ever fallen for.'

In fact, with his broad shoulders and tall, athletic frame, he looked positively edible in his evening wear. He smiled and held her hands out to her sides.

'And I thought you couldn't look more beautiful. But this new dress makes your already mesmerising green eyes shine like emeralds. And your red curls even more fiery!'

Her heart leaped with relief. Normally, she would have worn her signature green to a fancy cocktail party. Especially in Paris. It suited her, and she knew it. But she had decided it was time to be more adventurous with her wardrobe. So, instead, she'd risked a deep-mulberry silk cocktail dress.

He linked her arm in his and they threaded their way through the crowds, the many admiring looks she received confirming Paris agreed with her new husband. Although Seldon received just as many glances, she noticed.

At the base of the Eiffel Tower, he looked around. 'We can't have to queue, surely? The reception will be long over by the time we get to the top!'

He was right. One flash of the gold-embossed card Delorme had given her saw them escorted like royalty straight to the first of the three lifts. The walrus-moustached operator closed the doors, and the crowds receded below them. The fifty or so occupants held their breath, Eleanor and Seldon included as they reached for each other's hands. She had ridden in two lifts before. But only up and down a maximum of three floors in one luxury hotel on England's south coast and one apartment building on her New York trip. And even then, only for the first time two years ago. Seldon's grip tightening on her hands made her realise this was an entirely new experience for him. *Hardly a gentle introduction, poor chap, Ellie. We're going to shoot up the Eiffel Tower!*

They had to cross a walkway suspended six hundred feet up to reach the second lift, the Seine now a mere ribbon of winding greyish-blue. A few minutes later and their third lift operator announced they had reached the end of the line, and from there they would have to use the stairs. The uniformed guard lowered the gold-painted chain blocking the way and gestured them on up.

'I thought we were going to a cocktail party, not boarding a royal naval ship!' she joked, to cover her creeping nerves at the formality of it all.

He linked his fingers in hers. 'Don't worry. The other guests will be too caught up thinking how beautiful you are to expect any highbrow conversation.'

She laughed. 'Let's just go and have fun, Hugh. Honestly, what's the worst that can happen up the Eiffel Tower?'

The staircase corkscrewed around an iron pillar until it stopped at a platform manned by a slick-haired steward who inspected their invitation and then passed them a flute of champagne each. His formal manner was rather ruined as the wind at this height whipped his knee-length suit tails up behind him like two rearing serpents.

She held up the bottom of her cocktail dress. 'Get someone to sew some of those invisible hem weights we ladies rely on for maintaining our decorum into your tails, monsieur.'

His wide-eyed expression showed he was unused to being addressed by guests. 'Madame is too kind to offer this suggestion,' he said, trying to hide his amusement.

As they walked on, she looked around. They were on a metal-railed balcony deck, suspended more hundreds of feet above the ground than she dared think about. A little further along, two men were deep in discussion, seeming to care nothing for the stunning view of Paris lit up far below like an exquisite miniature replica. Nor the petite, flaxen-haired girl of about nineteen toying listlessly with the telescope fixed to the rail. One of the men waved his cigar at Eleanor with a smile before returning to his conversation.

Glancing down, she realised the public viewing platform was

only about fifteen feet below. It protruded out further than the one she was on, giving her a bird's-eye view of the sightseers milling back and forth. In front of her, a metal door reminded her of a ship's wheelhouse. Its bank of thick-glass windows was riveted so securely, it looked fit to survive the worst the elements could throw at it. Through the open door, however, she could see an incongruously cosy drawing room; velvet armchairs were set among a long-cushioned banquette seat and occasional tables. It even had orange and green patterned wallpaper. At the far side of the room, she could see another door through to a small kitchen where an aproned waiter and waitress were dashing about.

A man with sagging jowls and a portly waistline, clad in blue velvet, strode up to them. 'You must be Lady Swift and Mr Seldon? I am your host, Monsieur Jolivet. Delorme mentioned you would be coming in his place.'

'Bonsoir, Monsieur Jolivet.' She shook his hand. Seldon followed suit, thanking their host for the extra treat to their honeymoon.

Jolivet responded by offering a toast to their wedding. Then turned to Eleanor.

'Delorme told me you are something of an art connoisseur? He has sourced many fine paintings for my collection. He will do you proud.' Beckoning the steward over, he rapped out a stream of commands. Turning back to Eleanor and Seldon, he smiled. 'Perhaps you will forgive me leaving you in the care of my manservant, Gerard, for a while? I must attend to the other guests.'

As he left, the steward presented a selection of cocktails on a silver tray. Behind him, the waiter and waitress had started circling the room with delectable-looking canapés.

She eyed the array of glasses. 'Which is the least likely to have me dancing on the railings, Gerard? I heard it's quite a long way down to the ground.'

The steward hid a smile. 'Perhaps the byrrh and cassis, madame? A wine apéritif, flavoured with blackberry.'

'Perfect, thank you.'

'And for monsieur, the Armagnac *gingembre*? It is the more usual gentleman's drink.'

Furnished with a cocktail and plate of canapés each, they began to mingle. There were about a dozen other guests at most; diamond-encrusted ladies and black-jacketed men, chatting over the jazz being played at the piano. After passing pleasantries on the delights of Paris with the majority of them, she noticed the man, with the flaxen-haired young woman in tow, come in from the outer deck. He approached her, hand outstretched.

'Lady Swift? And Mr Seldon?' At their joint nod, he continued. 'Allow me to introduce myself. I am Victor Yves Archambault. And this is my niece, Odette.'

Before Eleanor could reply, their host appeared. 'Monsieur le Comte, puis-je vous présenter—'

'Too late, Jolivet. We have made our own introductions,' their new companion replied sharply.

Eleanor's ears pricked up. '*Le Comte*' was French for 'Count' she remembered from a favourite penny dreadful novel. Now she looked at him again, he had the distinct look of an aristocrat; his perfect Roman nose, the point of his prominent chin and the uncompromising wave of his lustrous fair mane, which was combed back from his wide brow like a crown. Some people had family. This man clearly had ancestors.

He half bowed. 'Please forgive me approaching you so directly. But Monsieur Delorme asked me if I would look out for you.'

'That was so kind of both of you,' she said, trying to include his niece in the conversation. 'Do you come to Monsieur Jolivet's receptions often?'

Odette sighed. 'We go to somebody's reception almost every night, Lady Swift.'

Le Comte laughed softly, but the glance he gave Odette was one of disappointment. 'Young people. They have no idea what responsibilities some of us have.'

Eleanor whispered loudly to the girl. 'Don't let on to your delightful uncle here, but I'm probably very close in age to him, and I still consider myself a "young person"!'

For the next twenty minutes, Le Comte engaged them with a raft of interesting tales about Paris and their host, Monsieur Jolivet. He had impeccable manners, was eloquent and amusing, and had a certain... enigmatic quality that left her disappointed when he excused himself and Odette.

'Interesting man,' she said to Seldon, once they were alone. 'I get the distinct impression there's more to him than meets the eye.'

He nodded. 'It was good of him to look out for us, though. I'll give him that. Saved me trying to make small talk. Which is not my strong suit at all.'

'Nor mine.'

It was only then, she realised the room had emptied, the other guests having drifted out to the balcony deck. Someone closed the door to the outside. She felt the pressure change in her ears. Pulling Seldon with her to the nearest window, she looked out at the burnished bronze- and lavender-streaked clouds scudding past. Suddenly, she felt claustrophobic.

'Let's get some air.'

'My wife leaving the nibbles table so soon?' he quipped.

Outside, the views from this side of the wrap-around deck were even more spectacular. The wind tugged at her curls and ruffled Seldon's against her cheek. She felt she had ascended to a celestial paradise. Their host reappeared, and though he had clearly seen it all before, pointed out the sights.

'And that dome is the roof of the Musee d'Art Contemporain.'

Eleanor shivered. 'Ah, yes, we have visited that.'

Once Jolivet had left again, Seldon said quietly, 'No thoughts about unpleasant matters tonight, my love.'

She nodded, watching the orange gold deepening against the thickening clouds. But somehow the very air seemed charged with a sense of foreboding.

Maybe there's going to be a lightning storm, Ellie?

Le Comte reappeared, the smoke from his cigar swirling around his head like a halo. 'I must take Odette home now, otherwise I would invite you to join me for dinner.'

'That is very kind of you, but we must be leaving, too,' she replied.

'Perhaps, instead, I can invite you to stay at my home, Chateau Archambault?' He held out a card. 'Any time.' Shaking both of their hands, she was pleased to note, he started down the stairs.

'I hope you will,' Odette whispered. 'We young people need to stick together. And... and we don't entertain much.' She smiled and darted after Le Comte.

Eleanor slid the card into her beaded evening bag, thinking that was not going to happen on her honeymoon. Besides, a niggle said to her, he was acquainted in some way with Delorme, and she neither liked nor trusted that gentleman. And Odette had said they went to somebody's reception almost every night. And yet, according to her, they rarely entertained themselves?

Strange, Ellie?

They returned inside, thanked Monsieur Jolivet for a delightful time, and then ducked into the kitchen to thank the waiter, waitress and steward. The three of them beamed back at her, clearly unused to praise and recognition.

At the bottom of the spiral stairs, the public viewing plat-form was crowded. As she struggled through the throng of eager sightseers, she heard shouting behind her.

'It's Clifford!' she cried.

'Wrestling with another man!' Seldon muttered. 'What in blazes?'

But before they could battle back through the crowd to reach her butler, he hurled himself down the nearest staircase in pursuit of the man.

Experience told her to wait there for him to return. When he did a good five minutes later, his usually inscrutable expres-sion betrayed hints of fury.

'My abject apologies for the disgraceful spectacle, my lady. Sir. And for failing to catch the bounder.'

She tutted. 'No need to apologise. I know you wouldn't have dreamed of shoving half the Eiffel Tower visitors out of your way unless you thought it vital. So?'

'A pickpocket, my lady. He was attempting to relieve you of the contents of your handbag.'

'The wretch!' Seldon growled.

Eleanor scoured through her evening bag. 'Phew! Nothing missing, anyway.'

Clifford sniffed. 'He was far from proficient at his reprobate trade. Hence my spotting him. But even without the usual encumbrance of Master Gladstone, who is snoozing in your hotel suite, I failed to apprehend the swine,' he ended self-reproachfully.

'Well, thank you for trying, my faithful guard dog! And I'm truly sorry you missed seeing Eiffel's private apartment. But maybe we've all had enough for one night?'

'Hear, hear,' Seldon said fervently. 'I fancy no more surprises of any sort.'

Clifford nodded and led the way to the lifts.

As the last lift deposited them at the bottom of the tower, a scream rent the air. Looking up, Eleanor instinctively stretched out her arms to hold the others back.

A split second later, a body struck the ground inches from her feet.

26

Eleanor covered her mouth in horror as the man landed so hard, his body fleetingly reared back up with the impact.

Instinctively, she dropped to her knees to check if there was any hope of saving him. But he was dead. Of course he was. No one could survive a fall from that height, whichever of the viewing platforms he had plummeted from.

'Eleanor, oh lord, not again!'

She felt the warmth of Seldon's body as he hunched down behind her and wrapped his hands over her eyes to shut out the image. But she shook them off, despite the electrified emotions coursing through her.

'Hugh, look under that hood covering half his face! I can't believe it, but it's... it's Officer Hacqueville, isn't it?'

Seldon eased the body over. Brow furrowed, he nodded slowly. 'It's him, alright. I'd never forget his face after he accused you of being the thief's accomplice last night in the hotel!' He ran his gaze slowly down the inert form, then lifted back the long overcoat. 'No obvious sign of foul play. It looks like suicide.' His tone softened as he scanned her face. 'It's probably not that uncommon, Eleanor. The height would at least give any poor soul who has reached such a desperate decision the cold comfort of it being certain. And almost instant.' Their gazes went up together to take in the crowd now closing in. Seldon shot up and tried herding them backwards. Her thoughts were reeling as much as her insides were churning. What had Hacqueville been doing here, up the Eiffel Tower? And out of uniform with his face concealed?

Despite the harrowing sight of what had been a living, breathing man only minutes before, she reached for Hacqueville's trouser hems. Emile's murderer had cut their shin up on her hotel's atrium roof, she was sure of it.

Raking back the cloth with trembling hands, she blanched.

'Where the blasted heck has Clifford gone? Ah! Finally!' Seldon's unusually sharp tone rang out. 'Where have you been? Oh, it doesn't matter. Now you're here, help me keep these gawkers at bay!'

Clifford strode up, shaking his head firmly. 'Regrettably not, sir.'

'What? Have you forgotten her ladyship is here, man!' Seldon thundered.

'Quite the reverse, sir. Which is why we need to leave. Now!'

Seldon's jaw tightened, but he nodded slowly as he took in her butler's uncharacteristically determined expression. He glanced back down at Hacqueville's body and flinched. 'Let's go!'

In an all-but-deserted café, Eleanor wrapped her hands around the glass of cognac Clifford had brought from the bar. He sat down and cleared his throat.

'It was not my place to speak so out of turn, sir.'

Seldon frowned at him. 'I suppose you had your reasons,

Clifford. But they had better be good because we just deserted the scene of a policeman's death. Blast it!'

'As her ladyship's butler, that is still troubling me far less than safeguarding the lady herself,' Clifford said crisply.

'Now, look here!'

'Chaps, whoa there!' she cried. 'Let's calm down and drink our cognac. The shock has got to each of us. That's all that's happening here.'

Clifford turned to Seldon. 'My sincere apologies, sir,' he said stiffly.

'Mine too, I suppose,' Seldon gruffed, drumming his fingers.

'That's hardly kissing and making up, boys!' she chided. At their joint silence, she added, 'We're supposed to be a team. The three musketeers. Like the novel Clifford is reading. Do I need to come around and knock your heads together to remind you of that?'

'"All for one, one for all." A good enough motto for Dumas's musketeers,' Clifford said, as if mulling it over.

Seldon's jaw relaxed. Clifford's lips twitched. They shook hands.

She let out a sigh of relief.

'Perhaps now you'd explain why you felt we had to race away from the Eiffel Tower, Clifford?' Seldon said, sounding more his usual self.

'Willingly, sir. As the... ahem... person landed, I recognised him as the pickpocket I chased.'

'The pickpocket who tried to steal from my handbag?' Eleanor said in disbelief. 'But that dead man is—'

'*Was*... Constable Hacqueville, my lady. I did not recognise him at the time as he had a hood pulled down over most of his face and was out of uniform.' The concern in his eyes deepened. 'But his identity is not the worst of it.'

'Gracious, go on.'

He took a deep breath. 'At the risk of rekindling the awful

moment, along with him landing, I saw something fall with him and land a little way off. On scouring the bushes a few feet away, I found this.' He reached inside his jacket and produced a slim leather bag with a shoulder strap.

'Looks like a messenger's bag,' Seldon said.

Clifford's lips pursed. 'Indeed. The very one I saw "the pickpocket" wearing, as I assumed he was at the time.' He unbuckled the flap and pulled out a wad of banknotes.

Seldon's brow furrowed. 'That is a lot of money for a policeman pounding the beat in any country.'

Clifford reached inside again and produced three cigars. Placing them on the table, he reached in a third time. She frowned and leaned forward. Where had she seen...? As her butler pulled his hand out and unfurled his fingers, she gasped.

'That! I recognise that from the Christophe Ury display at the museum! I noticed it because it reminded me of growing up on my parents' sailboat, forever crossing the oceans.'

Clifford passed her the miniature sculpture of a boat carved from some highly polished soot-black stone.

'And it was among the exhibits in Christophe Ury's personal effects, you say?' Seldon said.

'Yes. Right next to the space left by the pearl brooch that Emile took.' She shook her head.

'But what was Hacqueville doing with it?'

'I now believe, my lady, he was trying to hide it in your handbag,' Clifford said gravely.

Seldon rapped the table. 'The blaggard! So he wasn't pickpocketing?'

'I greatly fear not,' Clifford said. 'It explains why he seemed so nervous and had his fingers clenched while reaching into her ladyship's bag.'

Eleanor slumped back in her seat. 'But why?'

Seldon ran a troubled hand through his curls. 'To plant incriminating evidence that would strengthen the case against you as Emile Ury's accomplice. That's why. Just as he himself declared so publicly in the hotel dining room!'

Her brow creased. 'But the museum would have to have reported they'd found a second item stolen.'

'Yet who would question such?' Clifford said. 'Given the vast number of the museum's exhibits and the confusion of that night?'

Seldon leaned forward. 'Well, thanks to you, Clifford, his devious plan has been foiled!'

'For now, sir. But it strikes me that Hacqueville would never have been the one to "find" that stolen item in her ladyship's possession. It was too risky, given he was the one who planted it. I conjecture that another of his colleagues was lying in wait at the bottom of the Eiffel Tower. Or may still be waiting back at our hotel.'

Seldon nodded, his face grim. 'His partner, Constable Bernier, most likely.'

Eleanor pictured the page in her notebook where she had listed the suspects for Emile's murder. 'Originally, I thought Gripperel could have been involved because it was the *police nationale* that were on the atrium roof when Emile was pushed through. Or so I believed. Because Pronovost, overheard by Cass, the porter, blamed Gripperel for chasing the thief up there. But the two policemen we spoke to at the museum on our return visit both swore there had been none of their division up there at all.'

Seldon leaned forward. 'What are you saying, Eleanor?'

'That perhaps the police on the roof when Emile was pushed were *municipale*, not *nationale!*'

He thumped the table. 'Hacqueville and Bernier! Blast it, how did I miss that? Those two were the first on the scene in the dining room after Emile Ury fell.'

She nodded. 'At the time, we assumed they had come in answer to Pronovost's telephone call to the police. But, looking back, they can't have. They arrived almost literally on his coat-tails. In a matter of, what, five minutes?'

He nodded back grimly. 'That wad of money, Clifford? How much is there roughly?'

Her butler discreetly flicked through the notes under the cover of the table. 'I should say twelve thousand francs. Equating to close to one hundred and twenty-five pounds.'

Seldon whistled quietly. 'That's half a year's salary for a police constable in London! That suggests that money was payment to plant that second stolen item on you, Eleanor.'

'Or for killing poor Emile? Or both!' She shuddered, horrified by the thought of a policeman, the one person you were supposed to be able to trust, being a hired assassin. 'On paper, Hacqueville seemed to be the chief suspect, but now he's dead as well. The notion it was suicide isn't washing with me.'

Clifford nodded. 'Nor I, my lady. The modus operandi of the two deaths is too distressingly similar.'

'And,' Seldon said, 'it makes no sense he would be happy enough to plant that item on you one minute. Then leap to his death the next.'

'And that fits with the fact he had no cuts to either shin or calf.'

Seldon groaned. 'Eleanor! What in blazes were you thinking of? Pulling up a dead man's trouser bottoms to gaze at his legs in public!'

'Is it a consolation it probably isn't the first time, sir?' Clifford said.

'No!'

'Traitor!' she muttered to her butler. 'But, Hugh, I had to check. And I'm glad I did as it rules Hacqueville out as having killed Emile, in my mind.'

'Then it does in mine too,' Seldon said without hesitation. 'Until proven otherwise, at least. So, we're looking for one murderer who killed both Emile Ury and Constable Hacqueville, right?'

She frowned while nodding. 'Yes. And that person could still be anyone on our suspect list. But my money is tending towards Rion, or for the first time, Omfroy.'

'Why, Eleanor?'

'Because this carved boat was stolen *after* we were at the museum the night Emile was murdered. I specifically remember looking at it again as we retraced our steps to leave.'

Seldon tapped the table thoughtfully. 'Hmm, excellent point. Hacqueville wasn't part of Gripperel's team, so had no acceptable reason for being there. So Rion or Omfroy must have passed it on to him?'

'Or someone else with a connection to the establishment,' Clifford said. 'Monsieur Delorme springs to mind, seeing as his gallery is the one who loans much of the Impressionist paintings to the museum. I imagine he can come and go without anyone thinking it noteworthy at all.'

She pursed her lips. 'Or Gripperel. He could have taken it the following day. His men were still swarming all over the place. There's one silver lining in all this, though. Hacqueville and whoever he was working with can't have known I have the pearl brooch. Otherwise, they would have had no reason to try and plant this second item on me.'

'The second item which you are still currently holding, Eleanor,' Seldon said soberly. 'Which means, along with the brooch, you now have two reasons to be indicted as the thief's accomplice!'

'Or his murderer,' her lips let fly before she could stop them. 'A falling-out between thieves. We said exactly that ourselves!' she groaned. 'I've just realised, a whole crowd of people up the Eiffel Tower saw Clifford wrestling with Hacqueville only minutes before...'

'He was thrown to his death,' Clifford finished for her gently. 'And there is still a further matter to consider.'

Seldon closed his eyes. 'Go on, Clifford.'

'We do not even know for sure that Monsieur Pronovost made that call to the police after Monsieur Ury died, sir. Maybe he was in on whatever Constables Hacqueville and Bernier were really doing to be close enough to have arrived so swiftly?'

Seldon rapped the table. 'Right. That does it. We can't return to the hotel.'

'Or stay in Paris herself, I suggest, sir.'

Eleanor nodded. 'It feels like we're caught in a deadly web that's being spun around us. And fast! Going to Inspector Gripperel's no good either. We still have no idea about him, as we said.'

'Then where can we go, for Pete's sake?' Seldon said. 'Any contacts here, Clifford?'

He shook his head. 'Regrettably not. Not after so many years since his lordship was here.'

'Well, I say first one of us has to sneak into the hotel and grab Gladstone. Which I'm—'

'Not going to do, Eleanor!' Seldon said with a stern look.

Clifford pointed at himself, then held a deferential hand up. 'Unless you feel it should be yourself, sir?'

Seldon grimaced. 'I want to say, categorically, yes. However, your highly questionable skills will see you in and out in a blink. Whereas my lack of them would likely have me caught red-handed.'

'I'll take that as a compliment,' Clifford said nonchalantly.

Eleanor opened her handbag and promptly spilled the contents onto the table. 'Dash it! This is no time to go to pieces!' she muttered.

Clifford helped collect her belongings, but paused in handing over the card Le Comte had given her at the cocktail party.

'My lady?'

'Oh, that?' She waved it away. 'It's a chap we met tonight who invited us to stay at his chateau. But it's no good thinking we'd stay there. He's a mercurial sort of fellow, to my mind, and an acquaintance of Delorme. And anyway, we need to be somewhere where we can keep investigating somehow.'

Clifford's brow furrowed. 'Hmm, "mercurial" the gentleman may be, but any port in a storm, as the saying goes. And, ahem, his chateau is perfectly placed for continuing the investigation.'

He laid the card on the table and ran his finger under the last line of the address.

She gasped. 'Magnes-sur-Oise? That's where Sabine said Emile lived!'

27

Chateau Archambault was every inch the fairy-tale castle Eleanor had gazed dreamily at in storybooks as a child. Its enchanting cream stone turrets and towers called to her inner Rapunzel. Its romantic corner balconies further stirring her already captivated Juliet. Inside the four-storey mansion, however, she was finding the vast echoing halls and scantily furnished rooms with faded wall tapestries rather soulless. Though she was also struggling to shake off the feeling, the souls of those passed were watching wherever she went.

She mentally chided herself for giving in to her over-fanciful imagination after the two recent murders. Instead, she dragged her focus back to their host, Le Comte, who was waiting to lead her courteously in to dinner.

In truth, she was itching to ask him a raft of questions. Not that she necessarily suspected him of anything untoward just because he knew Delorme. She imagined most people of money or wealth in Paris knew a man like Delorme in one way or another. But Le Comte was a hard man to read. And he did have rather unpredictable mood swings. She'd overheard him twice already haranguing a bewildered member of staff as if he'd caught them stealing the silver.

But he had welcomed her earlier telephone call. She had explained they had shuffled some of their honeymoon plans around to take him up on his gracious offer. And, on their arrival, he'd received them warmly into his chateau.

'It really is too kind of you, Monsieur le Comte,' she said, arranging the folds of her amethyst silk evening gown.

He smiled. 'The pleasure is all mine. Though please forgive us dining in the family salon. We are only four and either of the banqueting halls would feel like I was entertaining you in one of the barns.'

Four, Ellie? That means Odette isn't coming. Dash it!

She'd hoped to talk to her, too. Remembering Odette's remark about Le Comte rarely entertaining at Chateau Archambault, she wondered when those banqueting halls had last been used.

'It's positively charming,' she said, admiring the duck-egg blue of the flock wallpaper, matching drapes and upholstery.

'Mr Seldon, please.' Le Comte gestured at the chair next to Eleanor. Then to the one opposite, as he cocked his aristocratic chin in Clifford's direction. 'And your... secretary is welcome too, Lady Swift.'

Clifford had agreed to go along with the ruse as she wanted him next to her, as extra eyes and ears, not stuck in the servants' quarters. Besides, with the expert hand with which he officiated over her affairs, including her financial accounts, he genuinely fulfilled the role of a private aide, and so much more besides. And as he hadn't made it up to Eiffel's 'secret' apartment, Le Comte would be none the wiser.

Gladstone gave up trying to scrabble his portly form up onto the seat beside her, sitting down instead and licking his lips at the delicious aromas coming from the serving table.

'Good job we didn't bring Tomkins, too!' Seldon murmured.

Eleanor hid a smile. She had conceded to Clifford's concern that Le Comte was clearly a powerful man in the area. And accepted his reminder they were there to lie low. Thus, she intended to tread carefully.

'You have the most remarkable chateau in such a peaceful setting. It's hard to remember Paris is only an hour and a half away by motor car.'

'Peaceful?' Le Comte seemed to consider the question gravely. 'Now, yes, Lady Swift. But it has not always been this way. Not for much of its history.'

She nodded. 'Which my boffin of a secretary has likely deduced already. Honestly, he's as insatiable about learning as my cheeky bulldog there is at devouring sausages.'

'You find time to study among your duties?' Le Comte asked him with a hint of suspicion.

Clifford bobbed his head respectfully. 'As your illustrious *écrivain*, Alexandre Dumas noted, "One's work may be finished someday, but one's education never." I find it assists my role in advising her ladyship soundly on antique, art and property matters.'

To her dismay, Le Comte's gaze turned more scrutinising. 'Tell me, then, Mr Clifford. What have you deduced about Chateau Archambault?'

Looking unfazed, Clifford folded his hands. 'That it is an exquisite example of High Renaissance craftsmanship built during Le Grand Siècle between 1665 and 1672, unless I am mistaken? And if I might be forgiven for rendering an opinion, sir? The Verdure aux Oiseaux tapestry in the east gallery leading to our accommodations you have so graciously assigned is one fit to have graced His Majesty, Louis XIV's Versailles Palace itself.'

Le Comte's eyes widened. Then narrowed. He nodded slowly. 'It did. Once. By some accounts.' He looked at Eleanor.

'I see now why you brought your secretary with you on your honeymoon to Paris.'

'Oh, absolutely. And your house has that wonderfully grounded feel of generations of your family having lived here since it was built, yes?'

'Not exactly,' he said, glancing away.

She spotted Clifford's wince but had no idea what faux pas she had just made.

'I'm sorry if that was insensitive of me.'

Le Comte shrugged. 'Lady Swift, during the first French Revolution, many chateaux were stripped or destroyed simply to denounce and deny my class. Or sold, with no claim left to the owners. When my ancestors returned under the Second Empire, the inside of Chateau Archambault was looted completely. And much restoration work was needed, naturally, after sixty-three years of it being left only to the birds who nested in the broken roofs. And the vagabonds who had enjoyed playing *noblesse* among the rotten timbers!'

Ah! That probably explains why it feels so bare, Ellie! Restoring the building itself must have cost a fortune.

'Praise be to the providence of Napoleon the third's decree reinstating noble titles, then, sir,' Clifford said.

'Exactly!' Le Comte reached for his champagne. 'Now, before we begin with our *soupe aux palourdes*, I wish to raise a toast to your wedding.' He held his crystal flute aloft.

'I must warn you, the last time someone did that, it ended very badly!' she said without thinking.

She caught Seldon's quiet groan.

Le Comte looked at her oddly. 'I did not have the impression that you are a lady of a superstitious nature?'

She felt Seldon's knee nudging her leg under the table. Before she could back-pedal, however, Le Comte shrugged dismissively. 'Do not let the suicide of a man at the Eiffel Tower last night spoil your honeymoon. It happens sometimes.'

Wishing her evening gown was long-sleeved to hide her goosebumps at his indifferent tone, she stroked Gladstone's head where it had appeared in her lap.

'I thought you had already left with Odette before it happened?'

He looked up sharply. 'I read the news of him jumping in the newspaper this morning.'

'Do you know who he was?' Seldon asked.

'A strange question. Why should I?' He lifted his glass again. 'To your marriage. May it be long and happy.'

'It will,' Seldon said ardently. 'Thank you.'

Eleanor tipped her glass up, unable not to peer hesitantly at the ceiling before taking a sip.

The toast drunk, the first course arrived; clams in a butter, onion and parsley stock accompanied by a ring of gold, ochre and bronze banded shellfish drizzled in a crisp white wine and garlic sauce.

'Goodness, these shells are too beautiful to discard afterwards,' she murmured aloud. At their host's quizzical look, she smiled. 'I grew up on a sailboat. Shells and pebbles still always call to me.'

'*Amandes de mer*, my lady,' Clifford said. 'Or "almonds of the sea", due to their nutty, yet fishy, flavour. To compare it to our English cockles would be a gross injustice.'

She nodded, only then realising this first course was purgatory for him. Amongst his fastidiousness over food, he found seafood a total anathema, she knew. She sent him a sympathetic wince, receiving an imperceptible martyrish shudder in response.

Over the sublime caramel, hazelnut and soft orangey hints of the Madeira wine which followed, she restarted her earlier conversation.

'What was it like growing up here in Chateau Archambault, Monsieur le Comte?'

He hesitated, then shrugged. 'This I could not say. I spent much of my younger years elsewhere in Europe. Receiving my education.'

'Ah! That explains why your English is so impressively fluent, perhaps?' Seldon said.

'Perhaps, Mr Seldon.'

He waved to his waiting staff to serve the next course, which was the intriguingly named *profiteroles d'escargot*. In her travels, Eleanor had eaten many exotic unusual foods, but had never yet tried snail. She had to admit they were delicious; infused with shallots, red wine and garlic and encased in savoury choux pastry. As the *entremet* of celery mousse with anchovies came and went over more frustrating general topics, she was becoming increasingly itchy.

How to bring the conversation with this mercurial man back to the least suitable dinner topic of all, Ellie? Murder!

As they neared the end of the main course of *blanquette d'agneau*, lamb served in a creamy braised mushroom sauce, she decided subtlety would have to take second place. Picking up her glass of Marsanne wine, she enthused over the notes of pear and honey overlaid with tangy citrus, then held it aloft. 'I'd like to propose a toast, if I may?'

'But, of course.' He raised his glass, Seldon and Clifford following suit.

'To... keeping only good memories.'

Le Comte tipped his glass to her, but looked confused.

'On account of what you mentioned earlier,' she explained. 'About not forever associating that poor man's suicide with our honeymoon. Although, when I mentioned before the last toast that hadn't gone well, I wasn't referring to the death at the Eiffel Tower. But the earlier one.' She feigned a horrified gasp as if just realising something.

He frowned fleetingly. 'I am unaware of any other deaths, Lady Swift?'

'It happened in our hotel,' Seldon said, glancing in concern at Eleanor. 'My wife tried to save the poor fellow.'

She nodded. 'Yes, but gracious, my apologies. I should have offered my condolences the moment we arrived.'

'To me?' Le Comte said.

'Yes. He was from here, you see. Magnes-sur-Oise. Emile Ury was his name.' She watched him closely.

'Ury... Ury?' he repeated, tapping his forehead. He shrugged. 'I do not know this name.'

'Really?'

'Really, Lady Swift. It is just a coincidence if he lived in the village. Everyone has to come from somewhere. However, I do not mix with the locals. It is my policy.' With that, he rose. 'My esteemed guests, I must ask you to excuse me.'

'Of course. Not a pudding man, I see. More for us then,' she said, much to Clifford's evident horror and Seldon's amusement.

'I meant I must leave on a business matter. Which I had arranged before you telephoned me,' Le Comte elaborated.

'But we wouldn't have dreamed of coming if we'd known,' Seldon said.

'Naturally. Which is why I did not say.' He dropped his napkin on the table. 'I will be back tomorrow evening. And will bring Odette with me. Until then, please enjoy my home. It is entirely at your disposal. My staff will see to your every need.'

He strode from the dining room.

The three of them agreed to take dessert with an after-dinner cognac and were shown to a room with a pair of old-fashioned pink and blue settees. Once the door was closed and they were alone, she let out a long whistle. 'Well, how peculiar was that? He practically reached down the telephone to bite my arm off when I said we were free to take up his invitation. And then, even before we've been served dessert—'

'He deserts us,' Seldon finished for her. 'Seemed odd to me, too. But it still suits our urgent need to get out of Paris. Although I agree with your description of him being rather temperamental, Eleanor.'

'"Mercurial", I believe it was, sir. If you will forgive the correction,' Clifford said with a sniff.

She tutted. 'Before you complain about my character assassination, Clifford, tell me what word you would use?' She bent to feed her eager bulldog a piece of her fig and apple tart pastry crust. 'Hang on, though. Why does Gladstone smell of garlic?'

'I really couldn't say.' Clifford topped up her brandy.

'You scoundrel! You fed him all the shellfish you couldn't stomach! And the snails! I shall have hours of fun ribbing you about that.'

'Are you sure, my lady? A tournament of trumps regarding maintaining propriety is unlikely to go in your favour.'

'Oh, I don't know, Clifford. I could start with the fact that you snuck back into our hotel last night to rescue Gladstone and the perfect set of weekend-away togs for each of us. Because I meant to thank you for choosing just the right underfrillies for me.'

He ran his finger around his collar. 'Sir, I did no such thing! I enlisted the help of Sophie the maid for that... area of packing. Cass, the porter, then helped take everything out the back way while Jules, the waiter, recommended an alternative and very discreet hotel for the night before causing a distraction.'

Seldon smiled. 'I believe you, Clifford. But I'm in no doubt her ladyship has placed you in far more compromising situations I have no wish to hear about... I think,' he ended, looking suddenly undecided.

She laughed. 'Don't worry. There'll be plenty more, Hugh. Which you'll have more chance to witness for yourself from now on.' She wandered to the window. 'Ah! There goes Le

Comte. He's just marched over to his chauffeur, about to harangue him, no doubt.' She frowned and squinted harder. Something about the scene seemed familiar.

Oh gracious, it can't be, can it, Ellie?

28

The next morning, Gladstone led the charge down the grand staircase into the orangerie, which doubled as the breakfast room.

'Bravo for beating our mistress to the comestibles for once, Master Gladstone,' she caught Clifford murmuring as she entered with Seldon.

Her witty response dried on her lips as she spotted the wraith-like man whose black suit seemed to be all that was holding his angular frame together. Le Comte's valet and butler, she assumed, given only a skeleton staff were employed at Chateau Archambault.

'Bonjour,' she called cheerily.

'Bonjour, madame,' his gravelly voice replied, rather chillingly. His hooded, dark-eyed stare was unnerving too. However, he pulled a chair out for her, something she knew Clifford had needed to restrain himself from doing in his guise of being her secretary.

With a wave of his bony hand at the enticing array of breakfast fare spread across the table, he slunk back out through the door, closing it behind him.

Only not quite. Eleanor cocked her head to check for his footsteps receding.

Clifford rose, clearly reading her mind. Having closed the door forcibly, he poured her a coffee and an orange juice. Turning to Seldon, he held up both options questioningly.

He shrugged. 'Whatever there is, thank you. Might as well enjoy our absent host's generosity.'

'If not his staff's lack of subtlety,' she hissed. 'I'm pretty sure they have been told to watch us. And not because we might pinch the silver!'

He sighed. 'So much for trying to salvage some honeymoon romance by staying in a fancy French castle. Even if it is because, secretly, we're hiding out, blast it!'

'Chateau, sir,' Clifford corrected respectfully. 'This one was not built for defence, but purely to impress.'

'Well, like all of our time in Paris so far, it's going to leave quite the impression!' Seldon muttered.

Eleanor sighed into her coffee.

He shook himself. 'Sorry. At least nothing happened last night to get in the way of enjoying...' He broke off with a groan as she winced.

Clifford slid the notebook Seldon had bought her from his jacket pocket, along with his fountain pen.

Seldon nodded resignedly. 'Alright, let's hear whatever I'm in the dark about this time. Who'll start?'

'I am no more in the know than you, sir,' Clifford said.

The two of them looked at Eleanor expectantly as she flipped through to her suspect list.

She began adding notes as she explained. 'Well, when I saw our illustrious host leaving so unexpectedly last night, something unsettling struck me. And having slept on it, I'm even surer now. There's a strong chance he was lying at dinner. About not knowing Hacqueville was the man who died falling from the Eiffel Tower, I mean.'

Seldon's brow furrowed. 'What makes you think so?'

'His car. And his chauffeur, Hugh. I saw both at the Eiffel Tower. And I'm pretty certain that it was the same driver and fancy vehicle I saw Hacqueville lean in the rear window of the evening Emile was murdered. We were in a café, if you remember? The one with the old man playing the *musette* to his black cat.'

'When we wondered if he and his partner, Bernier, were following us?' Seldon nodded thoughtfully. 'But you didn't see Le Comte in the back of the car?'

'No. It was too dark to see who it was.'

Clifford added a small, oval-lidded dish to each of their plates. 'An unsettling thought has occurred to me, too, my lady. Maybe Le Comte had not actually left the Eiffel Tower before Constable Hacqueville's demise, as you imagined he had at the time?'

Seldon pointed at him. 'Excellent point! And now I think of it, he fudged answering that last night, Eleanor. By saying he read of the suicide in the newspaper.'

She shivered. 'But why?'

'Perhaps the coincidence of him living in the same village as Emile Ury is not coincidental?' Clifford said. He suddenly cleared his throat. 'If I might suggest my continuing to scribe the tasting notes for legibility, my lady?' He leaned across the table and leafed forward half a dozen pages in the notebook.

She glanced up, as the valet-cum-butler slunk in, followed by a maid, both of them carrying trays.

She looked back down. The sight of her butler's meticulous handwriting under the neat heading of 'Breakfast or *Petit Déjeuner*' would have made her smile in other circumstances. With his usual wizardry, he'd prepared for every eventuality.

'Quite right, Clifford. We were discussing that divine eggy toast.'

'*Pain perdu*,' he said slowly, as if explaining to a dim-witted child. 'Oh dear, I fear our French lessons will have to increase, my lady. Now, onto the *oeufs cocotte*.' He pointed to their lidded dishes. Seemingly satisfied, the valet and maid left their trays of more sliced fruit and a selection of honeys and retired.

Again, Clifford closed the door properly after them.

Seldon stared between them. 'Huh? "Tasting notes?" How does one of you come up with a ruse like that on the spot and the other always knows how to respond plausibly, blast it?'

Clifford's lips quirked. 'Oh, it is not purely a ruse, sir. Her ladyship's propensity for planning the next meal while eating the present one really knows no bounds.'

She rolled her eyes good-naturedly, mostly because it was true. 'Shall we continue?' At their nods, she wrote 'Bellamy Delorme', and looked up. 'It struck me before we were interrupted that he invited us to that cocktail soirée up the Eiffel Tower very readily, Hugh.'

Seldon shook his head slowly. 'Nothing strikes me as suspicious about it, Eleanor. He was just buttering you up because he believed you would buy some astronomically over-priced painting.'

She tapped the pen on her chin. 'Perhaps. Perhaps, not.'

'Most perspicacious, as always, my lady,' Clifford murmured.

She smiled at Seldon's confused look. 'He means "shrewd", Hugh. I only know because I looked it up once.'

Seldon glanced between them, frowning. 'Fancy explaining why to the supposed detective on the team?'

'By passing on the invitation, Monsieur Delorme may have been establishing an alibi, sir,' Clifford said. 'And one that would be backed up by the word of a gentleman of standing, Le Comte. Since he introduced himself to you specifically at the request of Monsieur Delorme.'

She nodded eagerly. 'It fits, Hugh. Delorme could have planned to be at the Eiffel Tower. But not to attend the soirée.

To kill Hacqueville after he'd planted that second stolen item on me from the museum!'

Seldon rubbed his hand along his jaw. 'I grant you, Delorme could easily have hidden among the crowds. But I can't see a connection with him and the first murder, as we still reckon there's only one murderer. Why would a high-class art dealer like him be involved with a petty thief like Emile Ury?'

Eleanor felt peculiarly bristled by his description. 'He wasn't a "petty thief", Hugh!' She squeezed his hand apologetically for that having come out so harshly. 'I'm sorry. I can't explain why I feel the need to defend him.'

'Because you believe you failed him when he died, my love, that's why. But you didn't,' Seldon said gently.

Clifford busied himself with feeding Gladstone a selection from the cold meat platter. 'Ahem, if we are including Monsieur Delorme, perhaps Monsieur Omfroy should be included for the same reason, my lady? He, of all people, would have been best placed to steal that second item that was intended to incriminate you.'

'Excellent point, Clifford.' Her pen flew across her page.

Seldon held his hands up. 'Hang on. Why would the director of a clearly prestigious museum get involved in any of this, any more than the owner of a fancy art gallery?'

She shrugged. 'Excellent point, too. I've no answer at the moment.'

'Ni moi,' Clifford said more loudly. 'Meaning, "me neither". Since we are combining your French lessons with tasting notes this morning, my lady.' He pointed at the door handle, which was slowly turning.

With the spurious delivery of more croissants and pain au chocolat than even Eleanor had no hope of finishing, the eerily silent valet left again.

She flipped back to her suspect list. Adding the last of their combined observations, she beckoned the two of them closer.

Alain Rion

- Lied about knowing Emile at first
- Lied about leaving his post
- Was seen coming back from direction of hotel by Officers Hacqueville and Bernier
- Easy access to steal second museum item found in Hacqueville's bag

Sabine Rion

- Lied about relationship with Emile?
- Lied about knowing about Emile robbing museum and his death?
- Related to museum guard (will find out exactly how) – did they plan murder together?

Pronovost

- Didn't appear immediately Emile fell – told staff in office – could have had time to push Emile and then come down service stairs – would have had key
- Refused to send for doctor – maybe hoped Emile would die?
- Tried to put blame on to Gripperel
- Easy access to steal second museum item found in Hacqueville's bag

Inspector Gripperel

- Lied about thief tripping while running across roof
- Had his men chase thief up on roof? (2 of his men say none went up there)

- Was surprisingly keen to let me go along to museum late last night – keeping an eye on me?
- Some access to steal second museum item found in Hacqueville's bag

Hacqueville

- At scene of Emile's death. Had time to kill Emile before entered restaurant
- Accused us of being accomplices!
- Seen leaning in window of what is very possibly Le Comte's car

Bernier

- At scene of Emile's death. Could have killed Emile, same as Hacqueville
- Was there when Hacqueville seen leaning in car (see above)

Le Comte

- His car the one Hacqueville was leaning in rear window of?
- Still at Eiffel Tower when Hacqueville murdered?
- Denied knowing Emile Ury but lives in same village
- Denied knowing name of Eiffel Tower 'suicide' man but if it was his car Hacqueville was leaning in... almost certainly a lie

Odette

- Same as for Le Comte?

Delorme

- Easy access to steal second museum item found in Hacqueville's bag
- Invited Hugh and me to Eiffel Tower where Hacqueville killed

Omfroy

- Best access to take second item to give to Hacqueville

Seldon sat back. 'Everyone seems to have had the opportunity. But no one has an obvious motive. And we're stuck here, having to hide out. Even from the servants now, blast it!'

She spotted her notebook being inched away. 'My scallywag bu— secretary is right, Hugh. How about a break to clear our thoughts?'

'Perhaps a tour of the chateau's grounds, my lady?' Clifford pocketed the notebook. 'While I play decoy here to keep the staff busy with a game of cat and mouse?'

She laughed. 'Perfect! Let the games begin!'

29

A whisper of a breeze drifted on the otherwise still morning air as she and Seldon slipped out of the chateau. The wrap-over folds of her favourite sage wool cape felt a snug defence against the damp as the pair of them and Gladstone were swallowed up by the mist.

They headed across the terrace, tripping on the uneven flagstones until they reached a colonnade of weathered columns. It fronted a seating area which probably offered lovely views of the chateau on a clear day. They followed a frolicsome Gladstone down the long sweep of balustraded steps at the end to find themselves in an extensive formal garden. Elaborately shaped flower borders were surrounded by low box hedging. The swirls, teardrops, radials and even knot patterns gave the scene the illusion of having not been planted, but embroidered. A network of paths radiated out from a central fountain around the whole garden.

She interrupted Gladstone as he prepared to dig excitedly in the nearest flower bed.

'Odd,' Seldon said distractedly. At her tug on his arm to explain, he rubbed his chin. 'Le Comte's speech at dinner about how proud he is of his family clawing back their ancestral home? I'm struggling to match that with the feeling it's just him and Odette who rattle round here with only a handful of servants. Maybe I'm wrong.'

'I don't think you are, Hugh. I've had the same feeling since we arrived. The house has that air of no one ever coming and going, as Odette hinted. I peeped in a few doors along the guest wing we're in and all the furniture was under dust covers. Which makes it feel all the more peculiar he was so keen for us to come and stay.'

Their musings had taken them to the end of the ornamental gardens. A shorter flight of steps led down, this time to a water garden. Then, yet more steps led steeply upwards to a viewing platform. The remains of what must have once been a spectacular maze spread out below them. But it was what lay beyond that attracted her eye.

'What do woods mean, Gladstone?'

He let out a round of excited barks and spun in an erratic circle.

'Rabbits to chase?' Seldon said.

She laughed. 'Mr Soppy there would rather cuddle up with them than chase them, Hugh. Unlike sticks. The next best thing as we've no balls to throw for him.'

'Ah! Then we can still run some fat off the sausage monster. Excellent idea.'

By the time they had navigated around the maze rather than risk getting hopelessly lost in it, the sun was high enough to pepper the woods with blinding orange shafts. In sharp contrast to the rest of the estate they'd seen so far, the woods had been left to nature's own devices. It made sense as no one would come tramping all the way out here, except occasionally in hunting season, maybe.

Normally, like Gladstone, she would have been in her element. But something gave the area a feeling of isolation.

No, Ellie. Desolation.

But only to her, it seemed, as Seldon strode cheerily along a slight narrow indentation on the forest floor, which had the hallmarks of an animal track. Badger maybe? Or deer more likely, as it would take their agility to leap the series of thick fallen trunks strewn across it at intervals. Seldon, with his long, athletic legs, slid over each one without too much trouble, even with Gladstone in his arms. She insisted on clambering over herself, the folds of her skirt hitched up over her arm.

'No point wasting time being ladylike when there's no one to see,' she said in reply to his amused expression.

'Except your husband!'

'Oops! You mean you thought you'd married a lady?'

'Only by title,' he said chuckling. 'I pity those knights of old who tried to rescue damsels in distress with a stubborn rhinoceros streak like you though. I'd have crept off quietly and left you to the dragon.' He chuckled again as he dodged the swipe she aimed at his head. 'Come on, there's a rocky outcrop over there. We can have a pause while Gladstone gets up to something he probably shouldn't.'

Making their way over to it was more of an obstacle course than they'd imagined, with more fallen trunks, clumps of protruding roots and scattered rocks. But it was just what they needed, she thought. A proper distraction. Their bodies working, not their minds. And Gladstone was in doggy paradise as he dashed around, under and over, his stumpy tail a constant blur of excitement.

Eleanor's natural competitiveness turned it into a race which left her and Seldon rosy cheeked and breathless by the time the three of them reached the rocky mound. Gladstone drank noisily from a small pool, spraying them with water as he lapped with gusto. She smiled as Seldon insisted on laying his coat down on the flattest rock for her to sit on.

'So there is something of the gallant knight in you still,' she teased. Her stomach let out a loud gurgle.

'Eleanor, you cannot be hungry!' Seldon cried. 'Not after the amount you devoured at breakfast.'

She tutted. 'That was just to fool the staff we weren't up to anything. Besides, according to Clifford, the official term is the amount I "laid waste to". But still, after our exertions getting here, I could eat a horse. Clifford would usually have packed one automatically for me. But I bet he's chuckling away to himself in the chateau now at not having done so because I asked him to pretend he's our secretary, not butler.'

'Indeed, my lady. In light of my new duties, I failed to pack you a morsel,' Seldon said in a remarkably good impression of Clifford. She laughed, then harder as he patted his coat pockets with a smug sniff. 'Hold on, what's this...' He frowned as he pulled out two waxed-paper parcels. 'It seems you were wrong!'

The first parcel turned out not to be a horse, but a selection of ham and cheese chunks with slices of pineapple. The second, a hearty portion of Gladstone's favourite liver treats. As she turned to show it to her bulldog, her foot slipped, toppling her sideways. The treats flew out of her hand, landing in a wide arc.

'There's a new game for you, Gladstone. And a treat for me, too,' Seldon said, helping her back up. 'Snuffling out your biscuits while I cuddle up with my wife away from anything dangerous or unpleasant for a change.'

The three of them did just that. Gladstone barking with delight each time he found one of his treats.

How long had passed before she realised his excited woofs had changed, she couldn't say. But at some point, they'd morphed into one insistent bark. She jerked upright. 'Hugh, where's Gladstone? He sounds like he's calling for help.'

They both leaped up from the rock. Listening intently as they went, they hurried around the base of the mound. The vegetation was much thicker this side, the dense bush of brambles snagging at her clothes and hands as she called and whistled.

'He's obviously not hurt. Probably just got his sausage-belly wedged somewhere,' Seldon said.

They listened again, her worries growing now. She clawed through the undergrowth, heedless to the scratches. 'If he's gone down an animal burrow, like a badger's set, we'll have to dig him out. But we've no tools! Oh Gladstone, where are—' She broke off as her fingers felt metal among the thorny vegetation. 'Quick! Here, Hugh.'

Seldon hurried to her. 'It's like the iron barriers the old storm drains in London have been sealed up with. You can drive a truck at those and they won't cave in.'

She pressed her mouth to the metal and yelled, 'Gladstone, we're coming!'

Throwing themselves at the barrier did nothing, except leave her winded and Seldon rubbing his shoulder.

'Hang on, there's a blasted padlock!' he said. 'It's very rusty. But it's still strong enough to need a key to open it.'

'No, it doesn't!' she cried, scouring under the brambles at her feet. Grabbing a small stone and the largest she could swing, she wedged the first into the gap between the bar and the padlock's body. 'Stand back!' Holding the large rock high above her head, she brought it down on the point where the bar entered the padlock. The whack reverberated through the door, making Gladstone bark more keenly. She swung the rock again. And again.

'Eleanor, let me,' Seldon said.

'No need. I've sprung it!' she cheered. 'Let's go get our hapless bulldog.'

He held up his hand. 'At least let me do the manly part of opening the door!'

As it swung back, Eleanor turned her face away with a gasp. She'd felt something... escape. Something more than just stale air. Something...

She frowned. 'It smells like an old bonfire.'

They peered inside. Some steps seemed to have led down once, but their mountings were now nothing more than charred remains. 'Hold on, Gladstone,' she called, glimpsing the whites of his eyes below as he let out another volley of barks. 'He's not that far down, Hugh.'

'Yes. But how are we going to get back up after we've got him?' Seldon said, looking around.

Before he could stop her, she grabbed the pair of thick chains he hadn't seen attached to the wall, yanked to make sure they were held fast, and slithered down them.

'Hugh, stay there a moment. I'm fine. And I'll need you to grab Gladstone from me. The technique for climbing up ropes I learned on my parents' sailboat as a child will work on chains.'

'I don't like it. You're really alright?' Seldon called down, sounding far from happy.

'Fine. I just wish we had some source of light, so I can check there isn't an easier way out that my daft bulldog hasn't spotted. Like however he got in!'

'Ah! I've got some matches, I think.'

She was baffled. He didn't smoke.

'I thought we might at least enjoy some romantic candles, so I borrowed some from Clifford.'

'Perfect. Throw them down.'

The sound of something landing at her feet told her he had. She struck two together and peered around. Her heart clenched.

'Oh my goodness!'

'Eleanor! Don't move,' Seldon called out. 'I'm coming straight down!'

'No, Hugh. Don't!' In the eerie glow of the spluttering lit matches, she could see she was in a small cavern. It looked as if, long ago, it had once been a boys' den. Along one wall, three rough seats, or thrones perhaps, had been made from fallen rocks and stones. It was hard to tell as everything was charred and blackened, including the walls. On one, she could just make out the letters "Fort Archambault" carved crudely, as if with sharpened flints.

She felt an inexplicable rising panic. 'Throw me your thick scarf, Hugh. I'll tie Gladstone to my front with it and start climbing. Haul hard on the chains as I do. Quick!'

As Seldon's muscular arms grabbed her at the top, she fell against his chest, cradling Gladstone.

'What is it?' Seldon said, his eyes filled with concern. He steered her out into the open. Only then did her pounding heart begin to calm. She took a deep breath.

'Hugh. Something bad happened in... in there. A long time ago. I... I could feel it the minute we opened the door. Let's get away from here.'

As she stumbled back the way they'd come, Seldon's arm wrapped protectively around her waist, she tried to forget what she'd seen, and felt, down in the cavern. For now, at least. Because her knotted stomach and intuition were telling her that if she was ever going to unravel what really happened the night Emile died, first, she would have to unravel the tragedy of what had happened in that dark place long ago, six feet underground.

30

They must have been gone from the chateau even longer than Eleanor thought. As they cleared the last of the woods, Clifford appeared on the viewing platform which looked down onto the neglected maze, clearly searching the grounds for them. A few moments later, he joined them. Scanning her face, his usually inscrutable expression faltered.

'Where to, my lady?' he said softly.

'Home to Henley Hall!' her wrung-out emotions wanted to answer, but her resolve to seek out justice for the murder victims answered instead. 'The village. We need to get away from Le Comte's house and his staff before I can tell you everything I discovered in those woods. You too, Hugh.'

He blanched. 'You mean there's more than you told me?' At her look, he nodded sombrely. 'Let's find somewhere first with coffee for you at least. If not something stronger.'

Consulting the plan Clifford had busied himself sketching of the chateau and its grounds, they made for the estate's forbidding boundary wall and an ancient iron gate. Emblazoned in the middle was the lion of the Archambault family crest.

Seldon twisted, then yanked on the heavy iron ring. 'Blast, it's locked!'

'Not for long, sir.' Clifford reached inside his coat.

Outside the grounds of the chateau, Eleanor found it easier to breathe. Not that she had realised quite how constricted her chest had been since lighting the matches, which illuminated the distressing scene in the cavern.

Seldon pulled her in tighter and linked his fingers with hers. 'I can't bear you being caught up in all this,' he said self-reproachfully.

'Well, I am. We all are. And I'll tell you the part that's troubling me most now as we walk to the village. Because I want everything I have to say to float away into the ether.' With Gladstone falling into line beside her, Clifford having done so unbidden, the four of them walked on as one.

First she filled Clifford in on how they had found the padlocked iron barrier and her feeling that something terrible had occurred in the cavern below. 'And somehow we'll have to find a way to return and reseal that door. Because whatever happened in there needs to be left in peace.'

'Hmm, "we" as in Clifford and me,' Seldon said firmly.

'Unquestionably, sir.'

'Thank you, both,' she said with feeling. 'But you'll have to be extra careful. Because what Hugh also doesn't know yet are two things.' As the village rooftops came into view on the narrow road below, she lowered her voice. 'The first is, I'm pretty sure Le Comte lied about knowing Emile. And the second is...' The four of them paused in unison. Even Gladstone stared expectantly up at her. 'I'm certain Emile knew about that cavern. I'd even say there's a good chance he'd been in there.'

Seldon's brow furrowed. 'How can you be sure?'

'There's a painting on one of the walls. And even with the fire and smoke damage, it's unmistakable. It's the exact same animal that Emile had tattooed on his arm. A porcupine, I'm pretty sure now.'

He blanched. 'That's not good—'

'And Magnes-sur-Oise is known for its many small production vineyards,' Clifford said, sounding suddenly like a tour guide as he gestured discreetly that they were no longer alone. An elderly man with his equally elderly horse had appeared from around the corner in the road, only yards from where they were. Clifford approached him with a genial nod.

'Bonjour, monsieur. Une belle journée pour une promenade.'

The man doffed his brown cap to Eleanor, his eyes scrutinising their faces.

'Les invités du Archambault?'

'Invités?' Clifford tapped his forehead. 'Ah! This gentleman is asking if we are guests at Le Comte's chateau.'

She nodded keenly, wishing she could say in French what her jumbled thoughts were struggling to articulate in English. Quite how did one ask if their host, and local dignitary, was likely to be a murderer?

Before Clifford could open his mouth to ask another question, the old man shook his head. 'Le Comte!' Putting his hand on the horse's harness, he hurried on his way, calling, 'Bonne chance!' over his shoulder.

Seldon sighed. 'Even I've grasped that means "Good luck!"'

They continued down the road into the village of Magnes-sur-Oise, a huddle of brown-red-tiled roofs tumbling down to the greeny-blue ribbon of the river. Every hundred yards or so, a set of stone steps cut down between the houses. Somewhere amongst the hotchpotch of houses was the church, the tip of its spire protruding above the rooftops.

They continued, only stopping to rescue Gladstone from the feisty cockerels and irascible geese, hissing and honking at them as they ran out from the front yards. Seldon flapped his coat at a particularly vicious goose.

'That racket will let everyone know we're here. I imagine in a moment half the locals will appear nonchalantly on their doorsteps with a broom or pipe in hand!'

'Good. Then we can find out about Emile. And Le Comte,' she said eagerly.

But this wasn't England. The lace strips serving as curtains did twitch in several windows, but the doorsteps remained frustratingly empty.

The first person they did meet was the village postman.

Surely that has to be the same as back home, Ellie? The postman knows everything, including all the local gossip.

He may have. But after exchanging polite greetings, he nodded sadly at the mention of Emile Ury's name and clambered back on his bike. Before she had even finished uttering Le Comte's, he was shaking his head apologetically and freewheeling away down the hill. Next they enquired of a man in farmer's overalls with a handcart of hay who immediately feigned an urgent rendezvous with anyone but them. The brace of middle-aged women with baskets filled with muddy beetroots and spring greens clucked sadly at Emile Ury's name, but hastily clutched their hats and muttered their '*au revoirs*' at Le Comte's.

After three more attempts had failed, despite being more subtly executed by Clifford and Seldon, Eleanor sighed in exasperation.

'I can understand Le Comte's staff clamming up out of loyalty. And fear of his rather temperamental moods. But none of the locals seems happy to say a word after hearing his name. And all we've learned about Emile is that news of his death has reached his village and on the whole people seem sad about it.'

Clifford cleared his throat. She waved for him to get whatever it was off his chest.

'Le Comte is clearly the most powerful man in Magnes-sur-Oise, my lady. And possibly this side of Paris. The number of aristocratic titles restored under Napoleon the third's decree in 1852 was by its retraction in 1870 but a fraction of those in existence before the French Revolution. So Le Comte is—'

'Quite the grand Camembert, or whatever the expression is,' Eleanor interrupted. 'I'm sure you're right, Clifford. The locals are just being cautious.'

Or maybe there's more to the mysterious count than we know, Ellie?

At a fork in the road, she turned left.

'I'm no expert on the layout of French villages,' Seldon said, pointing the opposite way, 'but the river is at the bottom of the valley. So it's more likely the main hub of the village will be downhill, surely? That way is uphill.' He nodded questioningly to Clifford for support.

'Most assuredly, sir. Shall we?' Clifford gestured left pointedly.

A minute later, a short flight of steps led up to an unexpectedly Gothic church. Eleanor climbed them and stepped to the vaulted entrance and bowed her head. Laying her hand on the stone, she whispered a prayer for Emile. She didn't need to go inside to trust that her plea he might forever rest in peace would be heard. Neither did she quite trust her emotions if she did. Instead, she sent another for Hacqueville and rejoined the others.

Clifford nodded to Seldon as the four of them set off to the bottom of the valley. 'There is always a reason for her ladyship's seeming whims, sir. Even if sometimes one cannot fathom what it is.'

Seldon smiled tenderly at her. 'I'm learning, Eleanor.'

'Thank you, Hugh. Now, let's go try our hand where we might do better. Where money talks.'

His mouth fell open. 'Clifford! Tell me my wife is not actually proposing to bribe people to give us information?'

'Her ladyship is not, sir.' His lips quirked. 'At least not until it is necessary.'

Seldon let out a long breath. 'I shall follow with my eyes shut and my hands clamped over my ears, seeing as I am still a policeman! Even if one breaking the law over harbouring two stolen items and deserting the scene of a policeman's death!'

Her hand strayed to her jacket front, but she said nothing.

The main street's narrow-fronted shops included a baker's, cobbler's, butcher's, tobacconist's and even a florist. The largest building of all, however, seemed to be the liveliest.

'Auberge Gravoux,' Clifford read the name painted in large red letters on the cream front. 'The local inn or hostelry. It could save a lot of time and unnecessary shopping elsewhere?'

She tutted. 'Tsk! Shopping is never unnecessary. Still, let's get a table and see what we can achieve in here.'

The *auberge*'s interior consisted entirely of dark wood; ceiling, floor, tables, chairs, and the bar. The man who came out from behind it to greet them had even taken on a similar hue himself. He escorted them to a table, placed a small chalkboard in a slotted stand on it and patted Gladstone on the head before leaving them to it.

'We're just having coffee, I assume?' Seldon said.

'We most certainly are not,' she whispered. 'Aside from something smelling irresistible, we need to spend proper money to get answers.'

'And only pull out the blackjacks and coshes when that doesn't work, I see.' He shook his head wryly.

'Actually, Clifford is an absolute whizz with both,' she said distractedly, trying to make sense of the chalked menu.

Clifford coughed. 'Ahem! Shall I order two of the only option available, my lady? That being *pot au fer*. A hearty stew of whatever meat is available with seasonal vegetables. The gravy is served separately as broth, followed by the meat and vegetables as the main course.'

She put the menu down. 'Order three. Because eating with us again won't actually finish you off, Clifford. And besides, now I know you're a dab hand at feeding Gladstone unnoticed... hmm?'

He sighed and went up to give their order. He returned with the barman, who was carrying a dark-wooden tray with a bottle of red wine and three brown glasses, plus a bowl of water for Gladstone.

'Get any useful information about Emile or Le Comte?' she whispered once they were alone.

'Perhaps, my lady.'

'And?'

'Unless my command of French let me down, I received a most courteously delivered warning to mind my own business!'

'Dash it! Well, we might as well enjoy the food and go.'

Their broth arrived, smelling delicious. As she lifted her first spoonful to her lips, a figure in a heavy black coat and hat slid out the door.

Clifford followed her gaze. 'My lady?'

'Hmm, oh nothing, I'm sure. Just a fleeting déjà vu. Again!'

'Searching too hard for answers can do that. I've taught myself to ignore it,' Seldon said to her surprise.

She ate, in between sipping the local wine, which was delicious sunshine in a bottle. Over the main dish of meat and vegetables, she asked the question the others had clearly been biting their tongues not to. 'Chaps, if we do eventually find anyone who'll talk to us about our host. And we learn something... untoward—'

'We leave immediately!' Seldon said forcefully. 'But don't ask me where to, because I have no idea. Gripperel will have alerted all the hotels to be on the lookout for us by now.'

They finished their food in a sombre mood, despite Clifford's best efforts at offering historical facts about Magnes he had gleaned from Le Comte's library. They then left with a guarded nod from the *auberge*'s proprietor.

That summed up the village's reaction to their presence and questions to her mind. No one was being unfriendly. Just... cautious.

Outside, she threw her hands up in exasperation. 'But they wouldn't be if they knew we were trying to catch the person who murdered Emile!'

'That is an obstacle we have to find a way around, Eleanor,' Seldon said. 'We can't show our hand. We've been over this.'

'I know, Hugh.'

'Take a break from it all for a moment, Eleanor. Enjoy some people-watching. It helps to remember that the bad, dishonest people are far outnumbered by the good, honest ones,' Seldon said, surprising her again. She was learning lots about him since they were married what was, unbelievably, only a week ago. And loving him all the more for it.

'There, see! That man with the umbrella just helped that lady with her heavy shopping bag up the steps opposite,' he said.

'Umbrella?' she repeated slowly. 'Which man, Hugh? The shortish one in a black coat and broad-brimmed hat... Oh, gracious, it is!' She spun them both by their jacket sleeves to face the cobbler's window in front of them. 'Look at the reflection. Remember him?'

Seldon shook his head. Clifford nodded. 'The very gentleman you teased me as being one I should likely enjoy swapping notes with on how to go about being "infuriatingly over-prepared", my lady?'

'Yes. The one we've seen twice in Paris.'

Seldon stiffened. 'In Paris? Twice?'

'Yes. First, when we were in Gripperel's car going to the museum immediately after poor Emile died. Then again at

Delorme's gallery. I thought he was just an art enthusiast, but now—'

'It seems he's been following us from the beginning!' Seldon interrupted. 'And knows we're hiding out here!'

She groaned, realisation dawning. 'Maybe everything that's happened since the moment Emile crashed through the atrium roof has been a set-up?'

Seldon rubbed his eyes in disbelief. 'But how? I only rearranged our honeymoon to Paris a month before we came. There must be some other explanation?'

'Only one way to find out,' Eleanor said, walking determinedly. 'It's time we took the fight to the enemy!'

31

Eleanor blinked. 'He's gone!'

While they had been discussing the 'umbrella man', as she had dubbed him, he had indeed disappeared.

'Dash it! He didn't look spritely enough to move that fast!'

'Unless that too was a ploy,' Seldon said gravely. 'Eleanor, I don't like this.'

'Neither do I, Hugh. But I dislike being set up and toyed with even more!'

Clifford's brow flinched. 'My lady, as Alexandre Dumas wrote so pertinently, "Haste is a poor counsellor." Perhaps we might—'

'Have heard enough of Dumas for now, thank you!'

She hurried across the road, narrowly dodging a horse and trap. Dashing up the steps where Seldon had noticed the man helping the woman with her shopping, she stopped at the top. Several benches were dotted around a grassed area, but there were no umbrellas. Off on the right, a group of old men were playing boules, the French version of lawn bowls, on a patch of gritty grey sand. But no one was wearing a heavy black coat and hat.

'Please remember, we're supposed to be keeping a low profile, Eleanor,' Seldon muttered.

She squeezed his hand. 'I hear you, Hugh.'

'Glinting, my lady. Ten o'clock.' Clifford tightened his grip on Gladstone's lead.

Seldon frowned and stared around the square. 'What?'

She pointed ahead. 'There, Hugh! The metal tip of our quarry's umbrella glinting in the sun. Come on!'

Trying to hurry, but inconspicuously, she paused at the corner. The man was looking over his shoulder. She flattened herself against the wall. When she dared peep again, he had turned left. She waved the others on and they continued to shadow their prey through narrow lanes between the houses hardly wide enough for a hand barrow. The uneven cobbles threatened to turn an ankle, even in her well-laced boots.

At the next junction, she paused.

'He could have gone into any of these houses,' she hissed. 'We—'

Seldon shushed her by pressing his fingers over her lips. He frowned and cocked his head. 'Listen!'

Dink... Dink... Dink...

'Ah! The tip of the gentleman's umbrella striking the cobbles as he leans on it like a walking stick up the slope, I believe,' Clifford murmured. 'Off to the left, just ahead.'

Hoping he was right, she turned in that direction in time to catch sight of their quarry's black coat disappearing up yet another lane. Only this time, the houses quickly ran out. Over the top of a long wall on her left, she could see a line of yew trees. And then...

'Is that the spire of the church you went up to earlier, Eleanor?' Seldon said quietly.

Clifford nodded. 'Indeed, it is, sir. I noted it as an exquisite example of Gothic tracery. One I believe was immortalised in a painting by the increasingly renowned Impressionist painter,

Vincent Van Gogh. Who... ahem, is not relevant at this juncture, of course,' he tailed off apologetically.

She smiled. 'We'd love to hear about him. But later.'

The path ran out. Facing them was a modest, two-storey house built in the local weather-beaten stone. And a flash of black disappearing through the front door.

'Right. Now, we wait.'

'Did I hear correctly, Master Gladstone?' Clifford whispered to her bulldog. 'Waiting surely involves patience? A new departure for our mistress.'

What felt like an age later, her feet numb from standing in one spot, she slapped her forehead.

'How blunt a brick are we? He probably just went in the front and straight out the back door!' Her expression hardened. 'Which means he's either already gone or we go with the only option we have left.'

'Which is?' Seldon said hesitantly.

She strode purposefully up to the door and raised the brass knocker. Before she had brought it down, however, the door swung open. Standing on the strip of brown mat just inside was her umbrella man!

'So you have followed me? And all the way from Paris.' The softness and musical tenor of his voice took her unawares. But not as much as his words. Or his clothes. A black calf-length cassock, paired with a white dog collar. For a moment she faltered, then shook herself.

He's the enemy, remember, Ellie? Anyone can dress as a priest.

'We haven't been following you, monsieur. It is entirely the other way around!' she said stiffly, closely watching his deeply lined face.

The man smiled disarmingly. 'Which ever it is, madame, here you are. And here is my home. Please enter.'

Seldon grasped her arm gently, but she shook her head. For,

as the man dressed as a priest had stepped back to let them in, she had seen the bronze crucifix dominating the hallway. If it was a trap, at least this man was putting the effort in.

'For Emile, I know,' Seldon muttered.

They were shown into a small, sunny sitting room with two mismatched armchairs and a pew-style bench set with a sprinkle of patchwork cushions.

'Please be seated,' their host said.

She remained on her feet. 'I'm not one for lounging, thank you.'

He shrugged. 'Then allow me to introduce myself. And tell you my story. After which, I hope sincerely you will lose the distrust that has walked into my house with you?'

She frowned. Something in his soft tone had hardened. He seemed... affronted? Somehow, it made her believe him a little more. She perched on the edge of the nearest armchair, Seldon standing next to her, while Clifford blocked the door back out into the hall.

The man spread his hands. 'My friends, I am Didier le Godine. The local priest of Magnes-sur-Oise. As I have been for thirty-nine years.'

'Then you knew Emile Ury?' she said quickly.

His expression fell. 'I knew him well.'

The sadness in his tone struck her as genuine. 'Then our sincere condolences.'

He nodded in acknowledgement. 'He is in God's hands now.'

'Can you tell us something about him?'

'Much. And with this telling, you will see why our paths were destined to meet.' He sank slowly into the other armchair, patting his lap for Gladstone to come to him. 'I knew Emile's father, Christophe. This was before he left for the tropics in 1886, of course. He was a friend of my church, my congregation. And of me. Sadly, his wife I never did meet. They met and married on the island Christophe settled his new life on. The lady died there before he returned to France.'

Eleanor tried to tally the date up with what she had imagined Emile's age to be. Evidently, her face gave her away as usual.

'Emile was born on the island,' Godine said. 'He was eight years old when Christophe brought him home here with him.'

'Do you know why Christophe left the island?'

'Yes. He was devastated by the death of his wife. And could no longer bear to be away from the village of his birth. Sadly for Emile, however, Christophe was called to Our Lord just over a year after he and his father returned to France.'

'It's not easy growing up an orphan,' she blurted out. Glancing fondly at Clifford, she added, 'Although I was the luckiest one ever.'

'And still are. I can see this.' Their host pointed at Seldon standing protectively near her and Clifford guarding the door. He put his hands together. 'Emile was a boy of good heart, like his father. But he needed the firm and guiding hand he lost when Christophe died. He grew wild. Then wilder still.'

'Let me guess, you want us to believe he got into the wrong company?' Seldon said sceptically.

'Yes. Because it is true, monsieur. His grandmother took him in and tried to teach him how to make good choices. But, we must remember, Emile had grown up to the age of eight on a tropical island where he ran free, especially after his mother's passing. To come here at that age, to him Magnes felt—'

'Like he'd been "brought to a prison built on pointless rules"?' Clifford glanced sideways at Eleanor, as that was exactly the phrase she had used to him one fractious summer as an angry and bewildered nine-year-old.

Again, Godine nodded. 'To shorten the story, Emile's grandmother came to me last week in a state of great upset. Emile had dreamed up a foolish plan to steal from the Musée d'Art

Contemporain in Paris. He would not listen to her.' He sighed sadly. 'Neither to me.' He rose and stepped to the window with his hands behind his back. 'So, I followed him to Paris to try and make him hear the sense of our words. But before I could reach him, he went to the museum. And then... then he was dead.'

Eleanor bowed her head as he muttered some words she couldn't understand into his hands held in prayer. Still, she kept half an eye open and watched him. Was this story all too pat? Too rehearsed? It sounded plausible, but then didn't all well-executed tricks? If only she could be sure. She glanced up at Seldon, who shrugged. Clifford arched a brow, but the fact he had silently beckoned Gladstone back to his side spoke volumes. None of them were sure how trustworthy this man was.

'It still seems odd that you and I have "bumped" into each other twice already before this meeting,' she said coolly.

Godine shook his head. 'Not to me. The hotel where Emile died. I was there because I chased after him from the museum.'

'Yet you left without talking to the police? Or even identifying his body?' Seldon said.

'Yes. To protect his name. And that of his grandmother. The police believed him to be a wicked man, a thief who steals only for money. But they are wrong.'

Eleanor rose. 'That still doesn't explain why you then followed us to the Delorme Gallery?'

'I did not. I was in the Galerie Delorme hoping to appeal to the owner's sympathetic nature. Alas, I did not find any. Then I overheard you asking Monsieur Delorme about Christophe Ury and also the young man who had died. So I followed your man there to tell him Emile's name. In the *urinoir*.' He shrugged at Clifford's horrified look. 'I am sorry, it was the best place I could find you alone.'

'Why did you think you could trust me?' Eleanor asked.

'Because I realised that Emile had.'

Her insides clenched. Had he seen Emile give her the brooch?

'I believe we've almost heard enough,' she said crisply. 'All that remains is your explanation of why you felt the need to murder Emile?'

Godine's jaw fell. His lips moved, but no sound came out.

'Oh come, come. I've no time for theatrics!'

'*Murder Emile?* Me? But—'

'Well, if it wasn't you, who was it?'

'No... no one. It was an accident that Emile fell through the roof!' Godine stared at her. His eyes held so much upset, she felt her suspicions waver. 'Wasn't it?' he said in little more than a whisper.

Seldon shook his head firmly. 'No. It was murder.'

Godine sank into the armchair, hand clamped over his mouth. 'And you are interested why?'

'For my part, largely because my wife here was the one who tried to save him,' Seldon said. 'And it's still haunting her that it wasn't possible.'

'And also, because the police believe it was an accident. So the murderer thinks they will get away with it. But they won't!' Eleanor said vehemently.

'You... you were the one who tried to save Emile?' Godine struggled up out of his chair. 'Then I will do all I can to help you. There is someone you must meet. It is very important. But you will need to come with me elsewhere. And to trust me.'

Seldon shook his head. 'Not a chance.'

'What choice do we have, Hugh?' she murmured.

He looked at Clifford, who in silent reply, stepped aside and opened the door.

She nodded to Godine. 'Let's go.'

32

The three of them with Gladstone followed Godine out of what she assumed was the vicarage and back down the path, and then through a winding maze of backstreets. Eventually, they arrived at a short alleyway which ended at a high stone wall.

'"*Impasse de la paix*" or "Dead end of peace", I believe,' Clifford muttered, doing nothing to dispel her growing fear she hadn't made the best decision.

A flash of movement made her jerk to a stop. A one-eyed black cat streaked through the open swing gate in the wall and launched itself up the front of Godine's cassock with the agility only felines have. The cat threw his paws around the priest's neck, purring loudly.

'Salut, Fifi!' he said softly, supporting the cat's back legs.

Eleanor frowned. Was this man friend or foe? Bad men didn't usually show such affection to animals so openly, in her experience. Gladstone strained on his lead to greet the new arrival. She shrugged at Seldon and Clifford's confused looks and followed Godine through the gate.

Set in the middle of a narrow timber-framed house, a faded,

yet newly washed, green door faced them, purple soap bubbles
shining as they winked and burst.

Eleanor scanned the front, but could see no one watching at
the windows. Or at either of the oval glass panes set high in the
boarding under the eaves of the moss-covered roof tiles.

Godine stepped into the house. 'C'est moi!'

The sound of slow, shuffling footsteps reached Eleanor's
ears. A silver-haired lady of not quite five feet in height
appeared. She was dressed in a black smock dress reminiscent
of the last century with a grey pinafore apron and worn brown
slipper boots buttoned up her swollen ankles.

'Mon Père, bienvenue,' she said a little breathlessly.

She blinked rapidly at Eleanor as Godine stepped aside. Up
close, she could see the woman's perhaps once striking blue eyes
were now milky, the right one so overcome by cataracts it looked
like a cracked mirror.

'Mon Père, qui est...'

The old woman broke off and pushed her face into
Eleanor's, hand outstretched. For a moment, she thought the
woman was going to grab her curls. Instead, she stepped back
and said, 'Bonjour, madame. Et messieurs.'

She muttered something to Godine Eleanor couldn't understand any more than the priest's reply. Evidently Clifford
couldn't either, as his brow flinched. The old lady looked the
three of them over again, her eyes lingering longest on Eleanor.
Finally, she nodded and shuffled away down the hallway.

Godine turned to Eleanor. 'This lady has invited you inside
her home.'

'Kind, I'm sure. But why should we be interested in taking
up her invitation?'

'Because this lady is Josette Ury. Emile's grandmother.'

*Like Godine, Sabine also mentioned Emile had a grand-
mother who brought him up, Ellie. And here she is, it seems.*

Eleanor followed Josette through a basic kitchen equipped

with a stone sink and a bread oven set in the chimney breast. The next room housed jars of pickles, jams, cheese – well aged, given the pungent smell – drums of kerosene and lamp fluid. The last room, obviously the parlour, was furnished with nothing but three armchairs and a neatly made day bed. Gladstone padded over to where Fifi the cat was now kneading a patchwork cushion on the small central rug and curled up with her.

'Madame Ury, je vous… er,' Eleanor began, cursing her lack of French.

'I can understand a little English, madame. And my name is Josette,' the old woman said with a formidable firmness that could have halted an invading foreign army not ten years back.

'Then, Josette, I'm so sorry for your loss. Emile, I mean.'

Josette tugged a thin handkerchief from her dress cuff as tears leaked from the corners of her eyes. 'He was a silly boy. But I loved him very much.'

'I hope it might help you to know he did not suffer at all.' Eleanor gently squeezed Josette's arm comfortingly. As her own tears threatened, she continued hurriedly. 'He was at peace immediately.'

Josette stared at her. 'But how can you know this?'

Overcome by the harrowing image of Emile breathing his last in her hands, Eleanor's words faltered.

'This lady knows because she tried to save him after he fell,' Godine said. He turned to Eleanor. 'I believe you. And all else you have told me. Perhaps now you can do me the same honour?'

'I'm starting to,' she said truthfully.

He smiled. 'Faith takes time, child.'

'Hush!' Josette took Eleanor by the hands, peering closely at her face. 'You tried to help Emile? Then thank you from the bottom of a grandmother's heart, dear girl. But tell me, why have you come here today?'

Eleanor hesitated. 'Well, that's a long and rather complicated story.'

Josette flapped her hand. 'Pah! All stories are. But there is always a short version. And it is this I want to hear.'

'What you might not want to hear is what... I don't really want to tell you,' Eleanor faltered again, unable to lie to this woman. Nor to add to her grief.

Clifford stepped forward with a half bow and held out one of his pristine linen handkerchiefs. 'Madame Ury, not all men are good and honourable like your son and your grandson. Emile met with one who was the very opposite of his kind,' he said gently. Gladstone crept over and laid his head on Josette's lap. Her hand trembled as she stroked his ears. After a moment, she reached for Clifford's handkerchief. 'You are saying my Emile did not die by an accident, monsieur?'

'I'm afraid that seems to be the case.'

Eleanor risked discreetly squeezing his elbow in gratitude. She could never have delivered such shocking news so sensitively.

Josette twisted the handkerchief in her fingers. 'Always, I feared it might end this way for him.'

'Because he often got into trouble?' Eleanor said.

'When he was young, yes.' Josette sighed. 'But even when he was older, I feared for him. Because he lived with his heart always. Never with his head.'

'Isn't that often the way with artists?'

'Oui. This is so. My son, Christophe, was the same. Only he learned early to know me, his mama, would reach for the broom if he did wrong or acted like a fool. But Emile.' She sighed again. 'Although he loved and cared for me, he came to me too late. He was eight when I first ever met him.'

'Nine would have been no easier, madam.' Clifford winked at Eleanor.

She smiled, which made Josette smile too. 'What my terror

of a butler, Clifford, is trying to say,' Eleanor said, 'is that I grew up very much like Emile. But Clifford learned on meeting me when I was nine, that if he tried the broom trick on me, he would have regretted it for the rest of the summer holidays. And still would be, even though I'm now in my thirties!'

Josette laughed, but it was mixed with a breathless sob. 'The wild child you were. And still are, I think. But your heart leads you well for the good of others, dear girl.' Josette patted her hand. 'Come, please. I need to show you something.' She rose stiffly and paused in the doorway, leaning on the frame. 'Something I think you will very much wish to see.'

She started slowly up the steep, narrow stairs with Gladstone and Fifi bounding on ahead, tails wagging and twitching. Eleanor followed behind, Seldon and Clifford too, with Godine bringing up the rear.

They emerged into the attic, the pitch of the eaves so steep, Eleanor could only just stand upright at its highest point. The floor was covered in paint splatters, the smell taking her back to her school art room. Looking around, there were a few scattered paint pots, and an easel repaired with clearly repurposed wood set in the centre of the space. She could see why. The two oval glass panes she had noticed from outside were set too far under the eaves to ever let in enough light to paint by. However, the space was bathed in sunshine, the mid-section of the roof having been swapped for glass.

Josette gestured around. 'This is Emile's studio.' She took a deep breath. 'It was. And before that, it was Christophe's.' She pointed to eight or so canvases leaning against the wall. 'I did not understand Emile's paintings. But I am old. And my eyesight was already fading when he began to paint.' She sighed. 'I liked Christophe's paintings. My eyesight was good when he was painting.'

'I like them too,' Eleanor said. 'The colours are so vivid. They seem to have been painted with such passion! And... and they reminded me of something. Like I'd seen them before somewhere. Perhaps you might let me look at one or two now to try and remember?'

Josette shook her head. 'This I would do, dear girl. If it was possible. But it is not. I had no choice but to sell all of Christophe's paintings.'

Eleanor frowned.

Why, Ellie, when her son's paintings are selling for astronomical prices in Paris, does Josette have the air of one living in penury?

'Josette, I don't mean to pry, but who did you sell them to?'

'To a wicked man.'

'Bellamy Delorme?' Seldon said.

Josette began to shake. 'That... that is the man!'

Godine hurried over to her. 'Josette, it is not good for you to remember this thing.'

'Let me be! I was the fool I told Emile he was so many times,' she said firmly, despite her more snatched breaths now. 'And Monsieur Delorme fooled you too.'

Clifford held out his hip flask, which Godine passed to Josette. She took a grateful sip. Then another. The colour began to return to her face. 'That man Delorme brought me a document to sign. To sell all of Christophe's paintings. I had no money and... He told me they were not very good, but he could make a few francs on them.'

'But he's selling them for a fortune!' Eleanor couldn't help blurting out.

'This I know. But too late. I signed the document. It also allowed him to take all the things in Christophe's studio.' Her face suffused with anger. 'This I did not realise at the time, either. He took everything I had of my son!' Her shoulders sagged. 'I am old and with my eyes so bad, I cannot even sew to buy food. Emile was good to me with the little he got from his paintings, but it was very little.'

'Couldn't he have got a job?' Seldon said tentatively.

Josette nodded. 'Oui, monsieur. But I would not agree. Emile was an artist in his heart. Like his father. How was he ever to live his dream if he spent all his hours killing his painter's hands and spirit working in the fields or the factories?'

'The document Monsieur Delorme brought to you?' Clifford said. 'Did anyone check it over for you before you signed, madame?'

Godine hung his head. 'I did. It was written I think by clever men with clever words. I showed it afterward to a friend who is a local lawyer, a good man. He assured me it was legal. And Josette could not withdraw. And it did not allow for...' He shrugged.

'Any further recompense?' Clifford said.

'Yes.'

Eleanor ran her fingers down the edge of the easel. 'Now I understand why Emile stole from the museum. He was trying to get his father's items back.'

Josette nodded. 'To make me happy. The silly boy.'

Eleanor hesitated. 'Do you... know why he took the pearl brooch particularly?'

Josette blanched. 'So that is what he stole? I thought so. Yes, I do know why, dear girl.' She managed a smile. 'I will show you.'

She flapped at Godine to step aside. Bending stiffly, she pointed at a section of the floorboards. 'Perhaps one of you gentlemen will lift these for me?'

Seldon strode forward and hunched down to where she was pointing. 'But they are nailed down, madame.'

Clifford was immediately beside him, pocket knife held out.

Eleanor watched with bated breath as they pulled first one, then two, three, and finally four of the floorboards free. Seldon looked up as if asking for Josette's permission. She nodded. 'Hand it to me, please, monsieur.'

Reaching down, he rose slowly, holding a large square item wrapped in a thin blanket.

Josette took it lovingly. 'This is the only painting of Christophe's I have left. Monsieur Delorme does not know I have it. Emile hid it in case that man might come again. I am cheating him by keeping this.'

Eleanor shook her head. 'No, Josette. He is the only cheat!'

Josette's stiff fingers fumbled with the ribbons. Then she handed it to her.

Eleanor stared at it, taking a moment to register what she was seeing. When she did, her mouth dropped. It was a portrait of a man with a striking resemblance to Emile seated in front of an open window which commanded a view of a tropical bay.

He must be Christophe, Ellie. And the young boy on his left knee, Emile! And the young...

Seldon and Clifford lunged forward in unison, grabbing a shoulder each.

'Are you alright, Eleanor?' Seldon said anxiously. 'I thought you were going to faint!'

She stared at the giggling, red-headed young girl on the man's other knee without replying.

And then at the two figures behind...

33

Eleanor felt herself swaying. Then Seldon's arms tightened around her shoulders.

'I'm alright, Hugh,' she breathed. 'It's just... seeing *myself* in that painting. Because it is me. And behind, that's... that's *my parents*.'

Seldon shook his head. 'That's unreal.'

She took a deep breath. 'Yes. And no. I thought I was having a moment of déjà vu when I was trying to help Emile. I felt we had some sort of connection I couldn't understand. But we'd met, I now realise. As children. And...' She kissed her two forefingers and pressed them to the two loving faces her heart had ached every day to see since she had been nine. Her eyes swam. Her tears spilled over.

Josette took Eleanor's hands in hers, her cheeks wet too. 'I am sorry to upset you, dear girl.'

'These are happy tears, honestly,' Eleanor whispered. It was true. Finding any link to her parents was like unearthing hidden treasure. 'I'm beginning to remember Christophe too, now. And his wife.'

'Then you had the treat I did not,' Josette said. 'I could never go out to La Réunion where they were living. She had a weakness of her heart, which they both understood she had when they married. And then she died.'

'La Réunion,' Eleanor repeated softly. 'That's it! Now, I remember more of it.'

Seldon cradled her as he looked at the picture with her. 'I should know, but is that a tropical island?'

'Yes. In the Indian Ocean.'

He looked embarrassed. 'Geography was never my forte.'

'Adjacent to Madagascar, sir,' Clifford said. 'Off the south-east coast of Africa. After only five years under English rule, it gradually became governed by the French authorities. Although it is not officially a French protectorate.' He glanced at Eleanor. 'Réunion is home to the most exquisite shells, I believe?'

Her heart swelled. 'I think in my beloved collection in my bedside drawer I've still got some of the very ones I collected along the shore shown in this painting. But, oh, how I wish I had made the connection when Delorme mentioned Christophe had lived on a tropical island!'

'How could you have? You're only what, six, in that painting?' Seldon said soothingly.

'Five. I remember we got caught in a terrible storm and were blown miles off course. We were sailing to somewhere else for Father's work. Mauritius, I think?'

She stared at the man in the centre of the painting. The one she now knew was Christophe. 'Yes. It was him. Mother and Father never used his surname which is why I didn't recognise "Ury" before. He helped Father make the repairs to our boat. On a beach of beautiful white sand.' Her hands flew to her chest. 'And Mother got ill. Very ill. For a while I was frightened she...'

Josette nodded. 'She was very sick. With the sickness of the island. It was rare, but serious. Christophe had some medicine. Only a little though, left to him by a painter friend from France who had returned here.'

'I remember Christophe gave his medicine to my mother!' Eleanor said. The full significance of that made her insides clench. If he hadn't she would have lost her mother aged five, not nine. Now even more grateful for her extra four years with both her parents, she smiled at Josette's nod. 'That was too kind of Christophe.'

'Yes. And your mama got better. And your father tried to give Christophe money for his help. But he refused. Your father begged Christophe to never stop painting. He told him his paintings were like no others, and they would be valuable one day.'

'He was right,' Seldon said with a frown.

Josette nodded. 'Now, yes. But all this happened in La Réunion. Christophe wrote to me at the time and told me. I was so proud of him to have helped your parents this way.'

Suddenly, everything fell into place for Eleanor. The fleeting déjà vu, the reason Emile had stared into her eyes, then reached out to her in his dying moments. 'He must have thought he was seeing things, too,' she murmured.

'He recognised you, my love. That's clear now,' Seldon said. 'Hiding up on the atrium roof from the police, he must have looked down and seen those beautiful fiery-red curls of yours. They're exactly the same now as in this portrait.'

'Yes. But when he put his hands on the glass to peer closer —' She broke off.

Josette let out a deep breath. 'Somebody terrible pushed him, didn't they?'

Seldon nodded. 'I'm sorry, Josette. But yes, that's exactly what happened.'

Eleanor wiped her eyes. 'My mother gave Christophe the pearl brooch to say thank you for all his kindness, didn't she?

That's why I recognised it! And that's why I couldn't bear to...'
Her hand strayed under her jacket. She smiled. 'No one could
say no to her.' She turned to Seldon. 'I'm sorry I didn't explain
anything about the brooch, Hugh. But it was such a jumble in
my head. And I didn't understand why it was precious to me. I
just knew that it was. And I didn't want to ruin our honeymoon
any more than I already had. It's only now I understand what
my subconscious knew and I didn't.'

He shook his head. 'I wouldn't have expected anything else
of you, Eleanor. Never apologise for being you.'

She fell into his embrace, caring nothing about etiquette
and composure. Just as he clearly didn't right then.

Clifford feigned horror, but his eyes were bright with
warmth. He was delighted for her. For her having Seldon. For
having regained a small part of her time with her parents. If
only in memories. Still, it meant the world. And he understood
that.

'Josette, I'm sorry,' Eleanor said, snapping to. 'Here I am
remembering happy times when you've just had terrible news.
That's unforgivable of me.'

Josette shook her head vigorously. 'No, it is not. I had the
feeling it was right to trust you when I see you at my front door.
I saw a halo around your hair.'

Eleanor bit back asking if she'd remembered correctly that
seeing halos was a symptom of cataracts. She might as well have
asked, however, as Josette tutted.

'A proper ring of sun shining around you. Not the stars
which forever blink in my way when I am trying to see up close.
Now, tell me, how are your parents?'

'I wish I knew.' Eleanor recounted how they disappeared
one night four years after that time with Christophe on the
island. Of the fear she'd felt. And how she wished with all her
heart to find out the truth one day.

'We will,' Seldon said gently to her surprise. 'Trust me.'

Josette smiled. 'I think you are very much like your mother, dear girl. Christophe wrote to me about her. And your father also. With their news after they left.' Eleanor's breath caught, but Josette was already continuing. 'This is why he kept the brooch your mother gave to him. It was very special to him.'

'Which made it special enough to you for Emile to risk stealing it from the museum, didn't it?'

'Yes. Always Christophe had it just here.' She tapped the ledge of the easel. 'He told me it gave him courage to keep painting, as your father said to do. And it kept alive the memories of the best times in his life. With his wife. And with his new friends on La Réunion – your parents.'

Eleanor's hand trembled, but it was the right thing to do. Reaching inside her jacket, she felt under her jumper, slipped the pin from its clasp and pulled out the brooch.

'Here. You must have it back.'

She put it into Josette's hand, holding it up to her milky eyes so she could see it clearly.

Josette's other hand flew to her mouth. 'This is the brooch!'

Eleanor nodded. 'Yes. And it doesn't belong to Delorme. It belongs to you. No one else.' As Josette traced the outline with her fingers, Eleanor hesitated, then continued. 'Can I ask you something? But it might sound rude.' Josette waved her on. 'Did Christophe or Emile ever sell the original pearls and have them replaced with fake ones?'

Josette gasped. 'Never! Neither would do such a terrible thing. This was a precious gift. Just like the medicine Christophe gave.'

'I didn't think for a minute they would have. But Monsieur Delorme told me they were fake. But if he was right, then the real pearls must have been swapped after this was taken with Christophe's paintings and the rest of his studio's contents.'

'By Delorme himself!' Seldon muttered.

'To be displayed with a fictitious claim the brooch was gifted to Monsieur Ury by a rich anonymous widow,' Clifford said with a sniff of disgust.

Eleanor frowned. 'But it makes no sense. You both saw the prices in Delorme's gallery. And not just for Christophe's paintings. The original pearls can't have been that valuable. Mother and Father never had that much money. They were far too bohemian about it.'

Josette tutted. 'What do we care about such things? You said this brooch is mine. But it was never mine. It was your mother's. And so now, it belongs to you.'

She pressed the brooch back into Eleanor's hand. It was so similar to how Emile had thrust it between her fingers, her breath caught. That same unfathomable feeling of comfort. She shook her head.

'I can't, Josette. This holds more sentimental value for you than I could ever bear to think of you losing. You must have this. No matter if the pearls are fake or real. Keep it. Hold it. Wear it. And feel Christophe's spirit smiling and at peace because you are.' She feared her voice might fail her.

Josette pulled her into a hug. 'Pin it to my dress, dear girl. My fingers are shaking too much.'

Eleanor laughed to disguise her sob at losing such a precious memento of her mother. But a small part of the hole in her heart healed. Her mother and father were smiling down at her. Wherever they were.

Josette patted the brooch. 'Perhaps I can give you something almost as precious?'

'Goodness, not the painting. Because I couldn't ever think of…' She tailed off at Josette's headshake. She watched as the old lady beckoned to Seldon to follow her back to the pulled-up floorboards. 'Feel to the end of the space, monsieur.'

He did as she asked, standing up after a moment. What he

had, if anything, Eleanor couldn't see. Until Josette turned around and placed a bundle of letters in her hand. The address on the top envelope was to Christophe Ury, in a house and street, somewhere on La Réunion. But the handwriting. That was her mother's.

34

The idea of hurrying away from Josette's house felt horribly like bursting a precious bubble that might never form again. But good friends never disappear, Eleanor's heart whispered. Because that's what Josette had become among all the unexpected revelations in the last few hours. All the shocking news and deep emotions had brought them together. And further steeled Eleanor's resolve to bring her grandson's murderer to justice.

Gladstone and Fifi were still giving each other kisses as she forced her feet to take her out through Josette's gate. They had been gone from Chateau Archambault for too long. Le Comte was likely to be back already. They didn't know his part, if any, in the two murders. So they couldn't risk arousing his suspicions.

Josette waved them off with the promise that tomorrow she would tell them all she knew about Emile and Le Comte, including when they were younger. It would wait until then. It had to.

What made it worse, hurrying back to the chateau, was that

all Eleanor really wanted to do was be alone. To curl up and read the bundle of letters tied with the green ribbon now protectively tucked inside her cape. Just to stare at her mother's handwriting would feel comforting. But that too would have to wait.

With Gladstone seeming to know instinctively this was no time for sniffing everything that moved, or didn't, the three of them made a hurried return to Chateau Archambault in pensive silence.

They were met by Le Comte's creepy valet-cum-butler and the news that his master would not be back with his niece for at least another hour. This was a relief. The valet further redeemed himself by providing a pot of hot coffee unbidden, although on leaving, he left the door slightly ajar as before.

Still deep in thought, Eleanor perched on the arm of one of the fleur-de-lis upholstered banquettes as Clifford went over and closed the door a little louder than necessary again. Gladstone scrabbled up onto the cushioned seat beside her and dropped his head into her lap as Seldon paced the floor. Door closed, Clifford poured them both a generous serving of the rich roast coffee, then added a dash from his hip flask to each cup.

'Merely a little fortification, sir,' he said in reply to Seldon's questioning look.

'For whatever thunderbolt this case is about to strike with next?' Seldon murmured, staring into his cup.

Eleanor sipped her coffee, appreciating its reassuring warmth. 'Clifford, please indulge as well?'

'Most kind, my lady. However, I am in fact swimming already.'

Seldon looked up. 'In cognac?'

Clifford raised an eyebrow in horror. 'In coffee only, sir. To disguise your extended absence from the house after breakfast, it became necessary to ring several times for the staff to bring a pot for three.'

'Gracious, thank you. It's a wonder you aren't climbing the walls!' she said.

'Aren't we all ready to do that, though? Quite literally.' Seldon sighed. 'Blast it, Eleanor. I wish I could take you away from this whole awful matter this second.'

'On your white charger? Ride off into the sunset?' She smiled wistfully at the thought.

But his troubled expression only deepened. 'Why did I have to bring us to Paris for our honeymoon? If only I'd left the plans as they were!'

Leaping off the arm of the chair, she spotted Clifford slipping out of the room. 'Hugh Seldon! Come here, right here, right now.' She pointed to the spot on the rug in front of her.

'Why do I suddenly feel like Gladstone is supposed to when he's caught doing something he shouldn't?' he said hesitantly, stepping over to her.

'Because you have! Hugh, you can't wish we'd never come to Paris. It was the most wonderful surprise in the world. And we've had some unforgettably special moments, too. Which we will add to in bucket loads the minute this is all over. Plus, it's only because of you arranging it all, that I now have' – she reached inside her jacket and produced the bundle of letters – 'these.'

He pulled her into his chest. 'I'm so happy for you, my love. And I'm sorry to have lost heart for a moment. It was watching you at Josette's relive that night your parents disappeared.' He cradled her closer. 'I couldn't bear that you'd been so afraid. You were so young.'

She didn't protest otherwise. It had been awful. Instead, she absorbed the warmth of his body and the love he was wrapping her in.

'Your coffee's getting cold,' she whispered.

'Who cares?' he murmured, but reluctantly released her.

'You can come back in now, Clifford. It's alright. I haven't guillotined Hugh's head off,' she called to the door.

'Just about, though,' Seldon said with a chuckle as Clifford returned.

'Rest assured, sir,' he said while topping up their coffees. 'My blanket stitch skills are serviceable enough should reattachment prove necessary in the future.'

Pleased that they were helping each other to keep their spirits up, she set the letters down on the side table beside her. From inside his jacket, Clifford produced the slim, leather bag Hacqueville had been wearing when he fell from the Eiffel Tower.

'Oh, good idea!' she said. 'Put the evidence we have where we can see it while we have another go at working through these awful murders. Any chance you've also got my notebook secreted somewhere in your impeccable togs, too, Clifford?'

'Naturally, my lady. What kind of *secretary* would I be otherwise?' He produced it with a flourish.

'Top-notch! Because I say we need to start from the beginning and re-evaluate everything.' She opened it and turned to a fresh page which she headed: *Who murdered Emile?*

'So, for all that we could dwell on what we haven't yet discovered about the murders, we at least understand now why Emile took that brooch. And why he gave it to me.'

Clifford bowed from the shoulders. 'It is not my place to say I know, my lady. But your returning it to Madame Josette when it was so precious to you as it had belonged to your mother was the act of a true Henley. His lordship would have been beyond proud of his favourite niece.'

They both knew she had been Uncle Byron's only niece, which made his words even more poignant. She mouthed him a thank you, not trusting her voice. The day had been a roller coaster of emotions.

From the bag, Seldon pulled out the small sculpture of a black boat Hacqueville had tried to plant on her. Then the wad of banknotes and the cigars.

'All and any thoughts, chaps. Because the one sure thing I have learned is that murderers don't stay idle for long!' she said.

The sound of a car drawing up outside had the three of them staring at each other.

'Let's hope my observation coinciding precisely with our host's return is no omen.' She grimaced.

Seldon dropped the items back in the bag and shoved it under a cushion before dropping down onto it.

A few moments later, she kept her expression neutral as footsteps approached the room. Too many footsteps?

'Ah, good afternoon, Inspector Gripperel,' she said smoothly, fighting a wash of unease.

What's he doing here, Ellie?

'It seems you've arrived a little ahead of Le Comte. He should be back soon, though. Whatever you've arranged to meet him about.'

Gripperel's dark-chocolate overcoat billowed out on either side of him like a vulture's wings as he advanced towards her, square-jaw set.

'No, Lady Swift. You are mistaken. I have no appointment with Le Comte.' His voice dripped even more honey than before.

'Well, if you've stopped off to cadge a coffee, it's divine. And his tobacco cabinet is just through there I imagine.'

'I have come for neither of these.' He clicked his fingers behind him. Three uniformed *police nationale* appeared in the doorway. 'What I have come to do is to arrest you, Lady Swift.'

She blanched. 'What?'

Seldon half-rose, but then hastily sat back down. 'Now see here! I—'

'And you also, Mr Seldon. And you too, Mr Clifford,' Gripperel said over the clunk of handcuffs being slapped on the three of them. 'I am arresting you all for involvement in the murders of Emile Ury and Gardien Thierry Hacqueville!'

35

The irony wasn't lost on Eleanor as she stood in the courtyard of the very building on which Clifford had pointed out the gold and blue clock two days before. Flanked by the two figurines representing law and justice, she had found them reassuring symbols. But now... now she was in La Conciergerie, Paris's infamous courthouse and jail. But not as an innocent victim. As a nefarious criminal!

From the outside, with its quarter mile riverfront façade, La Conciergerie looked a rival to Louis XIV's famed Versailles Palace itself. But once past its two forbidding central towers, all similarities ended. Inside, La Conciergerie was a vast fortified complex of unforgiving and endless high stone walls and iron bars. Unrelentingly grim, austere, punishing. She bent and stretched her handcuffed arms against her bonds to hug Gladstone closer to her legs. Not sure whether Le Comte was friend or foe, she'd refused to leave her bulldog at the chateau. And to her surprise, Gripperel hadn't argued.

She wondered how Seldon and Clifford were faring. They'd been marched off to the male side of the prison while she was left waiting there with two of Gripperel's men. She shook herself.

Don't worry, Ellie. They can both look after themselves. And hopefully, they'll be in a cell together.

A hatchet-faced woman in a grey warden's dress strode over.

Eleanor tossed her curls. 'Which way to the spa baths, then?'

The woman almost smiled. 'The cells for women are this way, madame.'

Forests of iron bars filled Eleanor's view at every turn as she was escorted to the female side of the prison, Gladstone trotting alongside. There, her name and address were written down and, to her surprise, she was subjected to only a cursory search. The only item the warden took was her beloved late uncle's pocket watch.

'If anything happens to that, I shall raze this place to the ground!' she swore through gritted teeth.

The search over, she was escorted again, this time deeper into the prison. As each iron-barred gate was unlocked, she had to duck under a spiked portcullis.

'Better than a guillotine, I suppose,' she muttered.

Her warden grinned. 'La guillotine? This is where Marie Antoinette was held before they chop off her head!'

She was led up a flight of dank-smelling stairs and along a series of corridors. The empty cells on either side were only just wide enough for a narrow bed and a stool, both of which were bolted to the floor only inches from the squat toilet.

On the second floor, her warden stopped in front of a wooden door with a small barred opening at head height.

'Welcome to your new home, madame.'

She inserted a long iron key from a bunch on her belt and the door swung open.

To Eleanor's relief and confusion, inside it was the size of a cell for three, but with only one bed. And an actual chair rather than a stool. There was a rudimentary table and even a screen hiding the toilet.

'An exclusive suite, how delightful, old chum,' she said to Gladstone, who was already snuffling in the corners. Her hand-cuffs were removed. The door closed.

As the sound of the warden's boots faded down the corridor, she slumped on to the inhumanely hard bed. Gladstone suddenly lost all interest in sniffing around his new home and joined her. She tickled his tummy as he rolled onto his back, seemingly having no problem with the quality of the mattress.

'Well, Gladstone, if I'm honest, this is a worrying turn of events.' She checked to see if he was paying attention. Unsure either way, she ploughed on. 'I can understand Gripperel being angered if he had somehow found out we... *I* had withheld evidence from him. But locking us all up is going too far. Mind you, this is France. Maybe their rules are really this strict?'

She sighed. Was Gripperel just doing his duty as a police-man? Or was he keeping the three of them out of his way while he finished concealing his own part in the murders?

If so, why was he treating her better than he needed to? The warden hadn't even insisted she stripped and put on the stan-dard prisoner's clothing of blue sackcloth. It seemed he had at least given orders she, and Gladstone, should be treated like human beings. And kept apart from the other female inmates, many of whom, she imagined, were hardened criminals.

A guilty conscience, perhaps?

She stared at the only window. High up, too small to get through, and criss-crossed with an uncompromising grid of iron bars, tunnelling out through one of the solid stone walls would be easier.

Her thoughts flew to Seldon and Clifford again. She hoped they were being treated as she was. If not!

If not, what, Ellie?

Her fight faded. The best she could do was hope again that at least they would be locked in together. Or at least in adjoining cells. That way, her butler's infallible calming presence might save her new husband from doing something rash. He'd been apoplectic when the policeman had slapped handcuffs on her. She groaned. A senior detective at Scotland Yard he might be, but it hadn't stopped him from being incarcerated. What hope for any of them, then? And the worst part was, she had got them all into this mess.

'Oh, Gladstone, old chum. What a hash I've made of this whole business,' she murmured, grateful for his snuffling kisses.

Think, Ellie, think!

Her first thought was to find a way to escape again. But how, in the depths of this iron-barred fortress with its confusion of passageways, wardens and guards at every turn? To say nothing of it being unlikely she could construct a convincing disguise that would hide her portly bulldog. And how would she then free Seldon and Clifford?

She shook her head. Better to work out how to persuade Gripperel he had the wrong person, or persons. After all, what evidence could he really have? Surely he wouldn't have arrested them with no—

Her heart faltered. The brooch! She'd given Josette back the brooch. Pinned it on her.

She shook her head again. Josette would never have told Gripperel where it came from. But what if he had found her with it? He wouldn't be so heartless as to lock up an old, half-blind woman in here, too?

Would he?

Realising she was getting nowhere, and panicking herself at the same time, she switched tack. The other piece of evidence Gripperel might have got hold of was the little black boat that Hacqueville had tried to plant on her. Along with the wad of money, of course! Had he found the bag Seldon had been sitting on when he'd burst in with the *police nationale*?

She realised her head was hurting from straining for answers. All she could do was wait to find out what he had on the three of them. And, more worryingly, what he was planning to do about it.

How long she had been sitting, thinking, she didn't know. But it was long enough for daylight to have slipped away, and night to have stolen in through the barred skylight window. That's why her pocket watch had been taken, she realised now. So time would seem as if it had stopped in here!

The stomp of boots outside jerked her out of her thoughts. A tray was pushed through a small flap at the bottom of the door and the boots receded once more.

She scooped up the tray, grimacing at the grey lumps of meat winking up at her from the gruel, next to which was a hunk of stale-looking baguette. In truth, it and the gruel were probably perfectly edible, but she had no stomach for it. Gladstone had never been known for his discernment, however, so she set the bowl down for him. Giving it the barest of sniffs, he lapped up the gruel eagerly. Once he'd finished, she filled the bowl with water from the carafe and shook her head fondly as he splashed the floor and half the wall as he drank. Toddling off with the baguette back to her cape, which she'd laid on the floor for him, he sprawled on his tummy. Gripping his improvised chew between his paws like an otter, he started crunching with gusto. She smiled at his tail wagging happily. Wasn't that the best thing about dogs? The simplest of pleasures were enough. And he was blissfully unaware of their plight.

She sighed. Hugh had tried so hard to make their honeymoon a romantic and luxurious trip they would never forget. But instead of dining in Paris's most gourmet restaurants and waltzing in its glitziest dance halls, they were locked in its grimmest prison. And not even together! Chateau Archambault, with its minimal furnishings and mercurial host, was better than this. As her mind ran over the scene of Gripperel marching in to arrest them, her heart faltered again.

Mother and Father's letters, Ellie!

She had put them on the side table just before Gripperel and his men had burst in. She hadn't dared draw attention to them and hadn't tried to take them with her as she was sure she would have been searched. But if Gripperel had spotted them as they were being marched out of the chateau, he would have taken them for sure. They were addressed to Christophe Ury, the very man whose two items had been stolen from the museum, and whose son was accused of the crime. The son Gripperel had seen her trying to save.

That did it! She needed to stop thinking about the hideous fix they were in and tackle what the three of them had been interrupted working out: *Who murdered Emile?* Because if she really intended to persuade Gripperel he had the wrong culprit, the best way was to work out who was the right one. And then present him with irrefutable proof. While hoping against hope it wasn't him!

Her shoulders slumped. Without Clifford and Seldon to bounce ideas off, and their input too, what would she actually achieve?

An unknown number of hours later, the answer was very little. Except to fry her brain to the point she was relieved when the warden appeared and escorted her down more miles of bleak corridors to an empty yard lit by blinding lights. Vertical stone walls with regiments of barred windows and walkways soared up on all sides. Happy in his belief this was just one more interesting adventure, Gladstone set off on a gambolling circuit, woofing at the shadows he made.

'Five minutes' exercise! Then bed,' the warden called, locking the gate behind her.

For a minute or two, she stood watching Gladstone. Then something soft hit her on the head.

'What the?'

Bending down, she picked up the object. And her heart skipped. It was one of Clifford's familiar handkerchiefs knotted in a ball.

She pretended to be fussing Gladstone so she could unknot it. Inside was one meticulously inked line:

> '~~Me? I~~, We prefer the wicked rather than the foolish. The wicked sometimes rest.' ~ *Alexandre Dumas ... All for one...*

She couldn't help smiling. This was his coded and ever-decorous way of saying Gripperel had behaved like a prize ass! But also, that he and Seldon were at least being held in the same wing, that was clear in the cryptic strikethrough in the quote.

Wishing she knew which of the sets of bars the handkerchief had flown from, she turned in a circle and waved it above her head.

'What is this you do?' the sharp voice of her warden barked.

'Just an English custom called morris dancing,' Eleanor replied smoothly. 'Fancy joining me?'

Back in her cell, the lights in the corridor went out as Gladstone curled up on her cape, now on the bed.

Dash it, Ellie!

Feeling her way across the cell from the facilities in the corner, she nestled in beside him, her back pressed against the inhospitable stone wall.

When she finally slept, fitfully at that, she had a recurring nightmare; Seldon and Clifford were being led to the guillotine, while she looked on helplessly as she fell from the top of the

Eiffel Tower. Tumbling over and over, the ground rushing up to meet her...

36

She was jerked awake by the sound of the key being thrust into the lock behind her. Struggling out of bed on creaky knees, she rubbed her stiff back and blinked, bleary-eyed at dawn filling her cell with pinky-orange fingers of light.

The door opened to reveal her warden and one of Gripperel's *police nationale*. As Gladstone stumbled up and shook himself, his hackles rose.

She grabbed his collar. 'Easy, old chum. No need for protection duties.'

As the policeman handcuffed her, she feigned horror. 'Tsk, monsieur! Creeping into a lady's quarters? And at this hour? Really! You might at least buy her breakfast first.'

The constable's stony expression softened, clearly impressed by her spiritedness. Catching sight of the warden watching him carefully, he cleared his throat loudly and marched Eleanor out, Gladstone following.

The room they eventually arrived at wasn't a room at all, she realised on entering, but actually a court. Complete with two raised but separated sections for the absent defence and prosecution. And one long pew for the equally absent jury. And facing it, an imposingly high judge's bench, from behind which Gripperel sat staring at her.

'Good morning, Lady Swift. I trust you slept well?'

She smiled frostily. 'Well enough. But no judge's wig, Inspector? Lacks a little gravitas without, I always think.'

'A "peruke", being the official term, my lady,' a familiar voice said as the door at the opposite end opened, the two faces being led through making her heart skip. And Gladstone woof excitedly.

Seldon shook off the policeman gripping his arm and raced to her side, his hair mussed as if he'd spent their entire time apart tearing it out. In his usual unfathomable way, Clifford looked meticulous, as if he just stepped in to serve her lunch.

Seldon fumbled to hold her hands with the restriction of his handcuffs.

'Eleanor, are you alright?'

'I'm fine, Hugh, really,' she murmured, leaning sideways momentarily to feel the warmth of his arm.

At Gripperel's wave, a policeman interrupted them, herding them into line in front of the judge's bench, her in the middle.

'Now,' she exclaimed, before Gripperel had a chance to speak. 'Let's see what preposterous nonsense this is.'

'Oh, that is hardly fair, Lady Swift,' he said in honeyed tones. 'I have justifiable reasons for detaining you, as you and your companions know very well.'

She wrinkled her nose. 'You can't have.'

'Why?'

She leaned forward conspiratorially. 'Because if you did, you wouldn't need to be sitting up there, playing God, to try and fool us into believing they're justified.'

His already square jaw tightened. Then he smiled. 'Alright, Lady Swift.' He rose and came down to stand in front of them.

She nodded. 'That's better, Inspector.'

'Care to explain now, precisely why, and on what grounds you arrested us?' Seldon said coolly.

Gripperel nodded. 'Where shall I start? You see, there are so many grounds that are "justified". First, I have an eyewitness who saw you at the Eiffel Tower, gathered around the dead body of the man who fell from there.'

'Constable Hacqueville, of the *police municipale*, you mean,' Eleanor said in a no-nonsense tone.

Gripperel nodded. 'Yes, Lady Swift. I do. You ran away. In France, it is a serious offence to leave the scene of a crime. Especially when it involves the death of a policeman!' He glanced at Seldon, who flinched. 'And second, when you ran, you took evidence with you. Again, here, this is also a very serious crime.'

She kept quiet, unable to deny any of it.

'Then,' he continued, 'when I came looking for you at your hotel to give you a chance to "justify" your criminal actions, you had run away again!'

She tutted. 'Not at all. We had simply taken Le Comte up on his gracious offer to stay in his charming chateau.'

'Without informing the manager, Monsieur Pronovost?' he shot back. 'Or taking most of your belongings? Except' – he glanced at Gladstone, who wagged his tail traitorously – 'your dog!'

Seldon opened his mouth, but Gripperel raised his hand. 'And then, the most "justified" grounds of all! When I come to Chateau Archambault to find you, what else do I find there?'

She stared back innocently. 'The exquisite wonders of baroque architecture?'

'Renaissance, my lady,' Clifford said as if to an errant pupil.

Gripperel snorted. 'What I find is the leather bag you took from Constable Hacqueville's dead body at the Eiffel Tower! And inside, one of the items stolen from the Musée d'Art Contemporain. Oh, and money. Lots of money!'

'And three cigars,' she said helpfully. 'In case you missed

those. But tell us, Inspector, how did you know we were at Chateau Archambault?'

'That is my business, Lady Swift.'

She opened her mouth to reply, but blinked instead. Seldon and Clifford shared a quizzical glance. Shaking herself, she stared at Gripperel.

'Inspector. I cannot understand why it did not strike me before. But you cannot "justifiably" arrest us for a murder that has not been committed!'

Seldon glanced jubilantly at Clifford, who was nodding slowly as Gripperel spread his hands.

'I confess, Lady Swift, you are correct. I did indeed arrest you, and your companions, for complicity in the murders of Constable Hacqueville *and* Emile Ury. So yes, for my own reasons, I am now treating both as murder.'

Eleanor groaned inwardly at the irony. She had been the only one convinced Emile's death was murder. Now, the police finally seemed to agree, the first thing they'd done was arrest her!

'Then please explain at least your declaration that "the thief", Emile Ury, fell through the atrium roof because he tripped "while running to escape the police"? And thus that was the reason he fell with such force?'

Gripperel shrugged. 'That was just a theory I voiced to the foreman replacing the glass the following morn—' He looked up sharply. 'How did you know this?'

'Ah, that is my business!' She was now thoroughly confused about whether he was the murderer, or simply an honest policeman doing what he thought was right. 'So, what's next, Inspector?' she said coolly.

He held her gaze for a moment, then turned away. 'You are to be released. Your bail bond has been paid.'

'Thank heavens,' Seldon said. He spun around to the

nearest policeman. 'You! Take those cuffs off my wife this instant!'

Gripperel nodded to the policeman, held Eleanor's precious pocket watch of her late uncle's out to her, then fixed Seldon with a steely look. 'My men will uncuff you all, but do not think this means you are free! You will remain under house arrest in your hotel. And if you try to leave, or are found talking to anyone of anything relating to either murder, you will be brought immediately back here. With no bail bond option.' He headed for the door, calling over his shoulder. 'And the next time we will meet, will be here with a proper judge. Wig and everything!'

As they were uncuffed, Clifford glanced at her and raised an eyebrow. She shrugged in reply, having no more idea than he did who had put up the bail bond. But her gut was telling her their reprieve was going to be short-lived. As they were escorted out of the courtroom, Seldon voiced what she was thinking.

'Out of the frying pan, into the fire?'

Being back in their honeymoon suite came with mixed feelings for Eleanor. Of course, it was a thousand times better than being in La Conciergerie. Or Chateau Archambault. But the armed policeman guarding their suite's door and his colleague stationed at the hotel entrance brought home just how much the 'romance' of their trip was in tatters. Clifford's discomfort was evident, too. Despite his horrified protestations, he had been forced to move into the second bedroom, disgracing his butler's code in his eyes by committing such an unforgivable crime against etiquette.

'Chin up, Clifford,' she said as he reluctantly joined them in the sitting room. 'It's far better than being in separate cells back in La Conciergerie! We'll need all three of us together to get out of this jam!'

'I'm glad you're with us too, Clifford,' Seldon said. 'Genuinely. And not only to help defend me against my wife, in case she starts in on me the way she did Gripperel in that courtroom!' He was clearly trying to be the one to lighten the mood this time. 'However, Gripperel still has the upper hand as' – he pointed at the door – 'here we are. Under blasted house arrest in our own hotel. And if we attempt to leave, or speak to anyone except the guard outside or the concierge, we will be marched straight back to prison and put on trial forthwith!'

She bit back asking who they thought might have bailed them out. They had more important answers to find. Seldon echoed her thoughts. 'I'd like to know who Gripperel's supposed eyewitness is.'

'Perhaps, Constable Bernier?' Clifford said. 'If he was the one at the bottom of the Eiffel Tower waiting for his partner, Hacqueville, to give the signal that he had planted the false evidence in her ladyship's bag.'

Seldon nodded. 'That's logical.'

Eleanor bit her lip. 'I'd also like to know who it was who tipped Gripperel off that we were at Le Comte's chateau?' She ran her hands down her arms. 'I've got a horrible feeling the eyewitness and informant are the same person.'

'The murderer,' Clifford said gravely.

'Or their accomplice, certainly. And there's one person who we discounted yesterday that I'm now doubtful of again on that score... Godine.'

Seldon winced. 'Eleanor, he's a priest!'

'I know, Hugh. But he has popped up three times in strategic places. And he could easily have been at the Eiffel Tower without us spotting him to make it a fourth! Plus, who's the person in a small village who hears and knows everything? The local priest! He certainly knew we were staying at the chateau.' Her thoughts flew back to their time at Josette's house. 'Dash it! If only we hadn't had to rush away yesterday, Josette would have told us about the connection she hinted at between Emile and Le Comte.' She pushed the thought of the precious letters she would probably never see again to the back of her mind. They had other, more pressing priorities. For the moment, at least. But afterwards...

Seldon cut into her thoughts. 'So much for us not showing

our hand. We couldn't have done a better job if we'd hired a marching band to announce our every move! Of course, Godine could have telephoned Gripperel just before he led us to Josette's house. Perfect timing for Gripperel to then drive out from Paris to the chateau.'

'Hence him arriving there but minutes after us leaving Madame Josette's house,' Clifford said soberly.

Eleanor threw her hands out. 'By fleeing to Magnes-sur-Oise and Le Comte's chateau, we thought we were escaping the deadly web we had inadvertently blundered into in Paris. But it simply followed us there.'

'Or,' Clifford said slowly, 'Magnes-sur-Oise, specifically Chateau Archambault itself, is the centre of the web?'

Eleanor nodded grimly. 'I think you're right, Clifford! Le Comte is almost certainly behind it all.' Her frustration propelled her off the settee. 'His invitation to the chateau was just to ensnare us in his lair.'

The three of them turned in confusion at the sound of knocking on the door. Gripperel had forbidden them any visitors.

Evidently not this one. Her eyes narrowed as Le Comte walked in.

'Good afternoon, Lady Swift.'

'You're not supposed to be here!' She folded her arms. 'No one is. Especially the person who had us arrested in the first place!'

He frowned. 'I did not have you arrested. You were my guests. This is why I paid your bail bond.'

'Oh! That was you?'

Her brow furrowed. What better ploy if Le Comte was the murderer than to have them arrested by tipping Gripperel off anonymously? And then swan in and bail them out, thus appearing as their saviour?

But then, why not just leave us to rot in jail, Ellie?

Now thoroughly confused, she opted for an ambiguous tone. 'So you've come to claim the bail bond fee back?'

Le Comte shook his head. 'That is not why I am here.'

To give her a moment to collect her thoughts, she peered past him. 'No Odette?'

He shook his head. 'I have left her at Chateau Archambault. I do not want her mixed up in this business. It has nothing to do with her. It is better she stays there until it is concluded. One way or the other.'

Eleanor held his gaze. 'So why are you here?'

'I came because I went to Monsieur le Curé, that is Didier le Godine, when my valet told me that you had been arrested.'

'Why go to him?' Seldon said.

'Because he is the priest of Magnes. And I needed someone to persuade Josette to see me. I did not think she would see me if I went alone.' He hesitated. 'You see, I thought she knew the secret between myself and Emile.'

A chill ran through her. 'The secret of Emile's tattoo? And what went on in that cavern in your woods?' she said breathlessly.

He blanched. 'I did not realise you had discovered that... that place. I see I greatly underestimated you, Lady Swift.'

'Most people do, sir,' Clifford said crisply.

'Go on.' Eleanor hesitated. 'What happened at Josette's?'

'I learned a very hard lesson,' Le Comte said penitently, to her surprise. 'After speaking with her, I realised Emile had never told her the secret. His own grandmother who raised him like her own son after his father died! And if he had not told her,' he held his hands out, 'he had never told anyone.'

'So?'

'So, I had him victimised needlessly.'

'And Constable Hacqueville?'

'Hacqueville got the justice he deserved!' Le Comte said

dismissively. He shook his head again wearily. 'But in truth, I probably deserve the same as him.'

'But he was mur—' Her words evaporated on her tongue. Le Comte's eyes had taken on an unnerving, feverish look. Was he more than mercurial? Maybe even a little... unhinged?

He turned to Seldon. 'Please forgive me disrobing in front of your wife. But she needs to see this to believe me.'

'I won't forgive that! You—' Seldon's ire dried on his lips.

Le Comte had shrugged out of his jacket and rolled his left sleeve up, revealing... a tattoo of a porcupine.

She swallowed hard. 'That's exactly the same as the one Emile had! And the same design as... as the painting on the cavern wall.'

He nodded. 'So now, please believe why I came here.'

He looked so pale, she waved him into a chair while Clifford poured him a brandy.

'We're listening.' She slid into the next chair.

He downed his glass in one. With a raised eyebrow, Clifford refilled it. Taking another swig, Le Comte cleared his throat.

'I came here to tell you a... a secret. A terrible secret I have carried since I was a young boy. A secret I thought I would never tell anyone. Until today...'

38

'We were boys,' Le Comte began in a faraway voice. 'But we thought we were men. Musketeers, in fact.'

'There were three of you then?' Eleanor said.

He stared into his brandy. 'Four. Three musketeers and one would-be musketeer!'

Clifford nodded. 'Just as in Dumas's novel, my lady.'

They waited for Le Comte to gather his thoughts. 'My father was always away. His military career was all that mattered to him. His only interest, to become the great Maréchal de France,' he said bitterly.

'General of all France's armies,' Clifford translated.

'Exactly. My mother died when I was a baby. So, like Emile, there was no one to stop me doing whatever I pleased. Nor to stop those who came to play with me.'

'Emile?'

'Not at first. In the beginning, we were just three. Myself and two brothers of another noble family across the river. Although theirs had not regained their title under Napoleon the third's decree, and their chateau was destroyed. Still, they were of noble blood. It was my idea to get the tattoo. Out of sight, where our shirts could hide our secret.' He wrenched his sleeve down. 'I made them do it. In a back street in Paris.'

'Why a porcupine?' Eleanor said.

'Because it is an ancient noble symbol of invincibility.'

'And you thought you were invincible?'

He choked on the sip of brandy he had taken. 'I am not proud of anything I have to tell you, Lady Swift! Then, I was fourteen, rich, a nobleman's son.'

She nodded in understanding. He had been a product of his upbringing.

'One day in the Archambault estate woods, we found Emile sneaking about.'

'So you let him join your musketeer gang?'

'Not at first. He was just a village boy. We threatened to give him over to the gamekeeper. Then I saw he, too, had the wild spirit. But he could not join as a musketeer. He had no noble blood. So I allowed him to join as our D'Artagnan. The four of us became bolder and braver, or so we told ourselves. In truth, we just became wilder and more uncontrollable. The people in the village tired of our outrageous behaviour, but we did not care. Emile's grandmother though, she did because the villagers came to her and warned her they would deal with Emile themselves, if she did not.'

'Just him?' Seldon said.

Le Comte laughed mirthlessly. 'I see you have never had a title or wealth, Mr Seldon. The other three of us were untouchable.'

'You were saying about Josette?' Eleanor said, leading him back to the story she needed, yet dreaded hearing.

Le Comte nodded. 'She threatened to send Emile away if he continued to see us.'

Eleanor's hand flew to her chest. 'Gracious, just saying those words must have nearly broken her heart.'

'I think so too now. But then' – he turned the glass in his

hand – 'I was young and arrogant enough to simply be furious that an old lady had stolen our D'Artagnan. So, me and the two brothers went to him and goaded him to come join with us again. For one last, glorious act of rebellion!'

'To do what?' Eleanor asked hesitantly.

'To be better than Dumas's musketeers! To defeat what they could not. The fire that burned down the Palais de Justice in the book.'

La Conciergerie's sister building, Ellie.

Her heart faltered. 'You re-enacted the scene... in the cavern?'

He nodded. 'But first we needed to set the scene, so it would be like the real palace! So we raided the chateau and carried our spoils to the cave. I knew my father would be furious if he ever found out.' His eyes looked increasingly feverish again, as if he was reliving every moment. 'The... fire got out of control. The stairs were ancient and dry. The flames, they... they tore up them as quick as paper. I made it to the top just before they collapsed. Emile too.' His voice shook, beads of sweat forming on his brow. 'It was the panic that made me do it. All I could see was my father's face. His... his fury.'

She forced herself to ask what her heart desperately didn't want to hear. 'What did you do?'

His expression was as blank as his tone. 'I locked the door. And ran away. Emile tried to persuade me to go back with him and... and unlock the door. But I was too scared.'

The three of them couldn't hide their horror at his admission.

Seldon swallowed hard. 'But the two brothers?'

Le Comte stared into the bottom of his glass. 'Their bodies were discovered a few days later. When my father found out, he gave out the official story that they had been messing around on the estate without permission. And without me.'

'That was disgusting of him,' Seldon said scornfully.

Le Comte shook his head. 'No, Mr Seldon. It was typical of
him. Reputation above everything.'

'And Emile?' Eleanor said.

'The villagers never suspected he had been part of it. They
thought he had stopped coming to the estate after Josette's
threat to send him away.' He shook his head again, as if in pain.
'And all this time, I assumed she knew it *all*. But she didn't. He
never told her what happened.' He slumped back in his chair.
'My father sent me abroad the very next day. I did not return for
years. Not until after he died.'

Eleanor didn't have the stomach to hear any self-pity from
him. 'Cut to why you said you're partly responsible for Emile's
death?'

He took a deep breath. 'Some years later, after I returned to
Chateau Archambault, I bought an apartment in Paris. Because
I tired of always driving back and forth to Magnes at all hours.
One morning, I was walking in the district of my apartment and
what did I see? But Emile! Selling his paintings along the river.'

'So?'

He gripped his glass, his eyes flashing with pure hate.

No, Ellie. Not hate. Self-loathing.

'Don't you understand?' he continued. 'I abhorred him for
what he knew! I never wanted to see or hear of him again! But I
did. Again and again. Over the months, it became like torture. I
found myself finding excuses not to leave my apartment in case
I should see him.' The glass in his hand shook. 'It was as if he
were haunting me.'

'So you murdered him?' Seldon said coldly.

Le Comte gulped down the rest of the brandy. 'No, Mr
Seldon. I did not. I only worked to drive him away. Away from
Magnes. And from Paris.'

'How?' Seldon said.

Eleanor's eyes widened. 'Hacqueville! You paid
Hacqueville.'

Le Comte nodded. 'Yes. To stop Emile selling his paintings so he would have no income and have to leave. By harassing him for petty offences, real or imagined.'

Seldon snorted. 'All you have done with these tales is to show you had the strongest motive to kill Emile Ury!'

Le Comte shrugged. 'You are correct. But I did not kill him. To this I swear.'

'Then who did?'

'Hacqueville,' he said flatly.

'But only because you paid him to!' Seldon retorted.

'No! I did not want Emile dead. Just gone. Now, I feel bad for trying to drive him away. And for his death.'

'Rot!' Seldon said. 'If that were true, why haven't you spoken to Inspector Gripperel and told him what you've told us?'

'Because I can't. It would destroy him.'

Eleanor stared at him. 'What do you mean? How?'

'Because he would quickly be guilty of a murder himself. But it is too long and complicated for now.'

'No. It is not,' she said in an uncompromising tone. She sat back. 'Take your time. We three aren't going anywhere. Thanks entirely to all this unpleasantness you started!'

'Perhaps. So alright. The two brothers. They had a third one. The youngest. He should have been our D'Artagnan, the fourth musketeer, rather than Emile. But he only ever wanted to study, never to play. And never to behave badly. You remember I said their family lost their title, their land? Well, also their money. So, they all had to work, eventually. The youngest worked his way up to become the chief inspector of Paris's *police nationale*.'

Eleanor gasped. 'Gripperel is the younger brother of the two who died in that cavern!'

Le Comte held his hands up. 'He is. But if I go to him with my tale, because he still has the blue blood of nobility running through his veins, he will be honour bound to avenge his brothers' deaths. By killing me.'

'Still a coward, I see,' Seldon said in disgust.

Le Comte shrugged wearily. 'Probably. But that is not why I will not go to him. If he kills me, he will go to the guillotine. Then I will be responsible for all the brothers' deaths.' He drained his glass. 'Two is too many for my conscience already.' He tried to get to his feet, but seemed genuinely unsteady. 'I have to leave now. To collect Odette. She knows nothing of this. And never must she.'

Eleanor stepped in his path. 'Was it you in the car I saw Hacqueville meeting with the night Emile died by Café...'

'Café Bohème, my lady,' Clifford prompted.

Le Comte nodded. 'Yes, it was. I met to pay him what I had promised for increasing his hounding of Emile. But I swear I did not know until later that Emile was dead.' He glanced at his watch. 'I must go. Even I can only get the police guarding you to look the other way for a certain amount of time. I will come again later. Because I want to help you catch Emile's killer. I know it is too little, too late, but it is all I can do to make amends. In the meantime, here, a symbol of trust between us, I hope?'

To Eleanor's amazement, he produced the bundle of her parents' letters and placed it in her hands.

The door closed behind him.

The three of them let out a long breath. Hers largely in relief at having the precious connection to her parents returned.

'That was all very unexpected,' she said shakily.

Clifford raised an eyebrow. 'I believe you have just taken back the very accolade you have so oft bestowed upon me, my lady. Master, or in this case, mistress of the understatement!'

'Did we trust what he said, though?'

Seldon shrugged. 'I kept blowing hot and cold, if I'm honest.'

'Well, he's shrewd enough to realise his confession would make him number one suspect for Emile's death in our minds.'

Seldon thumped his forehead. 'And convincing enough for us to fall slap bang into his trap again, if it was one!'

'What trap?'

'What was Gripperel's express edict? Strictly no visitors. And strictly no talking to anyone of anything relating to murder, or...' He waved a hand.

'We will be taken straight back to prison. With no bail bond option. Only a full trial in that very court,' Clifford said gravely.

Eleanor winced. 'Dash it, Hugh! You're right. He tricked us into doing just that.' She started pacing. 'But what kind of madness is that? To get us arrested, if he did. Then bail us out. Then to have us sent straight back there—'

'On much stricter terms.' Seldon groaned. 'And with possibly much less chance of being found innocent.'

'Truly Machiavellian. If that was the case,' Clifford said.

Eleanor's eye fell on her mother's handwriting on the top letter of the bundle Le Comte had given her. She made up her mind. 'I say, let's assume it wasn't a trick. His confession did seem to add up with the little we already knew, or guessed, didn't it?' She frowned. 'But he stopped short of admitting he killed Emile. Pointing the finger instead at Hacqueville as the murderer. But Hacqueville himself was murdered. So, unless there are two murderers, someone's wrong.' Her jaw set. 'There's one person we need to speak to next. The one who was right at the start of it all.'

The other two stared back questioningly.

'Alain Rion! The museum guard. My gut tells me he knows more than he told us. Much more! And remember, we're sure Sabine is related to him, Hugh.'

'Yes, Eleanor. But how are we going to "go" anywhere? Let alone to Rion. We don't even know where he lives. We're under house arrest, remember? We might as well just ring down to the reception desk and order up three lengths of rope.'

'There are easier ways to escape, sir,' Clifford said.

Seldon nodded. 'I know. I— Wait a minute. Whatever you've got, old friend, I don't want it shoved in my face, thanks.'

Seldon gently pushed the eager bulldog away.

'Master Gladstone. Stand down!' Clifford commanded. He bent and picked up the item the bulldog had reluctantly dropped.

Seldon frowned. 'What is it?'

'The soggy remains of a note, sir. I assume it was slipped under the door.' He peered harder at it. 'Written on quality vellum paper, I believe. And, despite Gladstone's administrations, still just about legible. Hmm, interesting.' He read aloud. 'Gripperel will be away from Paris until the morning.'

Eleanor stared at the others. 'That's great news!'

'If it's true,' Seldon said doubtfully.

'But it was delivered while the policeman was guarding the door. He still is! So, most likely it was Gripperel himself, surely? Who else could have sent the policeman off on some spurious task long enough to slip it under the door?'

'It could have been Le Comte? He obviously bribed the guard to let him in earlier.'

She shook her head, eyes wide. 'I'm sure it was Gripperel. He's giving us the chance to clear ourselves!'

'Or hang ourselves.'

'Hugh Seldon!'

He held his hands up contritely. 'Sorry. I'm just worried about you, Eleanor.'

'No time for that, Hugh. We've more pressing matters. Like, how to break out of here and track down a murderer by sunrise!'

39

Despite Eleanor's agitation, there was no time to lose. They needed to execute their escape just right. Anything out of the ordinary would arouse the suspicion of the policeman assigned to guard their door.

Finally, she heard voices outside. Flinging herself onto the settee, she grabbed a magazine from the coffee table. Clifford tutted and turned it the right way up before answering the officious rap at the door. The policeman looked them over, then stepped aside to allow Jules the waiter to wheel in the serving trolley filled with lidded dishes and two large pots of coffee.

'Ah, food,' she said. 'A long, leisurely dinner will sweeten this ridiculous incarceration!'

'And be entirely routine where her ladyship is concerned,' Clifford said drily to Jules as he tipped him with a folded note. 'And one pot of coffee is sufficient, thank you. Tempers in here are already testy enough without overdosing on caffeine.'

Jules nodded. 'Very good, Mr Clifford.' He ruffled Gladstone's ears, who'd come to see if there was anything worth snuffling out. Then he scooped up one of the pots and a cup and walked to the door, where he set it down in the corridor for the delighted policeman. He poked his head back into the room. 'Excusez-moi, madame. Perhaps you wish to make use of the hotel's dog walking service?' He gave her a discreet wink. 'Whatever the police find you guilty of, it is not fair that your dog miss sniffing outside?'

She nodded. 'Thank you. He can't cross his legs in here indefinitely.'

Jules bobbed his head. 'The doorman will see to him for the rest of the evening. Here, boy,' he called, patting his leg. Gladstone trotted over and they left together.

'Bon appétit!' the policeman said, closing the door. The sound of the key turning in the lock had the three of them racing off in different directions.

In her dressing room, Eleanor tore off her dress and hurled herself into her tweed travelling trousers. Disguising her far-too noticeable red curls with her most muted scarf, she shot back to the sitting room.

'Regrettably no ties, sir. Too English,' Clifford said, returning with Seldon a moment later.

Seldon wrenched his off with a grunt and reached for his hat.

'Even more English!' she hissed, holding up the darkest coloured berets she had bought for the party with her staff on the first night back home.

Clifford rolled his eyes, but took his along with Seldon. 'Your compact, my lady, if you please?'

Mystified, she grabbed it from her handbag.

Over at the door, Clifford listened carefully, then slid the slim mirrored case under the gap at the bottom. 'I can see the gentleman,' he whispered. He reached into his jacket for his trusty lockpicks. The three of them waited.

The pot of potent coffee Jules had left for the policeman had a very marked effect on their guard, who suddenly seemed to direly need the facilities. As he disappeared around the corner, Clifford withdrew the compact and picked the lock.

At the end of the corridor, they raced up the service stairs. The door at the top was unlocked. As they peered over the roof's edge, Sophie the maid glanced up from the yard below. She shook her head. A minute later, she reappeared, nodded, and disappeared back into the kitchen. Seldon went down the maintenance ladder first. Following him, Eleanor felt his muscular arms lift her and set her down as she reached the six-foot drop to the ground. A moment later, Clifford landed beside them as silently as a cat.

The gate was unlocked. The alley outside empty of policemen. Coat collars pulled up, they hurried away.

'Clifford?'

'Most assuredly, my lady. I will find a way to thank Jules and the others for their help. And ingenuity, particularly. The note I slipped Jules merely asked for some, ahem, strong coffee for our police guard, and that the service stairs be discreetly unlocked.'

'So he took upon himself to take Gladstone. And arrange about the gate and Sophie keeping watch,' she said, now even more grateful for their kindness.

'Hang on!' Seldon spun around. 'This isn't the way to the museum and Rion. Assuming he's on his shift?'

'No, Hugh. Change of plan. Because I've just realised Gripperel will have updated Omfroy. As the museum director, he'd have been told the second stolen item was recovered. And that we are under house arrest. So I think we need to avoid the museum for the moment.'

He nodded. 'Excellent thinking. But then where...?'

'Sabine,' she said determinedly.

. . .

The dilapidated door on the fifth floor of the weathered warehouse swung open with a shudder. Inside, Sabine, her eyes red-rimmed, looked Eleanor over with disdain.

'Whatever you want, I am not interested in it.'

'That's alright. I haven't brought anything,' Eleanor said airily. 'Which is terribly rude, I know.'

'Indeed, my lady. We really should have come bearing a bowl of calf's foot jelly or marrow fat broth,' Clifford said admonishingly.

'They would make me sick!' Sabine shoved her hands into the pockets of her plaster-splattered blue overalls.

Eleanor shuddered. 'As a long stretch locked in a cell at La Conciergerie will. Believe me. We've just tried it for a night.'

Sabine's mane of carefree raven waves swung as she shook her head. 'You expect me to believe that? You, the titled English lady?'

Eleanor turned her wrists over to show the still red marks from the handcuffs.

Seldon's jaw pulsed. 'My wife did it for Emile. What have you done for him lately, Sabine?'

A look of pain crossed her eyes. She hesitated, then turned and walked inside. They followed her in. The open-plan room was chilly. And damp, the gypsum in the air cloying. Sabine went over to where she'd been mixing up several large buckets of white plaster powder.

'What is it you want?' she said wearily.

'The truth,' Eleanor said simply. 'Before there is a third murder.'

'Third?' Sabine's dark eyes widened as they strayed over to the sculpture of the man hauling himself from the egg. 'I have kept the belief that was not how Emile died. But now you say another person has been killed?'

'Yes. Thrown off the Eiffel Tower.'

Sabine's gasp echoed around her studio. 'But the newspaper said—'

'A lot of lies.' Eleanor cocked her head. 'You should have spotted that. You're an expert at them yourself.'

Sabine threw down the large paddle spoon she had picked up. Running the cuff of her overalls over her face, she muttered, 'Why do you always have harsh things to say to me?'

'People being murdered must bring out the worst in me.' Eleanor wished she had never even heard the word. 'Now, let's talk straight. All I want is justice for Emile, and the man who was hurled to his death. That man was a policeman,' she said grimly. 'But that didn't save him from the murderer.'

Sabine's eyes flashed. 'And you think it is the same man who—'

'Killed Emile. Yes.'

Sabine buried her face in her hands. When she took them away, her eyes were even redder. She stepped slowly over to the egg sculpture and ran her hands gently over the man's face, then down his torso. 'You were correct before. Emile was... my lover. I knew his body so well, that is how I could sculpt it like this.'

Clifford ran his finger around his collar, while Seldon busied himself with his coat buttons.

'And you knew he was planning to rob the Musée d'Art Contemporain, too, I know that,' Eleanor bluffed.

Sabine let out a sob. 'Okay, so this is true also. I tried to tell Emile his idea was stupid. And dangerous! He did not even know the place. He had always refused to go there.' Her eyes closed as she kissed the sculpture's face. 'He hated the man who bought all his father's paintings. Not just because he robbed his grandmother and left her struggling, but even more because he broke her heart!'

'Which is why he needed you to help him, as you knew the layout of the museum,' Eleanor said pointedly.

Sabine shook her head. 'No, I do not. I have never gone. It is mostly paintings. Only a few sculptures. Why would I go there?'

'How do you know how few sculptures are on display if you haven't?' Eleanor shot back.

'When he did not listen that his idea was dangerous,' Sabine snapped. 'I told him I would have no part in his plan. The night he went there, I walked all over Paris. I was angry. And... and so scared for him.' She ran her cuff over her face again. 'It hurt too much to sit and wait to see if he came back.'

'Which he didn't. Because someone killed him,' Seldon said matter-of-factly.

The tortured look in Sabine's eyes struck Eleanor as genuine. 'But who would do such a terrible thing? Emile was not the kind of man ever to fight or make trouble for anybody.'

'Only to steal,' Seldon grunted.

Sabine's cheeks flushed. 'He had good reason for this!'

'We know,' Eleanor said in a softer tone. 'Who do you think might have killed Emile, Sabine?'

'I... I don't know. Really.' She folded her arms. But Eleanor didn't miss that her fingers were twitching.

This was the best chance they would get. She had to seize it. 'Well, chaps. It's painful to say, but I admit you were both right. And I was wrong. She just can't tell the truth, even to help bring Emile's killer to justice.'

The other two nodded.

'What? I have answered your questions!' Sabine cried.

'Yes. But only with more lies!'

'Like what?' Sabine said fiercely.

'Like you not knowing the Musée d'Art Contemporain, for starters. I bet you could tell me what's on every floor. Because it's a nice peaceful place... to chat with *Alain*.'

Sabine stiffened.

'We know Alain Rion is your relative. Don't bother to deny it.'

'Alain Rion is my father,' Sabine said reluctantly.

'And he just happens to be the guard who was on duty the night Emile broke in?'

Sabine shrugged.

'Very well. If you are determined that us trying to save your father's life is not our business, who am I to argue?' Eleanor said.

Sabine's eyes widened. 'Why do you say this? My father is in no danger!'

'Isn't he, mademoiselle?' Clifford had clearly caught Eleanor's drift. 'Because the two men who were murdered were killed over the same thing. And we have good reason to believe Monsieur Rion may be his next target.'

Eleanor crossed her fingers behind her back at Clifford's lie. They had no reason to think Sabine's father was in danger but this was no time for niceties. Not if they were going to catch a double murderer before Gripperel returned and threw them in prison!

Seldon nodded. 'The murderer threw a man off the Eiffel Tower whilst it was packed with visitors. Just imagine what he can do in a closed museum. To the night guard. Your father!'

'My father is not working tonight,' Sabine said breathlessly.

'Then he's even more vulnerable,' Eleanor said grimly. 'Now, where does he live?'

Sabine's head fell to her chest. 'I loved Emile. Now he is dead. I... I do not want to lose anyone else.' She hesitated, then looked up. 'Fifteen Rue Jessaint. Floor four.'

As Eleanor reached for the door, Sabine's eyes flashed again. Her hand curled around one of the chisels on the table. 'But when you find out who killed Emile, tell me first. *Before* the police!'

40

The area Clifford's map led them to was the dingiest part of Paris they had yet encountered. Under the faint pools of light from the few street lights still working, men in dishevelled clothing stared vacantly at them as they passed. The air was thick with soot from the endless passenger and freight trains clanking along the railway tracks behind the row of dilapidated tenement buildings.

Fifteen turned out to be the penultimate number in the street, the last having been partly demolished. The open carcass of the top floor was all that was now left of what had once been someone's home.

Seldon tightened his grip on Eleanor's arm.

'I'm fine, Hugh,' she said more brightly than she felt. 'Clifford and I have braved far less seemly places than this on occasions to get answers.'

Clifford nodded. 'Regrettably, that is the case, sir. Against my better judgement, naturally. However, without the option of padlocking her ladyship inside a guarded vault...' He left that hanging.

Seldon still looked far from happy. 'Even that wouldn't have worked, Clifford. Gripperel thinks he's done exactly that and yet here she is. Out and about in a dubious quarter of Paris, in the dark, to question another man about murder!'

'That's true. But I have you two with me for protection. And the three of us are the best detective team! And the way you got us into Sabine's studio was masterful, Hugh.'

He groaned. 'Hardly my finest hour for diplomacy, Eleanor. Honestly, I just blurted out my horror at the truth of you having spent a night in prison for Emile. Now, let's get in and out quickly. Before we're missed at the hotel.'

Counting up the line of windows, she was relieved there was a glow of light in the fourth one. The bells for each floor were all missing, however. Optimistically, she tried the door.

'Dash it! Locked. And it's a little exposed here for you to perform your unlocking magic, Clifford.' She peered back up. 'We can't throw stones four floors and hope to hit his window. We'll have to wait until someone—'

She broke off and stepped out of the way as the door opened, letting out a musty smell of stale cigarette smoke and over-boiled greens. The plump fiftyish woman who emerged eyed them darkly.

'Excusez-moi, madame,' Clifford purred, steering her to the edge of the broken pavement. 'Rue Pajol?' He pointed helplessly left and right.

Eleanor shoved the toe of her boot in the door just enough to stop it from closing. A raft of directions they didn't need given, the woman bustled away, muttering at the world in general.

The stairs up were narrow, the banister rail unpleasantly sticky. At the fourth-floor landing, Eleanor gestured questioningly between the two doors.

'No nameplates,' she mouthed.

Clifford grimaced as he pressed his ear to the left one, then the right. 'Only one person is home,' he murmured, pointing left.

'Then let's try that one.'

She raised her hand and rapped out a jaunty rhythm.

'Bah! Je suis fatigué. Que faire maintenant?' a man's voice grumbled from inside. Seldon stepped tighter into Eleanor's side at the sound of a bolt being drawn back.

'Monsieur Rion! How delightful to see you again.'

The ferret-like face of Alain Rion gawped at her, cigarette hanging from his bottom lip.

'You? What do you want?' he said tersely.

'To talk to you. And isn't it lucky? Here we are. And there are you!'

Rion's expression made clear he thought otherwise. 'I have nothing to talk with you about, madame.'

'Really?' She leaned closer, despite his glower. 'Your daughter, Sabine, seemed to think you might. Especially as you and her are both mixed up in two very nasty murders.'

Rion jerked so hard his cigarette fell to the bare wood boards at his feet. 'I warn you! You leave her out of any trouble you are making!' He retreated into the room as she walked in without waiting to be invited. Seldon followed quickly, then Clifford, who paused fleetingly to grind out the cigarette butt with his heel and a shudder.

Rion's apartment was little more than a bedsit with a tiny annexe for a kitchen. It was surprisingly neat and clean.

'My home is probably not good enough for you to sit in, madame,' he said gruffly.

'On the contrary, that's very gentlemanly of you.' She dropped into the nearest chair. 'I'll come straight to the point.'

'One mercy for me, then,' he said sarcastically.

Seldon stepped forward. 'Monsieur Rion. Kindly watch your manners. That is my wife. And believe it or not, she's trying to help.'

'Help me?'

'Perhaps,' Eleanor said. 'That depends. I'm definitely trying to help Emile. Because when I told you he was dead, I left out that he was murdered.'

Rion gasped. 'But... but I only intended—'

'Intended what?' she said quickly.

For a moment, she thought he was going to become defensive again. Instead, he covered his face in his hands and collapsed into the other chair.

'I did not intend for it to get him killed,' Rion mumbled.

Seldon and Clifford exchanged a glance, but said nothing, waiting for him to continue. After a few moments, she gently prompted him.

'What did you intend, then?'

Rion's mouth set in a thin line. 'To get him out of Sabine's life! He was not good enough for her. He made only a few francs selling his terrible paintings. And if he really cared for her, he should have got a real job. Like a real man!'

Eleanor shook her head. 'He had a real job. He was a painter. Following in his beloved father's footsteps. But now I see why you were so scathing about how few paintings you believed he sold.'

'Because it is true! He was going to give my daughter only a life of poverty. She needed to understand the other man was the one she should choose. And I did not believe it was love for Emile. Just a... a fascination that would pass.'

Eleanor thought for a moment. 'Tell us your part in Emile breaking into the museum.'

Rion hesitated, then all the fight seemed to leave him. 'He came to me with his foolish idea. At first, I did not want any part of it. But then I realised, if he was caught, he would go to jail. Then Sabine would stop thinking he was the man for her. So I told him I would help him and gave him all the times when I would check the Christophe Ury display. And the plan of where it was. And where the other guard would be at what time. On the night, I left the window in the coat room unlocked so it was easy for him to open with a metal bar. But I told him before, I would have to ring the alarm only a few minutes after he steals what he wants. It would be suspicious for me otherwise. And I was not going to be the one to get into trouble.'

'Rather misguided optimism,' Seldon said. 'But carry on, because you still seem the likeliest candidate for his murderer!'

Rion glared at him. 'I swear I did not kill him. But... but his death weighs on my shoulders. I told him to hide on the roof of the hotel. That I had a friend there who owed me a favour and he would leave the service stairs' door unlocked. And that there would be a bag of some clothes so he can change quickly and then wait quietly in the hotel like a guest while the police search for a man in different clothes.'

'Let me guess,' she said grimly. 'It wasn't unlocked? And there was no bag of clothes?'

He sighed heavily. 'And I have no friend at the hotel! It was all lies. I admit this. I planned for him to be trapped on the roof. So he could be caught when he came back down the outside ladder. And arrested straight away.' He hung his head. 'But Emile was not the only one to be betrayed. I was too. By the man I thought was good enough to marry my daughter! He was supposed to catch Emile and take him to jail like we planned!'

Suddenly, it all fell into place. Eleanor's breath caught. 'That man was Hacqueville, wasn't it?'

Rion nodded. 'He loved Sabine. He told me he wanted to marry her. But she told him no.'

'You said Hacqueville didn't do what he promised. What did he do instead?'

'He killed Emile,' Rion said flatly. 'But it is my fault. I see that now.'

. . .

In the street, she couldn't stop her feet from racing away from the place where Rion had conjured up his hideous plan to betray Emile. Seldon and Clifford kept pace, giving her time to be the one to speak first.

'What a tragic waste of life,' she finally muttered.

'And love,' Seldon said quietly.

She sighed, slowing slightly. 'How I stopped my hands from grabbing Rion by his shirt collar and shaking him I shall never know. And' – she threw her hands out in frustration – 'are all our suspects going to confess to everything except killing Emile! And then insist he was murdered by a dead man? Hacqueville!' She shook her head. 'So, were we wrong? *Are* there two murderers? Or are Rion and Le Comte lying?'

'Or is there another answer altogether?' Clifford said thoughtfully.

Eleanor pointed at him. 'Possibly. And there's only one man left who might know. And we're going straight to him!'

'Now? But we have to be back at the hotel before...' At her determined look, Seldon let out a long breath. 'Oh, well, might as well be guillotined for a sheep as for a lamb!'

Eleanor was acutely aware time was racing on. Every minute they were gone from the hotel was increasing the chance their absence would be discovered. And they would be hauled back, handcuffed, to La Conciergerie. Then she could never get justice for Emile. Nor Hacqueville.

But she had an even more immediate challenge. She had identified Bernier as the person they needed to interrogate next, but she had no idea where to find him.

Seldon rubbed his forehead. 'Well, given we're violating Gripperel's house arrest, we can't go to the police station and ask them where he is. Oh, and that we'd like to speak to him about a murder we ourselves have been implicated in!'

Clifford looked thoughtful. 'Indeed, we cannot, sir. For more reasons than that.' At his and Eleanor's baffled look, he continued. 'I was informed by Jules, unlike Inspector Gripperel's *police nationale*, the *police municipale* here operates from each of the city's district town halls, not from dedicated police stations. And they are under the governance of the mayor of Paris.'

She winced. 'Who wouldn't exactly welcome us with open

arms as we're being held on suspicion of involvement in the murder of one of his policemen, as you just pointed out, Hugh.'

Seldon groaned. 'Then we're on our own.' He frowned. 'Wait. Clifford, where's our hotel on the map?'

He examined it for a moment before pointing. 'There, sir.'

'And the museum?'

Again, Clifford pointed to a spot.

'Right. That identifies some of Bernier's beat as he and Hacqueville were near the hotel the night of Emile's murder. And the museum when they claimed to have seen Rion in the street before. So, Clifford, where is the nearest district town hall to this area?'

After a moment, he located that as well.

'Alright, now where's that midnight café we were holed up in when Eleanor saw Hacqueville leaning in what we now know was Le Comte's car?'

'Café Bohème, hmm...' He traced his finger along a raft of streets, then backtracked a few. 'On this corner, I believe, sir.'

'Excellent. Let's assume Bernier and Hacqueville weren't out of their assigned jurisdiction when at our hotel, the museum or outside that café. So, if I was drawing up beat routes for my men, I'd divide them like this.' Seldon gestured over the map. 'If Bernier's superior has an eye for efficiency, it means we'll most likely strike lucky in finding our man in this area.' He traced a section of the map.

'Hugh, that's brilliant!'

'Thank you, Eleanor. But he might not even be on duty. And even if he is—'

'We'll find a way to talk to him. Besides, I now think he's up to his neck in this so deeply, we'll be able to match any threats he might make about going to Gripperel,' she said resolutely.

'Marvellous. Now we're about to add threatening policemen to our Parisian crime sheet!'

The three of them hurried along the streets Seldon had

proposed they scour, eyes alert for the midnight-blue uniforms and tall pillbox caps of the *police municipale*. As they reached yet another junction, a crowd of men were drinking outside a bar. Clifford strode over.

'Avez-vous vu un policier?'

The men all agreed they had, but due perhaps to their inebriated state, couldn't come to any consensus how long ago or in what direction they went. The barman came out to see what was going on.

'Policier?' He flapped his cloth at his customers to quieten. Grabbing Clifford by the shoulder, he turned him left and pointed down the street. 'Il y a cinq minutes.'

'Fingers crossed,' Clifford murmured as they hurried the way the barman had suggested.

'Blue uniforms!' Seldon hissed jubilantly only a short while later. 'Just went round that corner up ahead.'

Having reached it, Eleanor peered around the corner, quickly ducking back out of sight. 'It's Bernier, alright,' she whispered. 'With another policeman I don't recognise. They've paused under a street lamp to light a cigarette. Hang on, they've changed their minds and are moving on.'

Seldon grimaced. 'I should have realised he'd have been given a new partner. We'll just have to wait for the right moment.'

They shadowed the two policemen until that moment arrived. They stopped outside a tobacconist and Bernier's new partner went in.

'Ah!' she said. 'That's why they never lit their cigarettes. Out of matches. That gives us our best, and possibly only chance.'

Before Seldon could protest, she hurried up to the solitary policeman.

'Good evening, Constable Bernier.'

Bernier stared stupefied back at her. She flapped a hand.

'It's alright, I'm not offended you don't remember me. You've only seen me before in my emerald silk evening gown at the hotel where Emile Ury was murdered.' She slapped her forehead. 'And then again, of course, in my mulberry silk cocktail dress with the exquisite beaded bodice. At the Eiffel Tower. Where your partner, Hacqueville, was murdered. You were there even though you rudely failed to say hello.'

The shocked look on Bernier's face told her they'd guessed right on that one. He glanced nervously at the tobacconist his partner had gone in to. She leaned closer.

'Exactly. You don't want your new partner in on this conversation, do you?'

At that moment, the other policeman left the shop and strolled over. Bernier turned to him. What he said, she didn't understand, but his new partner gave her a quizzical look, nodded at Bernier, and walked on. Once he was out of earshot, Bernier turned back to Eleanor, a sly grin on his lips.

'Lady Swift, I remember you, naturally. And Mr Seldon. But I also remember hearing that you are under house arrest in your hotel? Perhaps I should contact Inspector Gripperel and—'

'And maybe I should contact the mayor, your boss, who might be interested in learning a killer is roaming the streets in his blue uniform and pillbox cap?' She gestured at his hat. She sighed. 'You know, you were smarter than Hacqueville, Bernier.'

Bernier checked his partner was now nowhere to be seen, his expression a mix of unease and curiosity. 'Why do you say I am smarter than Hacqueville?'

'Because he was about to blow your cover when he started throwing his weight around in our hotel's dining room. You're clearly more experienced at concealing your crimes. I admit I didn't suspect you at all at first.'

Bernier's face twisted in exasperation. 'You have not one thing to suspect me of now!'

Seldon stepped forward. 'Maybe. But we know for a fact

that Hacqueville was paid to hound and harass Emile Ury. And Hacqueville is dead. Which means you're the only one left to take the blame, as dead men can't talk. And any wretch who would dishonour his uniform as you have is also eminently capable of murder, in my book.'

'Mine too. And the mayor's I'm sure,' she said. 'So, do you want to tell him all about it? Or shall we? Your choice. And we've got all the time in the world,' she ended, swallowing her panic as the truth was very much the reverse.

Bernier rubbed his hands over his face. 'Alright, we make a bargain.'

'Try me?'

'I tell you what happened. And you say nothing to the mayor. And I say nothing to Inspector Gripperel about you breaking house arrest. Deal?'

'Deal.'

'Then I tell you it all starts with a woman.'

'Cherchez la femme!' Clifford murmured.

Eleanor nodded. 'Let me guess. Sabine Rion. We know her well. Her father, Alain too.' She spotted the surprise on Bernier's face with satisfaction. 'That's right. We're privy to a lot more than you realise. So please don't waste time lying.'

He held his hands up. 'Alright. The short story is that Hacqueville was in love with Sabine. He was like a madman for her. And her father thought him a good husband for her. But she was in love with Emile Ury.'

She had to bite her tongue. All that was nothing they didn't already know.

Bernier shrugged. 'I have been in love once and I had nothing against Emile. So, when someone offered money to Hacqueville to hassle Emile so much he would leave Paris, I refused to help him. But he was my partner, so I did not try to stop him either.'

'Cut to the chase,' she said curtly. 'Who paid Hacqueville to harass Emile?'

Bernier's eyes widened. 'Not a chance, Lady Swift.'

Her expression hardened. 'Silly of you. Because I already know it was Le Comte Archambault.'

His mouth fell open, real fear showing in his eyes. 'Okay, okay. So you know plenty! But Le Comte was not the only man who wanted Emile gone. Alain Rion did too. It was his idea to get Emile sent to jail. Hacqueville liked this idea very much.'

Her cheeks flushed. 'Because then Sabine would choose him? Or so he arrogantly thought.'

'Yes. But also he liked the idea of making more money from the arrangement. Le Comte had paid him only to make life very hard for Emile. Hacqueville went to him and told him, he would do better. He would make sure Emile was sent to jail.'

'If Le Comte paid him a lot more money, I imagine!' Seldon said in disgust. 'Did Le Comte agree?'

Bernier nodded.

She shared a look with Seldon. Le Comte had conveniently left out that part in his confession earlier that afternoon.

She turned back to Bernier. 'Jump to the night Emile died.'

He nodded. 'Hacqueville had arranged with Rion he would wait in the street by the kitchen yard of your hotel. Emile had been tricked by Rion to go up on the roof, with no way down except back into the yard. I was waiting around the other side of the hotel because I told Hacqueville I wanted no part of his plan.'

'Keep going,' Seldon said.

'Hacqueville told me he would arrest Emile, like is normal for a policeman who happens to pass and spot a thief. He would then join me. But he did not come. Instead, a hotel waiter ran out of the hotel, shouting that a man had fallen through the dining room roof.' Bernier cleared his throat. 'I went to find Hacqueville. He was just coming from the kitchen yard. We ran to the front of the hotel together and went in.' He shrugged. 'And you saw the rest.'

'Which is when you gave yourself away. Although I didn't realise it at the time,' Eleanor said. 'When Hacqueville accused me of being the thief's accomplice, you hushed him because you thought it too obvious he was setting up an alibi for himself. Without any regard for you, it now seems, though,' she added pointedly.

Bernier threw his arms out. 'I told him, as I told you, I never wanted to be involved! But he got me involved in his stupid plan whether I wanted it or not.'

'And now only you can get yourself out of it,' Seldon said grimly. 'So, who pushed Emile Ury to his death?'

Bernier shrugged. 'Hacqueville! This is obvious. He was there. He hated Emile. He set him up to die. But I did not know that was his plan. And do not think I will ever say any of this again. Not to anyone.'

'So who killed Hacqueville? You should know. You were at the Eiffel Tower when he was thrown off it. We saw you,' she bluffed again.

Bernier shrugged. 'I do not know. If you saw me, then you know I was there, yes. But I was waiting at the bottom of the tower because Hacqueville told me he had information that meant we could recover the second item stolen from the museum.'

'And just what was your role?' Seldon said.

'To wait for Hacqueville. That is all.'

Seldon's eyes flashed. 'That's a lie! You were going to arrest my wife for being in possession of that second stolen item after Hacqueville planted it on her!'

Bernier's shoulders slumped as he nodded contritely. 'Alright, yes. I admit, I was supposed to arrest you, Lady Swift, the minute Hacqueville appeared.'

'Only when he did appear, it was face down. Dead. Every bone in his body broken!'

Bernier nodded again. 'I saw that still you tried to save him. That was brave.'

'Was it you that reported us to Gripperel as having been there at the time?'

He sighed. 'Yes. But anonymously. I reported I saw someone around Hacqueville's body. That they took his bag and ran. I describe you and your companions.'

'That's why you didn't arrest us at the time, then. Too scared your part in all of it would come out,' she said, making clear it wasn't a question.

'I'm asking you again.' Seldon held the policeman's gaze. 'Who killed Hacqueville?'

Bernier stared at his boots. 'I am telling you the truth. I do not know. It was not me. I was on the ground waiting for you as you saw.'

He's right, Ellie. He can't have been the murderer, unless he's called my bluff and knows we never saw him at the bottom of the Eiffel Tower.

She jumped at the sound of a clock striking the hour. They should have been back at the hotel long ago. She looked at Bernier, her disgust thinly veiled. 'Alright. We believe you. And we'll stick to our end of the deal. Enough of it tallies with what we were told by others who are also up to their necks in this.'

Like Le Comte for one, Ellie!

Rion flew into her thoughts. The story he'd spun still seemed doubtful at points. 'One last question. You told us you and Hacqueville both saw Rion coming back from the direction of the hotel just around the time Emile was killed. Where exactly was that again?'

'I cannot say.'

'Yes, you can,' Seldon said firmly. 'Or our deal is off.'

Bernier raised his arms up angrily. 'Alright! After I told you that we saw Rion, Hacqueville told me to keep my mouth shut. Because...' He looked away.

'Because?'

'Because it was not Alain Rion we saw! But I will never tell who it was. I have no wish to finish up like Hacqueville.' He jerked his chin at her. 'Now let me alone or I will tell Inspector Gripperel you have escaped from your hotel just to get you out of my hair!'

As he stalked off twelve sombre peals reverberated in the night air.

Midnight already, Ellie, and all's definitely not *well!*

42

'No!'

Two men in silver-buttoned uniforms were standing guard on either side of the gate into the hotel's kitchen yard. There was no mistaking the red piping and leather pistol pouch attached to their wide black belts.

'Gripperel's men!' Seldon hissed.

They beat a hasty retreat. Regrouping in the dark passageway opposite, they ducked behind a collection of empty crates.

'Blast it! They've not only discovered we've broken out, but exactly which way we managed it too,' Seldon said. 'Now what?'

'I'll check the other entrances and exits, sir.' Clifford melted away. In a heartbeat, he was back. The concern etched in his expression made words unnecessary.

Seldon hesitated. 'How many police are there?'

He winced. 'I stopped counting, sir.'

Eleanor felt terrible. 'Chaps, I'm so sorry. This is all my fault.'

Seldon managed a wan smile. 'No, it's entirely the murderer's fault. And having got us this deep in a desperate situation, on our honeymoon of all times, I'm going to personally double my efforts to bring that wretch to trial!'

'That's the spirit, sir,' Clifford said, momentarily abandoning the covert watch he was keeping on the hotel.

She shook her head firmly. 'No! We have to stop now.'

Clifford's ever-unflappable composure failing him would have made her laugh in any other circumstances. But this was no laughing matter.

Seldon's jaw had dropped too.

'Stop, Eleanor?' he said in disbelief. 'You've never stopped. Or given in. You're the most impossibly stubborn person I've ever met.'

'Maybe. But the fact Gripperel's men know we escaped isn't just about us any more. Jules and the others will be in the most fearful trouble if the police find out they were involved.'

Seldon squeezed her hand. 'What a fool I am. I forgot to add you're also the most compassionate. But giving ourselves up now won't help Jules and the others.'

Clifford stiffened.

'What is it?' she whispered.

'Monsieur Pronovost, my lady. Acting furtively. Given he is slinking out of the side window of the hotel cloakroom!'

'But what's he got to hide?'

'As you've shown me on many occasions, there's only one way to find out,' Seldon said. 'Follow him!' He held his hand out. 'Want to be my date and come too?'

She nodded, remembering again how reticent Pronovost had been to call a doctor when Emile landed on her table. 'Yes!'

Clifford half bowed. 'Welcome back, my lady!'

'Thank you. But you've got two dates, Hugh. Coming too, Clifford?'

'Willingly. As the chief inspector said; one might as well be hung for a sheep as a lamb. Or was it guillotined?'

As they set off, she shuddered.

Let's hope the only person who finds out is the murderer, Ellie!

Pronovost's darting way of walking had struck her as unusual when she'd seen him in the hotel. Now it felt a heaven-sent gift, as there was no mistaking his scurrying form. Or his pointed features each time his neat lapelled collar fell from his sharp chin. The three of them shadowing him had the harder job as they tried to blend inconspicuously among the few other pedestrians.

Suddenly he slowed. Then jerked to a stop altogether. She beckoned Seldon and Clifford into the shadows of a closed shop doorway.

'Look!' she whispered. 'He's signalling discreetly to that man in overalls over there.'

Clifford sniffed. 'Hardly discreetly, my lady. A touch of St Vitus's dance would have been less noticeable.'

'Only because we're watching him,' Seldon said, hands on Eleanor's shoulders as he peered over her head. 'To anyone else, I bet he looks like a man trying to give up smoking. Now arguing with himself not to dash up to the counter and buy some cigarettes from that tobacco kiosk.'

She couldn't deny he had a point. She thought back to Bernier's partner. Never had she been to a city where so many people smoked.

As the man Pronovost had signalled to stepped over to him, Clifford tapped his forehead as if trying to remember something. With the briefest of exchanges, Pronovost reached inside his smart suit jacket. Like an anxious rabbit, he thrust an envelope at the man and started hurriedly back in their direction.

'On three,' she whispered, ear cocked for his pattering footsteps. 'Three!'

She stepped out of the doorway, colliding with him.

'Oh gracious, how clumsy of me, Monsieur Pronovost. I do apologise.'

He flicked his handkerchief over the front of his jacket and down his sleeves.

'I should think so too, madame— Mon Dieu! It's you, Lady Swift.' He pointed at Seldon and Clifford too, glancing around him as if searching for a policeman. 'You are supposed to be in my hotel. Not sneaking about here!' he said stiffly.

'You too.'

'Me?' His thin lips pursed. 'I do not know what you mean. You three people left my hotel in such a manner as to deliberately evade the police!'

'So did you,' Seldon said firmly. 'Or do you usually slink out of the hotel's side windows like a thief?'

'Oh la la!' Pronovost's slim, white hands flew to his face. 'I was in the most desperate haste. And the police would have stopped me to ask so many questions.'

'Just as we have,' she said firmly. 'Monsieur Pronovost, we saw you give that man an envelope under the most suspicious of circumstances. I think Inspector Gripperel would like to hear about that.'

'Which man?' Pronovost replied unconvincingly.

Clifford clicked his fingers. 'The foreman of the glazier's company.'

At Pronovost's horrified look, she glanced questioningly at Clifford.

'I was trying to remember, my lady, where I had recognised him from while we were watching Monsieur Pronovost.'

'Spying, not watching,' the hotel manager said tautly. 'You were spying on me!'

She nodded. 'With good reason. Two men have been murdered already over the events which have centred around your hotel.'

Pronovost paled. 'But I have played no part in any murders!'

The three of them stared back at him, shaking their heads.

'Hopeless,' Eleanor said.

'Pathetic,' Seldon grunted.

'Pitiful,' Clifford tutted.

Pronovost looked from one to the other, wide-eyed. 'But I am telling the truth!'

'Then carry on,' she said. 'And tell us the rest of it. Why were you meeting clandestinely with the glazier company's foreman?'

'To pay him to stay quiet,' Pronovost mumbled. 'I knew the structure of the dining room roof was dangerous. I had been... economising on the repairs.'

'Blast it, Eleanor!' Seldon cried. 'I failed to stop you creeping about on that thing.'

'We both failed twice in that regard, actually,' Clifford said remorsefully.

She flapped a hand at them and turned back to the hotel manager. 'And not just the roof, either, Monsieur Pronovost. Other repairs you neglected while you pocketed the money you put through the accounts with fictitious invoices, I'll bet!' Pronovost's look said it all, but one thing was still puzzling her. 'Why did you risk being caught leaving the hotel so surreptitiously just now? The police would have got out of you what you were up to if they'd followed you. Just as we have.'

Pronovost groaned. 'Because I had no choice. I promised the foreman the money. But since you have been put under house arrest, my hotel has been swarming with policemen! But tonight, he telephoned to say he would wait no longer. If I did not come straight away and pay him, he would inform the owner of the hotel and the local civic building regulator!' He wrung his hands. 'Please do not tell the police about the roof and the money I paid to the foreman! And I will not say one word to them that I have seen you three. Yes?'

'No,' Eleanor said without hesitation.

Seldon groaned quietly, but didn't argue. Pronovost stared pleadingly at Clifford. Her butler, however, gestured this was Eleanor's call.

'Monsieur Pronovost,' she said. 'You keeping quiet about having seen us is not enough. I want your word on something else. Something far more important. I'm concerned some entirely innocent people are going to be caught up in the trouble we are in. Wrongly! So if the police even suggest that any of your staff had a hand in helping us escape, you will deny it flat out. And tell the police exactly where each of them was all evening, which was nowhere near our suite, the service stairs or the rear gate from the kitchen yard. Agreed?'

He nodded keenly and darted away.

Seldon let out a long breath. 'Well, that's bought us a bit more time to come up with something. Any ideas what, either of you?'

'Yes,' she said in unison with Clifford's firm nod.

He looked between them dubiously. 'Does it involve anything I should be struck off the police force for being part of?'

She nodded. 'Probably, Hugh. But we've run out of options. And time.'

43

Eleanor groaned. Stepping into Café Bohème was like the worst kind of déjà vu. It symbolised just how desperate things had become. The last time they had been there had been the night Emile was murdered. Which highlighted that they were right back where they had started. Literally. And possibly no closer to identifying the murderer. The only progress they could fairly claim, she thought, was that they were now fugitives of the law!

The barman smiled and nodded to Eleanor as they entered.

'Dash it! I didn't expect him to remember us,' she whispered once they were seated at the most out of the way table.

'No matter.' Clifford gave her a reassuring look. 'We are not actually on any "Wanted" posters pasted up around the city.'

'Yet,' Seldon muttered.

'Well, if we are, I shall make sure they capture my best side,' she said.

'Just let Gripperel try,' he gruffed. 'Blast him and his house arrest for tying our hands like this. I'd like to hang him up by his ankles and leave him to the vultures.'

'Me too, Hugh. But this is France, not the Wild West.'

Their order of cognacs and coffees arrived. The barman left

them, stopping off to talk to the old man with the *musette* and his black cat who were at the same table in the window as before.

Checking over his shoulder they wouldn't be heard, Seldon spread his hands. 'Right. To business then.'

Clifford tutted quietly. 'Sir, as her ladyship mentioned, we are in France.'

'Meaning?'

Eleanor pushed his glass and cup over to him. 'That you need to at least sip these first. Because here, nothing comes before fine drink or food. No matter what.'

'How her ladyship has resisted moving here permanently remains a mystery,' Clifford said.

Seldon groaned. 'I appreciate your attempt at trying to lighten the cloud of worry hanging over us, but blast French custom. Or any other. If we don't work out a solution, and fast, we will all be living here permanently. In jail!'

Finding it hard to argue, she nodded in agreement. 'Then let's start by working out what we've missed, chaps. Because something's eluded us.'

They each ruminated in silence for a moment.

'I'm still missing it,' Seldon said with a sigh.

'And me, sir,' Clifford added.

She grimaced. 'Me too, unfortunately. But we've managed to get a lot of confessions in the last few hours. From Le Comte, Rion, Bernier. And Pronovost too, just now. Even Sabine, to some extent. In fact, the only one we're really missing is someone confessing to having murdered Emile and Hacqueville. Which, I admit, is the big one.'

Seldon nodded. 'I say we don't waste time discussing who had the opportunity or means because, to my mind, any one of our suspects could have been on the roof when Emile was pushed. And the only physical clue we have, a cut or scar on someone's shin, has proved impossible to check.'

'Which is the crux of the problem,' she said forcefully. 'Now. I know we believe it is the most likely scenario, but can any of us say with utter conviction that there is only one murderer?'

Seldon shook his head. 'Eleanor, I wish I could give a rousing "yes!" But I can't.'

Clifford held his hands up. 'Nor I, my lady.'

She winced. 'Which goes for me, too. The big problem with the "one murderer theory", no matter how much we believe in it, is that so much points to Hacqueville having killed Emile. Yet his were the only legs I've been able to check so far and he had no scar at all. Although, I suppose I could have been wrong about how the blood got onto that broken roof strut?'

Seldon closed his eyes. 'Please don't remind me you raked up the trousers of a dead man to stare at his legs in public, Eleanor.'

'Perhaps you feel dubious about Constable Hacqueville being responsible for Emile's murder because so many of our suspects have pointed the finger at him?' Clifford said.

She nodded vigorously. 'Exactly! We've caught every one of them lying about something or other in their "confessions", so we know they're unreliable.' She spread her hands out on the table. 'We simply have to find a way to come at this from a different angle.'

The large black cat slid down the *musette* man's back and stalked over to them.

Clifford tickled its ear. 'Sorry to disappoint, monsieur, but Master Gladstone is not with us this time.'

Eleanor's arms were already aching to cuddle her absent bulldog. 'I wish he was too, pussycat,' she said, running her hand along its back as it jumped on the table. 'Anyway, I'm glad Gladstone isn't here. He's much safer where he is. Jules and the others will be spoiling him rotten.'

'I wish I could be so certain about you being safe too, Eleanor,' Seldon murmured.

'Well, the best way to ensure that we're all safe, Hugh, is for us to get back to working out what we've missed.'

Clifford drummed his fingers against his coffee cup. 'Perhaps we should shift away from considering the suspects and consider the events of Emile Ury's murder again? We have, to all intents and purposes, re-enacted the actual murder itself on the roof of the hotel. But what about the events that led up to his death? Maybe that "something" we are missing is to be found there?'

'Clifford, you clever bean!' she blurted out. 'That's it. I've been such a blunt brick.'

Seldon rubbed his forehead. 'Why do I feel more lost than ever?'

'Clifford's right, Hugh. We've concentrated so much on the suspects, we forgot about the missing ten or fifteen minutes while Emile was in the museum before he was murdered at the hotel. Which none of the information we've gleaned has accounted for.'

'Excellent reminder, Eleanor. Let's start with him breaking in,' Seldon said.

She looked around to check they still couldn't be overheard. 'Right. I'll be Emile. It only works for me if I actually go through the motions.' She reached around the cat, who was leaning against her front, purring. 'So, here I am jimmying open the window. Which Rion, the guard, said he'd make easy for me. I slide in over the sill. Then I quickly double-check the timings of the guards' rounds and the plan of the museum Rion gave me. I creep out of the room I've dropped into, which is the one used to store visitors' bags. I hurry across the oval hall with the amazing mosaic floor spoilt by the glass panels. And probably hope my heart isn't pounding as loudly as it feels it is as I then race silently down the passageways and negotiate the vast gallery rooms. I arrive at the Impressionists, and then the Christophe Ury display where I find the recreation of his studio.' She paused, running her hands over the cat's soft tummy.

'Eleanor?' Seldon said gently.

'It's alright. I just imagined the wash of sadness Emile must have felt in that room filled with all the things that had meant something to his father. The villagers of Magnes might have thought Emile was a troublemaker growing up, but I think he was probably feeling horribly lost. And raging at life for having taken both of his parents from him while he was so young.'

Seldon squeezed her hand. 'Sure you want to continue?'

'Absolutely,' she said resolutely. 'So, I'm Emile again. I know I've only got a few minutes at most, so I head straight to where Rion has told me the pearl brooch is. I break into the cabinet, grab it, and start heading back.' Clasping her hand around the imaginary brooch, she stiffened. 'I hear the alarm. And panic.'

'But Rion told us he didn't ring the alarm immediately, my lady,' Clifford said. 'And, in fact, he can't have. Because he would have needed to report he saw the thief in the recreated studio. But he didn't.'

'You're right,' Seldon said. 'So Emile had time to get back to the window he broke in through *before* the alarm sounded. It's not that far from the Christophe Ury display to the oval hall and that bag room. Plus, it's always quicker on the return because you're more certain of the route.'

'This is wonderful, chaps,' she said eagerly. 'So as Emile again, I've got the brooch I came to get clasped in my hand and seemingly nothing to stop me escaping. So what then causes me to stay there with each ticking second increasing my chance of being caught? Every fibre of my being wants to get out of there. What's stopping me? What's different on the way out to on the way in?'

Seldon pointed at her clasped fist. 'You didn't have the brooch, for one thing.'

'Excellent, sir!' Clifford said.

She nodded. 'Back to being Emile, having just grabbed the brooch. Do I look closer and realise the pearls are fake?'

Seldon shook his head. 'Neither I nor Clifford could be certain if those pearls were real or fake.'

She bit her lip. 'You're right, Hugh. Which means I, as Emile, have no way of knowing. So what else was so important I risk getting hauled off to La Conciergerie rather than get out scot-free? Do I decide to try and take something else before leaving?' She shook her head. 'No. Nothing else was taken.'

She watched the cat distractedly as it strolled across the table to the mirror in which she had first seen Hacqueville leaning in what she now knew was Le Comte's car. The mirror with the painted ladies in crimson plume-feathered hats and gold puffed skirts looking so gay and carefree. They reminded her of the women in many of the Impressionist paintings she'd seen in the museum. Although, obviously, the ones on the mirror weren't the real thing...

Her jaw dropped. Not the real... fake! She blinked and looked again... crimson plume-feathered hats and gold-puffed skirts. Crimson and gold...

No, Ellie. Red and gold!

44

'I do not appreciate games, Lady Swift. Particularly in the middle of the night.'

'Neither do I. Particularly when they are deadly ones, Inspector.'

Her gaze flicked past Gripperel at the sound of voices further inside the museum. Her stomach knotted.

'I trust this is not a game, then?' Gripperel's honeyed tone belayed the hard set of his square jaw.

She shook her head. 'I've kept my end of the deal we made on the telephone. I'm here. And, though I wish with every fibre of my being I could do this without involving them, so is my precious husband. And my treasured butler.'

Seldon and Clifford stepped forward to stand on either side of her.

The three of them held their wrists out.

'We're giving ourselves up as promised, Inspector,' she said soberly. 'But, as I told you on the telephone, you have two choices. You can arrest us immediately. Or you can indulge me for ten minutes and walk out of here with the murderer of Emile Ury and Constable Hacqueville.'

His eyes narrowed. For a moment she was sure he was going to call for one of his men to shackle them. But instead he nodded curtly. 'Handcuffs can wait. It would be a shame if these good citizens were dragged out of their beds to no purpose. You have the floor for the agreed ten minutes. Make the most of each one, Lady Swift. Because I shall personally escort you back to jail when they are over. Permanently this time!'

She hid how much that made her heart falter. 'In that case, have you brought everyone I asked for, Inspector? And searched them?'

'I have. They are all unarmed. Now. Except my men.'

'And have you done the other thing I asked?'

He nodded curtly again and flicked his hand for her to start walking.

The tension in the Impressionists Gallery of the museum, or, more accurately, the Christophe Ury display, was palpable. Her, Seldon and Clifford's appearance sparked an outburst of outraged and angry questions from the seated suspects. Gripperel strode in behind them, his commanding presence reducing the commotion to a general murmur of discontent. The armed policemen standing by gripped the pistols in their waist pouches tighter.

'Here goes,' Eleanor muttered.

Seldon gave her hand a discreet squeeze. 'For Emile,' he murmured.

'And Hacqueville,' she whispered. 'But, chaps, if I'm wrong...'

'You will have done your admirable best, my lady,' Clifford said softly.

She nodded and walked slowly around to face her unwilling audience of seven; Le Comte, Omfroy, Delorme, Pronovost, Bernier and Alain and Sabine Rion. An aristocrat, a respected museum director, a prestigious art gallery owner, a luxury hotel manager, a municipal policeman, a security guard and a struggling sculptress.

But there was an eighth. Gripperel. A chief inspector of the *police nationale* he might be, but he could be harbouring a secret as deadly as any of the other seven.

But did it relate to the murder of Emile? She hoped the next ten minutes would decide.

She took a deep breath.

'Good evening, all. Thank you for coming.' She glanced at Sabine, hoping she hadn't kept her unspoken threat and come armed with a chisel seeking revenge! But her face gave away nothing.

'Inspector Gripperel, what is the meaning of this?' Delorme thundered.

Le Comte said nothing, but regarded Eleanor quizzically.

Pronovost half rose. 'Yes! Explain yourself, Inspector. It is almost one o'clock in the morning!'

Omfroy mopped his bald pate. 'This is my museum! Not a... a cabaret stage for theatricals! As director here, I insist—'

'Monsieur Omfroy,' Gripperel said firmly. 'I regret you and everyone else here has been inconvenienced in this manner. But *I* insist you remain here and listen to what Lady Swift has to say.'

'I will have your job for this!' Delorme barked

'Fine. But a poor job you would make of wearing my badge,' Gripperel said genially. 'Now sit. All of you, please. The quicker you are quiet, the quicker this will be over. And then the quicker you may all return to whatever you were doing before my men so rudely interrupted you.'

Except the murderer, Ellie.

He nodded to her. She looked around the room. 'I understand none of us want to be here. I certainly never expected to be spending my honeymoon trying to solve a murder. Two, actually. Those of Emile Ury and Constable Hacqueville. So, for the sake of brevity, I shall stick with that of Emile. Because, once we unmask his killer, we will have unmasked Hacqueville's.' She raised a hand to quell the renewed clamour. 'You see, we' – she gestured to Seldon and Clifford – 'briefly thought there must be two murderers. But now I know there is only one heinous enough among you to have committed these terrible acts.'

She'd noticed Le Comte becoming more agitated as she spoke. Now he stood up sharply. 'Enough, Lady Swift! I will not sit here and be insulted!'

'Then stay standing. Although, I am sorry. No insult was intended,' she said. 'However, I realise the truth stings. Or even burns... evidently.'

Her insinuation hit its mark. Le Comte sat back down, crossing one leg over the other as he turned away.

Clifford arched an appreciative brow at her. Then she realised why Le Comte was getting so hot under the collar.

He thinks you are going to reveal his shameful secret to everyone here, Ellie.

Bernier, emboldened by Le Comte's outburst, stood up next. 'I cannot be under suspicion. I am an officer of the law!'

She shrugged. 'So was Constable Hacqueville. But I won't speak ill of the deceased here by mentioning his unsavoury actions. Besides, you know them already.'

With all eyes on him, Bernier sank back down.

Rion looked at his boss, Omfroy, then seemed to find his voice. 'But why go through all this here? Why not at the hotel where Emile died?'

'Because he might have breathed his last breath there.' Eleanor fought back the prick of hot tears, reliving the moment Emile's pulse stopped as she held his hand. 'But he was dead before he left this museum!'

45

Once everyone had settled down again, Eleanor explained. 'Emile physically died at the hotel because he'd been betrayed.' She turned to Rion. 'Do you want to tell the others how, Monsieur Rion?'

He stared at her for a moment, then, sensing all eyes were on him, mumbled something and sat staring down at his lap, avoiding Sabine's eye. She sat rigid, gaping at her father in disbelief.

Eleanor forced herself to focus again. 'I thought not. But in the end, his betrayal made no difference. He had already been marked for death. Possibly right here in this room! It took me a while to tune in to my intuition. But when I did, I knew that the missing minutes between here and where Emile broke into the museum were key to working out who his murderer was.'

'What "missing minutes"? Really, this is riddles, Inspector!' Delorme protested.

Gripperel pointed at her. 'Ask Lady Swift. She is the one holding court at the moment.'

At least for a short while longer before she is marched to a real one, his sharp glance in her direction suggested.

'The "riddle" as you put it,' she continued, 'is why it took Emile so long to leave the museum after he had taken the pearl brooch.'

'Stolen!' Omfroy said tersely.

'Taken back,' she countered. 'It should never have left his family in the first place. Should it, Monsieur Delorme?' Receiving only a hard stare in reply, she shrugged. 'Unfortunately, taking that brooch was the root of poor Emile's tragic fate. Which was ironic, sadly, because like the story that it had been given to Christophe Ury by a rich widow, it was a fake.'

Rion and Sabine both jerked upright as if pulled by the same string.

So they both knew nothing about that, Ellie.

Omfroy rose angrily. 'This is a respected museum. One which aims to leave every visitor a changed person.'

'As it did for Emile, Monsieur Omfroy. It left him a marked man!' She gestured pointedly to his seat.

He sat back down with bad grace. 'I was well aware the brooch's pearls were fake. Christophe Ury was not a rich man when he was alive. Naturally, he sold the originals and had them replaced with paste. There was no attempt to deceive the museum's visitors—'

'Who couldn't have known whether or not the brooch was fake,' she cut in smoothly. 'Just as Emile couldn't. He wasn't a jewel expert. But he *was* an expert in one field no one else could match him in. *His father's paintings.*'

All eyes were on her now. Those of Gripperel's men, too. She could hear someone's fingers drumming on the leg of their chair.

'Emile had watched them be painted,' she continued. 'He grew up with them. He knew them so well, they inspired him to become a painter himself.'

'And a brilliant one!' Sabine cried out.

Omfroy clucked his tongue at her. 'And how would you

know, mademoiselle? You only came to my museum to waste your father's time when he should be working!'

'At least she came,' Eleanor said. 'Emile could never bring himself to do so. Not until that night he felt compelled to honour his father's memory and console his grandmother by returning home with that brooch. He had never come here before because he could not stomach the despicable underhand way his father's paintings and possessions had been acquired.'

'*Bought*, Lady Swift.' Delorme waved an imperious hand at her. 'I paid for them all.'

'A pittance, yes. Despite the exorbitant prices you knew you would then be able to sell them for,' Eleanor said coldly.

'It is called commerce, dear lady.'

'No, it's called *greed*.'

Pronovost shifted in his seat. 'But what has any of this to do with these "missing minutes" you spoke of? And quickly, I do not have all the time in the world. I have a hotel to manage, madame!'

'If you hadn't refused to call for a doctor when I urged you to, perhaps Emile would have had time!'

Pronovost turned red and found some imaginary lint to pick off his trousers. While he did, Eleanor collected her thoughts. She believed she knew what had happened during those 'missing minutes'. When she had told them in the café, Seldon and Clifford had agreed it was the most plausible explanation. But, ultimately, she had no proof. Certainly that a jury would accept. So she had to sound completely convincing to trick the killer into showing their hand.

'Coming back to Emile while in the museum,' she continued. 'He had the brooch in his hand. He thought he had an escape plan. And not knowing he had been betrayed, he thought he had a minute at least to honour his father's memory. What he found in this very room, however, made him need to avenge it.'

'Well, what did he find?' Bernier said.

'We've established he knew the real thing when he saw it.' She gestured around the room at the paintings. 'But what he saw was far from the real thing. Just like the painting I saw on a café mirror earlier today. What he saw were... fakes!' She turned to face Omfroy. 'Emile couldn't spot a fake pearl. But he could spot a fake Christophe Ury, couldn't he?'

'Lies!' Omfroy shouted. 'Lies!'

'Well, you're the expert. Monsieur Delorme told me that himself. He said you were the most respected expert on Impressionist painters in France. Is that a lie, too?'

'No, of course not.' Omfroy swallowed hard. 'But you cannot march into a museum and accuse its director, me, a man of my standing, of not knowing a fake painting from a genuine one!'

'Oh, I wasn't,' she said contritely.

He flinched. Then frowned. 'It sounded very much like you were.'

She forced her voice to stay even. The next part she had no proof for either. But it all tied in. What other possible explanation could there be?

'Not at all. I am happy to reiterate that you categorically can tell a fake Christophe Ury from the real thing. Because you were the one having the forgeries made. And then selling the real ones on the black market as the prices soared.'

'What!' Delorme leaped up, knocking his chair backwards.

'That's right, Monsieur Delorme. Omfroy here was double-crossing you. It must have seemed the perfect arrangement. Him showcasing the paintings you had bought, here in this oh-so illustrious museum. Only the ones he returned to you once each exhibition was over were fakes. How many, I have no idea. Perhaps all of them?' She halted Delorme's reply. 'I pointed out your greed, but I have to admit I think Omfroy's was even greater. And more arrogant. I know for a fact that Christophe, or his family, never replaced the pearls in the brooch with fake ones. You did, Monsieur Omfroy, didn't you?'

The murderous look in the museum director's eyes told her she was right.

'And here's something else I learned during this investigation,' she continued. 'You see, Emile wasn't hiding from the police on the roof of our hotel. Nor was he meeting an accomplice.' She caught the wild look in Omfroy's eyes. 'He was hiding from his murderer! Because he ran into you, here in the museum while trying to make his escape, Monsieur Omfroy. And he told you your forgery game was up, didn't he?'

Omfroy lunged for the pistol in the policeman's belt beside him. Before the man could react, Omfroy had it out of the holster and pointing at her chest.

46

Eleanor swallowed her panic. She'd completely forgotten what she was saying.

Someone pointing a gun at you can do that, Ellie.

She saw Seldon bite back a cry. And somehow hold back from lunging at Omfroy. Like Clifford, his expression was harried, but the look they both gave her told her they weren't about to do anything stupid. Gripperel obviously had the same idea, as he had raised his hand as his men had gone to withdraw their own guns.

'Keep your pistols in your holsters. And stand to,' he commanded. Slowly he lowered his hand, all the while keeping his eyes on the palpably sweating museum director. 'I want to hear what Monsieur Omfroy has to say.'

'Actually, I don't,' she said calmly, looking directly at him. 'You see, you jumped the gun, Monsieur Omfroy. Literally.' She looked around the crescent of stunned faces. 'Anyone mind if I continue?' She swallowed hard.

Keep it together, Ellie.

'You have said enough!' Omfroy's left eye twitched, but he

held tight to the gun. 'No one is setting me up for a murder charge!'

She shook her head. 'Actually, they're not. Because there's more to this very sordid tale yet.' She forced herself to face the other people in the room. 'You see, the night Emile broke in, Monsieur Omfroy was here in his office. According to him, just working late as usual. But that didn't ring true. Alain Rion gave Emile the timings for everyone in the building because it was essential to him that Emile made it out of the museum. And onto the roof of the hotel so he would be arrested by Hacqueville. So, had he known his boss was going to be here, he'd have rescheduled the robbery. It would have been madness otherwise. However, because he didn't, it went ahead. Not surprisingly, the plan went very awry. And when that happens, split-second decisions need to be made. And they are never good ones.'

Rion's head fell back against his shoulders as he stared at the ceiling. Beside him, Sabine's dark eyes widened in horror.

'So why was Monsieur Omfroy there clandestinely that night in his own museum?' Eleanor continued. 'The answer is, because he had a meeting. A meeting he didn't want anyone else there to know about. It struck me almost too late, just how unlikely it was he would be drinking coffee, eating a biscuit and smoking a cigar all at the same time. Because those three things were all on his desk half-finished when I followed the inspector into Omfroy's office only a short while after Emile died. And they must have been recent, or they'd have been cleared away. But events moved too fast for Omfroy or his visitor to realise how incriminating those little things were to become.'

Pronovost shuddered. 'To eat at one's desk, ugh!'

The gallery owner jerked to his feet. 'What is this nonsense, Lady Swift? I was working late also.'

She nodded. 'Yes, Delorme. But here, not at your gallery as you told me! You were here working with Omfroy, on your underhand art scheme to buy paintings for next-to-nothing and sell them for a fortune! The scheme I realise now you two must have been arguing about in the private room of that restaurant.' She held his gaze. 'Yes, I saw you there. Smoking again. A cigar with the same distinctive red, or crimson, and gold band. I finally connected it when I saw those two colours in the same café mirror I mentioned earlier. It is the insignia of an unusual American brand, La Palina, my knowledgeable butler informs me.'

'So what?' He snorted. 'I am not the only man in Paris to smoke these.'

'Probably not. But something of a coincidence, as that red and gold banded cigar turns up again later in our story and links two murders. But for now, back to those missing minutes. You were, I believe, smoking your cigar waiting for Omfroy to return. Only he ran into Emile. Blinded, I imagine, by anger, Emile told Omfroy he knew the paintings were fake. And even though it was the last thing he wanted to do, Omfroy came back to his office to confess to you, Monsieur Delorme. Because he needed you to help save his sorry behind from the wretched mess he'd created.'

'"Believe"?' Omfroy said, his voice now as tremulous as his hand holding the gun. 'You obviously have no evidence of this!'

'Oh, haven't I? But I haven't finished with your disgraceful partner yet.' Eleanor mentally crossed her fingers. 'You're a flamboyant man by nature, Monsieur Delorme. Only the finest things in life are good enough for you. The truth getting out about Omfroy having faked the paintings would have meant the end of everything you hold dear; prestige, reputation and money. Lots of money. And, by the way, when I announced just now Monsieur Omfroy had been swindling you with fakes, your equally fake pretence that you still didn't know at that stage wasn't very convincing.'

Delorme's fists balled.

Out of the corner of her eye, she saw Omfroy's grip on the pistol tighten. 'I did not kill anyone!' he shouted.

'I know,' she said dismissively. 'I don't believe you have it in you. You're not the sort to get your hands dirty. You'd rather leave that to someone like Delorme who has a temper as black as his heart. He knew you had him over a barrel. If Emile had exposed the fakes, Delorme was sunk. No one would believe he hadn't known about it. Anyone who had bought a Christophe Ury painting from him would naturally demand their money back once the story became public. In a blink, his gallery, reputation and riches gone. Bankruptcy, dishonour and most probably prison in its place. None of which appealed.'

'Lady Swift, enough! I am completely innocent,' Delorme snapped. 'Omfroy is the Impressionist expert, not me. I am—'

'What? You foolishly told me yourself you were the second most-respected expert on Impressionist painters in France! You also told me Omfroy was the first. Which is another reason why, despite burning to get rid of him, I imagine, you didn't kill him there and then. Because he's too important a person in the art world for questions not to have been asked. An investigation might have led straight to your door. But Emile? An unknown painter? A petty thief? A nobody? He could be killed with impunity. And once he was out of the way, you and Omfroy could work out how to sweep this whole torrid mess under the carpet and keep the money rolling in. So, you followed Emile as he ran from the museum.' The words made her voice crack as she spoke. 'And up onto the roof of the hotel. And then you pushed him to his death.'

47

Sabine let out a soft sob, but shook off her father's arms as he tried to comfort her. Omfroy looked dazed, but still gripped the pistol.

'It's a ridiculous fairy tale, Lady Swift,' Delorme said smoothly. 'For one thing, what reason could I possibly have for the second murder?'

'Constable Hacqueville's?' she said scornfully. 'At least be man enough to say his name! To answer, because I believe he saw you, not Alain Rion, climbing back down off the hotel roof after you killed Emile.'

Delorme smiled smugly. 'Oh dear, you really are making a fool of yourself, Lady Swift. Because if that were true, why did he not arrest me?'

'Several reasons. Arresting a petty thief is not the same as arresting a respected figure with connections to the rich and influential. Secondly, he knew it wasn't you who had robbed the museum, so arrest you on what charge? And thirdly, he must have heard the glass shatter, and the horrified shouts and screams from the hotel dining room. I believe Hacqueville put two and two together and realised what you had done. And in his mind, he saw the possibility of blackmail and a large wad of easily earned banknotes.'

'Lies!'

'Really? Constable Bernier can confirm everything I just said.'

'Me? Now wait!' Bernier glared at her. 'How is that keeping to our deal?'

'How is staying silent now keeping to your police partner's code?' she said earnestly. 'If you can't do it for your conscience, at least do it for Hacqueville. Tell everyone who you saw!'

Bernier's eyes flicked to Gripperel. He paled. 'I didn't see anyone.'

She felt sickened by his cowardice. Or was it greed too? Was he looking at Delorme, thinking he'd carry on the black-mail Hacqueville had started?

Let Bernier get himself killed if he wants, Ellie. You've still got a murderer to catch.

Delorme sneered triumphantly and sat back down. Grip-perel held his watch up to her pointedly.

Time's almost up, Ellie. La Conciergerie awaits. For all three of us. One last push.

She tried not to focus on the gun Omfroy still had aimed at her.

'I thought it over presumptuous when Hacqueville announced he believed the man who had fallen to his death, Emile as we now know, was a thief. And that I was his accom-plice. Later, it became clear Hacqueville was a quick thinker, if nothing else. He was setting me up as a patsy to reinforce his hand in his upcoming blackmail. Delorme would think he only had to pay to be clear of suspicion because Hacqueville would make sure I would be the only one under scrutiny.' She cocked her head thoughtfully. 'Either he then came up with the idea to plant the second stolen item on me at the Eiffel Tower, or you did, Delorme? Either way, it was no problem to get the black sailboat sculpture from Omfroy. He wasn't going to say no to what looked like an easy way out for him, too.'

Despite his former smugness, she noticed Delorme shifting uneasily in his chair. She continued with renewed purpose.

'Standing here now, I realise something else as well. Hacqueville was probably somewhere out of sight in Galerie Delorme when I went there. By sheer coincidence, I made it easier for you both. He pointed me out to you, Delorme, didn't he? Hence the eager way you thrust that Eiffel Tower cocktail party invitation into my hand. All Hacqueville had to do then was plant that stolen boat sculpture on me and arrest all three of us at the base of the tower.' She slapped her forehead. 'No, silly me. That was to be the job of the man who has just disgraced his partner. And in death, too.' She threw Bernier a hard stare.

'And the money?' Inspector Gripperel said, making the whole room turn as if they had almost forgotten he was there.

'Ah, yes. The wad of banknotes tucked inside Hacqueville's bag. Money paid by Delorme to Hacqueville. Although, at first, I incorrectly thought they were the ones you paid him, Le Comte. My apologies.'

He jumped to his feet. 'I did not kill Emile. I did not want him dead.'

'I know,' she said. 'But you were happy for him to go to jail! But let's stick with Hacqueville blackmailing Delorme. Blackmail is a hideous crime. It becomes addictive. The blackmailer gets their money. Then wants more. And more. And they can get it because they still have the same hold over their victim. The only way out for the victim is to eliminate their blackmailer. Ironically, we've got Hacqueville to thank for pointing out his murderer, albeit posthumously.'

Delorme's shoulders were rigid, a muscle in his jaw pulsing.

'You see, along with the money in that messenger bag Hacqueville was carrying were three cigars. All with a red and gold band. All American La Palina brand. I imagine he helped himself to them from your office at the gallery while he was there putting the squeeze on you for even more money, Monsieur Delorme.' She shook her head. 'You realised Hacqueville's demands would never stop. So, you followed him to the Eiffel Tower. After all, you'd already killed once and the second time is always easier, they say. And, thinking Hacqueville had successfully planted the stolen boat sculpture in my bag, you pushed him off the tower.' She pointed at the gallery owner. 'There's your murderer, Inspector Gripperel. Monsieur Bellamy Del—!'

Delorme lunged at Omfroy and wrenched the gun from his grasp. 'So clever of you to work it all out, Lady Swift. But not so clever now. I've killed twice. Now it will be three times.' He pointed the gun at her. And fired.

As the sound died away, she shrugged. 'It's loaded with blanks. Did I forget to tell everyone that?'

Delorme threw it at her, narrowly missing her head. Having ducked, she launched herself at his ankles and toppled him over backwards.

'Dear, dear. That is a nasty scar on your shin, Monsieur Delorme!'

48

Even having got justice for Emile, and Hacqueville, Eleanor was feeling distraught. She had made a deal with Gripperel. But now, the thought of Seldon and Clifford being incarcerated as well was too awful.

Out in the museum's courtyard, her heart sank further at the sight of two police vans with barred windows. The very sort that had carted the three of them off to jail before. She turned pleadingly to Gripperel.

'Surely, you could allow just me to be jailed, rather than all three of us? After all, the charges now can only be leaving the scene of a crime, withholding evidence and, possibly, interfering in a police investigation?'

'Gripperel, no!' Seldon barked. 'Do the right thing, man, take me and leave my wife out of it!'

Clifford darted for the nearest van as if Gripperel might be satisfied with the first one in only. He was brought back in the grip of two stern-looking policemen.

'All for one, one for all,' he said sombrely. 'Had we but known how direly Alexandre Dumas's words would come to haunt us!'

Gripperel frowned at the three of them. 'And I thought an Englishman, and Englishwoman's, word was their bond! I will not settle for one of you!' He pointed to the sorry-looking men being filed out. 'As the murderer, Delorme will be taken to La Conciergerie in the first van and Le Comte, Omfroy, Pronovost, Rion and Constable Bernier in the second. They have a lot to answer for. Which means I have no room for all three of you.' His square-jawed face broke into a grin. 'And I will not settle just for one. So, there is no room for any of you.'

'You mean...?' she breathed.

He nodded. 'It was my fiercest hope from the start of your show inside the museum that I would be able to say at the end... you are all free to go!'

Eleanor had to fight the urge to hug him. 'Thank goodness! Though if I'd known you were expecting a show, I'd have worn my cabaret tail feathers.'

Clifford pinched the bridge of his nose, but his eyes were twinkling as much as Seldon was trying not to laugh.

Gripperel didn't even try to contain the honeyed chuckle that escaped him. 'But before you leave, I wish to thank you all. But Lady Swift the most. What I witnessed you do in there, I will remember long after I retire from the police force. It was...' He held his hands up, clearly lost for words.

'Inspired. Brilliant. And heart-stoppingly too close to the mark,' Seldon said, pulling her into his side.

'Yes. All of this.'

'I believe you left out deviously wily, Chief Inspector,' Clifford said.

'Devious... wily?' Gripperel gaped at her. 'You did not know for certain all the accusations you made?'

'Oh, that depends on one's definition of "certain" really,' Eleanor said airily. She smiled. 'Inspector, thank you for having your men search all the suspects for weapons before we started.

And particularly for having two of them load their own with blanks.'

'My pleasure.' Gripperel cocked his head. 'What made you believe you could trust me, though, Lady Swift?'

'The fact I finally realised it could only have been you who slipped the note under the door of our hotel suite. No one else could have made the armed policeman on guard stand down long enough. And you leaving Paris and not returning until the following morning all just felt a little too... good to be true?'

The inspector nodded. 'I confess I did slide the note under your hotel door. And I only left Paris on the belief that you would break out of your hotel room. From the beginning I had doubts about Emile Ury's death not being an accident. Then when Hacqueville died too, I was sure.'

'Then why, Chief Inspector, did you arrest her ladyship and Mr Seldon at Le Comte's chateau, along with myself?' Clifford said.

'Because I had a concern it might be Le Comte who had killed at least one of the victims. And, it was most evident to me that Lady Swift was too stubborn to back off and listen to a mere policeman attempting to prevent another murder – hers!'

She rolled her eyes at Clifford, who was trying to hide his amusement. 'The more ladylike word is "tenacious", Inspector.'

He nodded with a smile. 'Yes. This is why I use "stubborn".' He turned to Seldon. 'I do not expect you to ever forgive me for doing this to your wife, but it kept her safe. And stopped any suspicion I was not doing my duty. Now, before I forget something. In Chateau Archambault, I found the bag you took from the crime scene at the Eiffel Tower.'

She held up a halting hand. 'Oh no you don't, Inspector! You've told us off for taking it from the scene of a crime already. You can't admonish us twice for the same misdemeanour.'

Gripperel laughed again as he reached inside his coat. 'I am trying to say that in the same room as the bag, I found this. It contained some very interesting information. Like my name on your suspect list!' He held her notebook out to her.

'It is a wonder you could read any of it, Chief Inspector,' Clifford said mischievously. 'A spider dipped in ink running over the page would be more legible.'

'Very droll.' She laughed, taking it. 'So, Inspector, you really placed us under house arrest, hoping we would escape and find the murderer? Or fail, having woven enough rope to hang ourselves with?'

'Yes. Hoping it would be the first, I promise you. But this is France. Our laws are fierce but fair. You understand, do you not... *Chief Inspector* Seldon?'

Eleanor's heart faltered.

Of course, Gripperel would have checked up on all our records in England, Ellie.

Seldon was holding Gripperel's gaze, his thoughts unreadable. But she was mortified. He would be in no end of official trouble when they reached England. He'd broken French law repeatedly; deserted a murder scene, taken and withheld evidence, to say nothing of breaking house arrest. There would be hearings, a tribunal...

Gripperel handed the bag back to the waiting policeman. 'When I get to my office after taking these six to jail, I will write my report. Which will include the names' he turned to Seldon – 'of all three of you, naturally. And all the events. Well.' He winked. 'Perhaps not all the events. Only the ones which tell how a chief inspector from Scotland Yard helped his wife solve two murders here in my city. With their butler also, of course.' He offered Seldon his hand. 'No hard feelings? From one policeman just trying to do his best to another?'

Seldon held his gaze. 'For what you did where I was concerned, none at all. Maybe even where Clifford is concerned. But in regard to what you put my wife through? Come to England, Gripperel. And allow me to repay the hospitality you've shown her. I shall be delighted to extend the full might of the English legal system in return.'

'Ah, another deal we have made then, yes?'

Both men smiled as they shook hands.

Gripperel whistled to the policeman standing by the passenger door of the nearest van. 'I have not returned all of your property yet.'

The door opened, and Gladstone raced over, looking his ever-exuberant self, fresh from another adventure. Eleanor dropped to her knees to accept his enthusiastic greeting. 'Oh, boy, I missed you that much, too!'

'Now, my friends,' Gripperel said. 'You are probably thinking you'll never visit Paris again. But if—'

'On the contrary, Inspector.' She slid her arm into Seldon's. 'We'll be here for our anniversary every year. There's a certain rose tree we need to keep an eye on.'

'Then, please, remember to call on me.' He looked between the three of them. 'You are a formidable team. If ever you were to work together permanently, that would be a very bad day for criminals.'

'Inspector, it's been a bumpy ride knowing you.' She paused as he laughed. 'But overall, it's been an honour. Have I redeemed myself enough to make one request, please?'

'Does it involve the tail feathers of the cabaret?'

She laughed again. 'No. it involves...' She caught sight of Sabine who was heading towards them. 'Ah, it's two requests, actually. But one minute.'

She turned and held her hands out to her. 'I'm so sorry it all turned out this way.'

Sabine managed a wan smile. 'Me as well. But as we say in France, *c'est la vie*. You were right, Lady Swift, you were a very good friend to Emile. Thank you.'

'You too, Sabine. I realised rather late that you were only trying to protect Emile in... in death, as you had done in life.

And that you painted over Emile's tattoo on your egg sculpture because he hated what it represented. Even though you didn't know what that was.'

Sabine squeezed Eleanor's hands and walked away.

'You wanted to ask me for some things?' Gripperel said.

Eleanor nodded. 'Yes. First, do you think if I pay for Josette's legal representation there is a chance she could recover Christophe Ury's paintings and effects? As his mother, she should have them. She was all but swindled out of them to begin with.'

He smiled. 'I know the best man in all of Paris for this. He owes me a favour. I cannot guarantee the courts will agree, but I think it very likely for the ones hanging in the *musée* and Galerie Delorme that are not fake. And certainly for any genuine ones recovered from the forger. I promise I will get the name from Monsieur Omfroy. He has already been "spilling the beans", as I believe the expression is, to try and shift as much guilt as possible from himself. And the second request?'

She gestured towards Sabine. 'As soon as a new director is appointed to replace Omfroy, could you help her get at least a showcase there for her sculptures? They are absolutely amazing.'

'And, ahem, striking!' Clifford added, running his finger around his collar.

'And, er, detailed,' Seldon said, fiddling with his buttons.

Gripperel nodded. 'I will do my best, Lady Swift. I promise this.'

He ruffled Gladstone's ears and was gone in the swirl of his dark-chocolate coat.

Eleanor beamed at Seldon and Clifford. 'Well, chaps, it's over.'

Seldon shook his head. 'No, Eleanor. I've learned with you, it is never over. There may be a temporary lull until the next bolt of lightning strikes, but that's all.'

'Amen, sir,' Clifford said.

'It's not my fault things happen,' she huffed, hiding a smile.

'It isn't. But you have an uncanny knack for it. Which is why' – Seldon took her arm in his, nodding for Clifford to fall into step with them – 'I want to have words with you both!'

She shared a wince with her butler. 'We could just get back to honeymooning, Hugh?'

He nodded. 'We will. The moment I've got your thoughts on whether or not we could do what's eating me up?'

She was intrigued. The quizzical look Clifford gave her showed he was, too.

'Which is, Hugh?'

'Well, remember I mentioned I was seriously thinking of leaving the police force after we were married, Eleanor? If I do, maybe we should team up permanently, as Gripperel hinted at?' He gestured around the three of them. 'A retired Scotland Yard detective, with a highly respected record. An impossible titled lady with an uncanny knack for solving murders. And a scallywag butler with more dubious skills than most of the criminals I've put behind bars. If we all wanted it to, it could happen? I mean, what could possibly go wrong?'

HISTORICAL NOTES

IMPRESSIONIST PAINTERS

Christophe Ury wasn't the only early Impressionist painter around Paris in the middle-to-late nineteenth century. Works by other painters such as Renoir, Degas and Monet later outstripped even his paintings in terms of fame and value. The most famous, and expensive, Impressionist paintings are often thought to be those of Van Gogh (*Orchard with Cypresses* sold for $117 million in 2022). But in art circles he is usually labelled 'Post-Impressionist'. The term 'Impressionism' was actually first used as an insult, but later became a badge of honour. Incidentally, the village of Magnes-sur-Oise is loosely based on Auvers-sur-Oise, just outside Paris, where Paul Cézanne lived and Van Gogh died.

MONTMARTE

As Eleanor found out, painters stuck together in Paris in the 1920s (they probably still do today). And the largest commune could be found at Montmartre, nowadays a suburb of Paris. But up to the late 1800s it was a separate entity, as Clifford rightly mentioned. You could only enter Paris itself from there via a tollbooth, the town being surrounded by a wall. And as you passed through, you had to pay Paris's taxes on goods. But not before. So anyone wanting a cheaper life, or, perhaps, one away from too much official scrutiny, chose Montmartre as their base. Which included many artists.

CIGARS

One way Eleanor learns Delorme is the killer is by following the 'trail of the cigar'. Cigars were first popularised in France by Napoleon, who made it a tradition to smoke them with his generals after a military victory. The actual brand of cigar Delorme smokes, La Palina, is fascinating in that it was made of Cuban tobacco in America by a Ukrainian. Its distinctive red and gold band gives the game away when Eleanor finds them in Hacqueville's bag after his murder. It is said the first cigar bands were made for Empress Catherine II of Russia, who wanted to avoid staining her fingers while smoking. And Clifford's favourite French author, while in Paris, Alexandre Dumas, said: 'A cigar is a divine pleasure. It is the fruit of the union between fire and air. It must be savoured with respect.'

WOMEN'S RIGHTS

Being an independent minded and thoroughly modern girl, Eleanor struggles with the inequalities between men and women in Britain. In France, a country who had overthrown their monarchy and ruled under the banner of 'liberty, equality, fraternity', you would imagine women would have fared better. After all, during the French Revolution, the National Assembly published the Declaration of the Rights of Man and of the Citizen, declaring royalty and title abolished and all equal. Except, that is, women. Indeed, when the women's petition was presented to the National Assembly, it wasn't received well. The petition suggested they might want to give women the same 'liberty, equality and fraternity' they were bestowing on their fellow men. The Assembly, however, rejected the idea and suggested instead that the women who had proposed it were suffering from hysteria. Maybe one of the real reasons the women's demands for equality were rejected was the 'outrageous' clause they included insisting that all women should have the right to wear breeches!

THE POLICE

As Clifford points out, to non-French, the police of the time (and still today) are quite confusing in their organisation. There are three types of police, again established by the Declaration of the Rights of Man and of the Citizen in 1789: the *police municipale*, the *police nationale*, the *gendarmerie nationale*. Hacqueville and Bernier belong to the *police municipale* which secures public peace and order at the local level, and answers to the mayor. The real confusion comes with the *police nationale*, Gripperel's province, and the *gendarmerie nationale*. Even though they deal with the same matters of law enforcement and crime, the first are civil servants and deal with urban areas. And the second are part of the military and deal with rural areas. However, even today, they have the same emergency number, and it is decided on a situation-by-situation basis which will be called out. For the sake of simplicity, I reduced it to two and stuck with the *municipale* and *nationale*.

NOBILITY

Le Comte's family were one of the lucky ones. After the French Revolution, many of his fellow nobility were either dead or in exile. And those that weren't had no chateau left to live in. Or officially privileges to enjoy. Because even though titles of nobility were restored in 1852 by Napoleon III, they were declared by the courts incompatible with that pesky Declaration of the Rights of Man and of the Citizen. Because of this, most noble families chose to relinquish their titles (or simply ignore them). The only one still in existence today is the Baron de Longueuil, who lives in Canada, but gets his right to the title from when Canada was administered by the French.

EIFFEL TOWER

Most people have heard of the iconic Eiffel Tower. It is still the most visited man-made structure in the world (that you pay to enter). Around seven million people a year ascend its stairs and lifts. At the time Eleanor visited, it was also still the tallest man-made structure in the world and the first over one thousand feet. It has over two and a half million rivets, all placed by hand, and weighs over ten thousand tons. And the likes of Alexandre Dumas's son tried to stop it from being built, declaring it would be an eyesore. And, unfortunately, quite a few people die there like Hacqueville. Over three hundred and seventy since it was built. Most have been accidents, suicides and attempted stunts. Including trying to fly a plane through the centre of the tower – it didn't go well – and jumping off using a parachute made of cloth – which went even less well!

A LETTER FROM VERITY

Dear reader,

I want to say a huge thank you for choosing to read *Death at a Paris Hotel*. If you did enjoy it, and want to keep up to date with all my latest releases, just sign up at the following link.

Your email address will never be shared and you can unsubscribe at any time.

www.bookouture.com/verity-bright

I hope you loved *Death at a Paris Hotel* and if you did I would be very grateful if you could write a review. I'd love to hear what you think, and it makes such a difference helping new readers to discover one of my books for the first time.

I love hearing from my readers – you can get in touch through social media or my website.

Thanks,

Verity

www.veritybright.com

facebook.com/veritybrightauthor
x.com/BrightVerity

ACKNOWLEDGEMENTS

My thanks to the amazing team at Bookouture for helping this book see the light of day and be as good as it is.

PUBLISHING TEAM

Turning a manuscript into a book requires the efforts of many people. The publishing team at Bookouture would like to acknowledge everyone who contributed to this publication.

Audio
Alba Proko
Melissa Tran
Sinead O'Connor

Commercial
Lauren Morrissette
Hannah Richmond
Imogen Allport

Cover design
Tash Webber

Data and analysis
Mark Alder
Mohamed Bussuri

Editorial
Kelsie Marsden
Nadia Michael

RAISING READERS
Books Build Bright Futures

Dear Reader,

We'd love your attention for one more page to tell you about the crisis in children's reading, and what we can all do.

Studies have shown that reading for fun is the **single biggest predictor of a child's future success** – more than family circumstance, parents' educational background or income. It improves academic results, mental health, wealth, communication skills, and ambition.

The number of children reading for fun is in rapid decline. Young people have a lot of competition for their time, and a worryingly high number do not have a single book at home.

Our business works extensively with schools, libraries and literacy charities, but here are some ways we can all raise more readers:

- Reading to children for just 10 minutes a day makes a difference
- Don't give up if children aren't regular readers – there will be books for them!

- Visit bookshops and libraries to get recommendations
- Encourage them to listen to audiobooks
- Support school libraries
- Give books as gifts

Thank you for reading: there's a lot more information about how to encourage children to read on our website.

www.JoinRaisingReaders.com

Made in the USA
Monee, IL
02 July 2025

20389332R00187